# A Scandinavian Summer

Helga Jensen is an award-winning British/Danish author and journalist. Her debut romcom, *Twice in a Lifetime*, was published in 2021 and she is currently studying for a Creative Writing MA, whilst continuing to work as a freelance journalist.

D0231555

# Also by Helga Jensen

*Twice in a Lifetime*
*A Scandinavian Summer*

# A Scandinavian Summer

Helga Jensen

**hera**

First published in the United Kingdom in 2022 by

Hera Books
Unit 9 (Canelo), 5th Floor
Cargo Works, 1–2 Hatfields
London, SE1 9PG
United Kingdom

Print ISBN 978 1 80436 020 0
Ebook ISBN 978 1 912973 99 6

Look for more great books at www.herabooks.com

Printed and bound in Great Britain by Clays Ltd, Elcograf S.p.A.

1

*Dedikeret til min far*

*Dedicated to my father*

# Prologue

I walk out from the kitchen holding Anthony's mug.

'Here's some tea, love,' I smile.

'You know I don't like that mug. I'm sure you only used it to provoke me,' he says.

His words take me by surprise and wipe the smile from my face. My eyes fill up with tears at his unexpected reaction to a welcoming cup of tea upon his return from work. All I've ever wanted is to make my little family happy.

I don't understand him. Last week the bone china mug was his favourite; now it appears only the hand-painted Portmeirion is good enough.

How can one man be so difficult over a mug?

I should tell him to make his own tea, but he hasn't been in the best of moods since Anna at work was promoted over him a couple of weeks back, and I need him on side when I tell him how much Rosie's school holiday is going to set us back. At sixteen, I feel it's important she gets out and sees the world, unlike me. Hopefully Anthony will agree.

I nervously wrap my long cardigan around me, pulling at it from either side. It cocoons me and acts as a comfort blanket, helping me remain composed.

'Snappy little crocodile,' I mutter quietly enough to ensure he won't hear me.

This flippant remark gives me strength somehow. I could think of much worse words than crocodile, but my mother brought me up to believe that if you don't have anything nice to say then you shouldn't say anything at all.

I transfer the tea into Anthony's other mug and count to ten to calm my nerves. I smile as I re-enter the living room with his drink.

'Here you go,' I say, handing it to him. Some may think I should have poured it all down his crotch, but then he'd never agree to the school trip.

His mood appears to improve as he looks at his phone. He then takes hold of his favourite mug. I watch him eagerly as he takes a sip.

'Lovely,' he says.

The man from Del Monte says 'yes', I think to myself.

I breathe a sigh of relief when the living room door flies open. Rosie bounces in, easing the tension further.

'Hello Mam, Dad,' says a cheery Rosie.

Anthony smiles up at her as if nothing was wrong. He probably hoped she would sit beside him, but Rosie walks across to my armchair instead and places herself on the arm. The strawberry smell of her familiar shampoo wafts over me.

'Gosh, is it six o'clock already? How was your after-school club?' I ask.

'Great,' says Rosie.

She shifts about on the arm of my chair and whispers into my ear, 'Did you tell Dad, yet?'

'No, not yet,' I whisper back, feeling nervous at the thought.

We must tell Anthony about the trip to Kenya this evening. Hopefully he will realise how fortunate Rosie is to have been chosen to visit a conservation area after raising money to help save rhinos from poachers. He knows how much Rosie has always loved animals, ever since he brought home a stray kitten he found on the side of the road when she was a toddler.

I notice Anthony glance at his phone again.

'Six o'clock,' he says to himself.

'Yes, why?'

'I'm only saying,' he says.

'Okay, well, food won't be long. I'm making your favourite,' I say.

'I'm not hungry,' says Anthony.

'But can't you smell the slow cooker? The delicious aroma of coq au vin?' I smile.

'Martha, are you trying to get around me for something? What are you after?' says Anthony.

Rosie and I look at each other uncomfortably. He could at least attempt to be a bit nicer in front of Rosie.

'Well, I just wanted us all to sit down for dinner so we could tell you about Rosie's school trip. We need to pay the deposit tomorrow, and the rest in a few weeks,' I explain.

Anthony explodes at this. I know he is never keen to part with money, but this is extremely out of character, even for him. Rosie has always been his little princess, surely he can't deny her a trip like this.

'You know we don't have any money spare. I should have had that promotion. I'm an excellent accountant, can't they see that?' He stares me in the face, as though I have the answer. It's as though he blames me for him being unsuccessful in his promotion.

For a moment, I wonder how he can be the great accountant he claims to be when we don't appear to have any money. Surely, he should have managed it a little better. I don't understand where it all goes. I curse myself. A forty-seven-year-old woman, letting her husband manage the finances! From now on I am going to make sure I know where every penny is going.

'Look, I'm sorry you didn't get the promotion, but it's not our fault...' I say.

Anthony glares at me and storms out of the room. I try to stop him, but he rushes to put his shoes on and grabs his coat from the hallway.

'I'm going out. I need some space. We can talk when I get back.'

The door slams shut, leaving me and Rosie bewildered. What on earth is wrong with him? These past few months he has changed so much. Perhaps he needs to look for a new job. It's obviously too much for him where he is. He and Anna never got along that well. He probably hates the fact that he now works for her.

'He'll cool down. He's just a bit stressed with work.' I try to reassure Rosie. 'Come here, why don't we plait your hair?' I say.

Rosie huddles in beside me and I take strands of her beautiful silky hair in my hands.

She always loved having her hair plaited as a little girl. Although she is now a teenager, it seems to offer her comfort when Anthony is volatile. I'm sure she wouldn't want her friends at school seeing her like this.

'Ah, this is nice, Mam,' she says.

'Lovely, isn't it?' I reply.

In this moment, we feel closer than ever. I think back to my parents, who were so conservative and never showed any emotion. I sometimes wonder if that is why I ended up with a staid husband who shows similar traits.

'I wonder if Dad will notice my hair when he gets back?' says Rosie.

'Yes, I'm sure he will. It looks so pretty in plaits,' I smile.

'He'll be in a better mood when he returns, won't he? I really want to go on the trip, Mam,' says Rosie.

'Oh gosh, yes. The trip will be fine. He just needed some space, that's all.' I say.

Four hours later the police arrive to tell us the shocking news.

# Chapter One

*Two Years Later*

My obsession with Scandinavia all started with a pair of colourful Nordic socks. Thick, cosy and ever so warm, they brightened up my life. With nobody to put my cold feet on in bed, they were a life-changing discovery. I even slept slightly better. Amazing what a pair of good quality thick socks courtesy of a Facebook advert can do.

From one pair of socks, I wondered what else the Scandinavians had got right. I already knew they had amazing meatballs; I had visited IKEA in Cardiff enough times to know that.

Then there was all this *hygge* talk. Goodness knows I could do with a bit of hygge in my life. So, next, I invested in some candles and prayed the house wouldn't burn down. It hasn't so far, and for the last year, I have lit a candle every night in front of a lovely photo of Anthony. It is a photo of him on Rosie's fourteenth birthday, before he started having trouble at work and became the stressed-out person he was.

I hug my big fluffy hygge cushion as I try to stop any further memories flooding through. Since Anthony died in that terrible car accident, I have locked all the bad memories away in a part of my mind that I don't wish to access. If anything ever creeps through, I quickly distract myself with my favourite Danish television programme, *Drabet på får*, or *The Killing of Sheep*, as it is called in English. It always takes my mind off Anthony and the loneliness I suffer, especially now that Rosie has moved in with her best friend and I struggle with an empty nest. I wish she would have stayed at home with me, but she was determined to sit in front of Netflix with Amy every night. With her share of her dad's life insurance, she could now easily afford it. I also suspect she wanted to leave home to forget the image of Anthony walking out that night, but who knows?

I tuck my Nordic-socked feet underneath me as I settle down alone with my cocoa for the night. The telly jumps to life with subtitles. I wish I spoke Danish so that I didn't have to depend on the screen to tell me what they are saying. Maybe I should consider lessons as a treat for my looming fiftieth birthday. Although I can't imagine many people around Llanelli could teach me.

'*Jeg slår dig ihjel!*' screams out the telly.

'I will kill you!' the subtitles announce moments later, as the murderer attacks.

Gosh, he's very handsome for a nasty murderer. A strapping blond with the most piercing blue eyes. He is making me feel a bit hot under the collar. His big, strong, Viking hands feel like they are lurching through the screen at me. Imagine those tracing up and down your body. His firm grip on your thigh.

*Oh, Martha, what is wrong with you? Is this the menopause kicking in? Am I having one last hormonal surge?*

I open the top button of the anti-allergenic cotton blouse I have been wearing all day. That's better.

The television suddenly focuses on the actor who plays the victim. The man who acts as an office worker, attending to some late-night work, now pretends to be dead. His computer flashes in red with some strange message in a language I don't understand.

*Du må ikke dræbe fåret.* Whatever does that mean?

This is dreadful. So gruesome. I don't know what has come over me recently. Anthony wouldn't recognise his 'nervous nelly', watching murders on TV. I never liked anything gruesome before. Perhaps it is because when I am immersed in my Scandinavian TV dramas, I am comforted by the fact that the victim's life is actually worse than mine. Reality slips away. Of course, for other characters on the programme, their lives are far better than mine and much more glamorous too. I could only wish for the policewoman's exotic life in *The Killing Of Sheep*. Sometimes I sit and imagine I am the sophisticated Gretchen, my skinny thighs being hugged by a pair of skintight black leather trousers, driving a vintage Aston Martin as she does. I purposely avoid looking at my strong thighs in my trusty elasticated black corduroy trousers when my imagination takes me far away. Unfortunately though, when the programme ends, so does my fantasy. I am once again me. A widow who certainly doesn't own a pair of fancy leather trousers. I have no vintage Aston either; instead, I am the proud owner of a battered old Renault Duster with more dents than I care to think about. I am not a bad driver really; it's just that my glasses steam up from time to time when I reverse and I get flustered.

The programme ends with Gretchen driving off. She certainly doesn't have any dents in her car.

I feel sad as yet another episode draws to a close, but then an advert takes me by surprise. I sit up straight and listen carefully.

'Win a visit to our studios in Copenhagen!' blasts out from the TV.

'Text this number now to win an all-expenses-paid trip to our studios and meet the cast. You just have to answer this simple question,' says Gretchen.

I clamber for a pen and paper and note down the phone number. Not that I'd ever be brave enough to go if I did win.

'Where is *Drabet på får* filmed?'

'That's so easy!' I scream at the TV.

'Is the answer A) Copenhagen, B) Oslo or C) Stockholm,'

'It's obvious it's Copenhagen,' I shout at Gretchen.

I write down 'A' on the paper. Of course, I would never enter in case I won. Rosie might need me, not to mention the panic attacks I've been having since Anthony died. I would be texting the number non-stop if circumstances were different.

I pick up my latest Scandi noir book to take my mind off the fact that there is an opportunity to go to Denmark and meet the handsome murderer along with the rest of the cast. However, I am only on page two when I am startled by the sound of 'Dancing Queen'. It is Rosie's special ringtone. It is 10:30 pm. What on earth does Rosie want at this time? It must be an emergency. This is the reason I never switch my phone off at night. You never know what can happen in the dreadful hours of darkness.

'Mam, Mam! Guess what!' she screams.

'Are you okay?' The adrenaline pumps around my body as I await her response.

'Yes, I'm better than okay, Mam. I just got an email from Borneo.'

'An email from Borneo, at this time? It must be very late there now. Who on earth would email you in Borneo? You don't know anyone in Borneo. It must be a scam.'

'No, Mam, only now I'm checking my emails. Typical. They messaged this morning. I had to call you straight away… I'm going to help orangutans.'

'Orangutans? There's no orangutans in Wales, are there?'

'Noooo, I'm off to Borneo. I'm leaving next week for six months. I'm going with this fabulous organisation and…'

I sit up straight. Is Rosie actually telling me this, or has the thought of a prize to visit the studios in Copenhagen sent me doolally?

'Borneo? Next week? Surely you're not serious? You couldn't arrange something like that at such short notice.'

'Oh, Mam. Look, I didn't want to tell you before, okay? I applied ages ago but didn't think it would get approved. The paperwork just arrived with the email, and they want me to fly next week. I told them I was available at short notice… I didn't expect it to be *this* short. Lucky I had my jabs, just in case.'

'You had your jabs without telling me?'

'Yes, Mammy. I had my jabs alone. I'm a big girl now. I don't need you to take me for my injections any more.'

'No, of course not.' I forget Rosie is eighteen. An adult in the eyes of the law, but just a baby to me.

'But I thought you wanted to do a hairdressing course at college? What happened to that? And what about your girlie movie nights with Amy. Isn't that why you wanted to move in with her?'

'Amy said she doesn't mind. She's met someone and he's always hanging around now, to be honest. Besides, the careers advisor told me that volunteer work always helps your CV, so it's an investment in my future.'

'An investment? I thought you said this was charity work?'

'It's only three grand.'

'Three grand! This is getting worse, Rosie. What on earth, love?'

'Don't worry. I've still got more of Dad's life insurance left. It's what he would have wanted.'

I don't mention it, but I think how he reacted to the school trip to the conservation area. I don't know what he would have wanted, quite honestly.

'Do you not think he'd have preferred you go to college?' I say.

'Of course, he'd want this, Mam. Remember when Dad got me that fluffy monkey thing? After that, we sponsored Oliver the Orangutan. That was Dad's idea. Oliver even sent me a birthday card one year. Bless him.'

'Oh my goodness, Rosie. Yes, I remember. Although, it's one thing to get a fluffy toy and a card. What if they're vicious and you get attacked?'

Since Anthony's death I seem to worry about the most random things happening. Perhaps the grief and shock changed me. Although it isn't only me who changed through the years. I think how Anthony was a different person just before he died. He and Rosie had always been so close, but he was becoming so much more distant to both of us. Still, his death affected us terribly; I should be grateful that Rosie is finally excited about something. When someone has an accident just like that, you're so unprepared and you not only have to deal with the grief, but the shock too. I don't know how we would have managed back then if it wasn't for good friends. Although

I won't forget how Mrs Roberts from next door didn't even bother to express any condolences to me. Even though there isn't much neighbourly love between us, I would never have done that to her. However, no matter who it is, it doesn't take long for everyone to stop rallying around and you're once again left to your own devices. Suddenly people stop calling and bringing around casseroles and cakes and that is when it hits you the hardest. Now it's just the two of us left and one of us is heading to the other side of the world. How on earth am I expected to cope?

'Don't be silly, Mam. They are gorgeous and fluffy and cute. I may even get to bottle-feed one. Like a baby. Aww. Can you imagine? It'll be worth every penny.'

'Rosie, I've not spent any of the money from Dad, and you're racing through it. Dad would have wanted us to use the money sensibly and not on a jolly to Borneo.'

'It's not a jolly, Mam. I'm going to help the orangutans. They are dying in the rain forests… *Dying.* Have you not heard about the palm oil scandal?'

'Yes, of course, Rosie. It's terrible what's happening, but Borneo? Can you do something over here for them instead? You might get malaria or a vomiting bug. I've already lost your dad; I don't want to lose you too.'

Immediately I feel guilty for saying this as I know how much she missed out on not being able to go on the trip to Kenya. I should be delighted for her, but I can't help worrying about such a big change in our lives.

'Stop thinking the worst, Mam, I'll be fine,' says Rosie.

I don't respond as I know I won't be able to hide the concern in my voice. I can just imagine her sitting there with her lips all pursed, a habit she has when she gets annoyed. She squeezes them so tightly together, her mouth looks like a little duck's bottom. I bet she is even twirling her finger around her chestnut hair extensions like she normally does when she can't think of anything else to say. Well, she won't be able to manage her hair extensions from the Borneo jungle. I bet she hasn't thought of that.

'Mam, Mam… Are you there? Look, Dad's been gone a while now. I'm grown up and going away. Perhaps you… Well, you could do something too. Would that make you feel better about me going? I don't mean meet a man. Obviously, nobody would ever replace Dad. But you could take up a hobby. What about Salsa dancing? You might need to swing your hips a bit now you're getting older. You don't want to need a hip replacement,' laughs Rosie.

'Hey, cheeky thing. I'm not that old quite yet, young lady.'

'Well, you've plenty of time for Salsa dancing then. Listen, I've got to go, Josh is calling for me. Oh, and can you look after Gazza for me while I'm gone?'

'Who's Josh? I hope you're not thinking of having my grandchildren with him. I'm too young to be a gran.'

I am talking to myself. She has already gone, and a tear makes its way down my cheek. I am selfishly sad that Rosie is off on an adventure.

As I walk into the bathroom, I notice my reflection in the mirror. When did I become older than my time? I'm only in my late forties and acting like an old woman. I am beginning to see my mother when I look at myself. It's the eyes I suppose. The hooded eyelids are creeping in and I look like the crotchety woman who lived for her husband. The woman who spent her life trying to be the perfect housewife, believing that children should be seen and not heard as dad would need his peace and quiet when he walked in from work. Dad was older when I was born and only really cared for his cricket. So, between the two of them, there wasn't much time for me in our family home; something I tried to make sure never happened when I had a daughter. Even when mother died of ovarian cancer at sixty, none of us dared shed a tear. She was more of a matriarch than a mother. Now my life is passing me by and I don't want history to repeat itself. I should do something that doesn't involve staying in and watching murders at night but I am also terribly afraid of the big wide world. I have my crossword puzzles to keep me company; I suppose they are a hobby. I certainly wouldn't be brave enough to join a salsa class though. I wouldn't even know what to wear. I'm sure throwing on an old pair of leggings would never do! My friend Suzy has taken up knitting. But I have never been one for knitting, not since I dropped a stitch at Granny's one school holiday and managed to unravel a whole stripy scarf. Goodness knows I could do with a holiday right now. If only I was brave enough to enter that competition…

Oh, how wonderful a trip to Scandinavia would be, seeing where *The Killing of Sheep* is filmed! I might even be able to visit Hans Christian Andersen's house. Perhaps if I visited a home full of fairy tales, my life would become one.

I am hit with an adrenaline rush as I consider how exciting it would be, but I'd never be brave enough. What if I won? I'd have a panic attack right then, for a start. Indeed, what am I thinking? I can't go on holiday. I have responsibilities. A home to run, a job in the library that I love and besides, who would look after the goldfish? No, I can't leave poor Gazza in the lurch.

What am I thinking? I shiver and put on my dressing gown. I was never destined for adventure. I was put on this earth to wear comfortable clothing and look after others.

–

I am climbing the stairs for bed when the chime of 'Dancing Queen' rings in my ears once again. Maybe Rosie has changed her mind. That was quick, even for her.

'Mam. Oh, Mammy.' Rosie's crying, and I want to wrap my arms around her.

'Aw, it's okay, love. Don't be upset. What's up?'

'It's Gazza, Mam.' Rosie breaks into big sobs now.

'He's been murdered.'

# Chapter Two

It all seemed like a normal day at the library, but I should have realised that it was too calm. Maggie, our library manager, wasn't sneaking about checking up on us, like a teacher in the middle of an exam. Her shoes weren't creaking as she walked up and down while peering over everyone's shoulders. She was nowhere to be seen.

'Excuse me, do you have a copy of *Fly Fishing* by J.R. Hartley please?'

'Ha ha, Suzy. Very funny.'

'You do?' Suzy laughs.

'There's no hope for you. Are you bored? You can help me log these books in if you like,' I suggest, glancing wearily at the mountain of new arrivals in front of me.

'I'm actually swamped, I'll have you know. I'm on a mission. I've been asked to round everyone up. Maggie thinks I'm some kind of cattle hand, I think.'

'Oh, what's going on? Any idea?'

'Nope. She just said to "round everyone up". All the team to be in the staff room at one pm…*Sharp…*'

Maggie despises lateness, along with anything IT-related. If anyone is late, her mouth twitches and I am convinced her left eye does too. As for IT, we try not to mention anything to do with it in front of Maggie. She had to take a month off sick when the library introduced a centralised computer system some years back.

'Wonder what this is all about, then?' I say.

'Goodness knows. You know Maggie – doesn't give anything away. That's the trouble with resting bitch face: it's hard to tell if she's in a bad mood or not. Shall we walk into the meeting together? Safety in numbers and all that.'

'That might be wise if Maggie's in one of her moods,' I reply.

I love my job, promoting books to children and chatting to the senior citizens who visit for the company, rather than the books. However, I can be having a nice quiet chat with one of our regulars, such as the lovely Mrs Morris, when Maggie will appear over my shoulder. Just like that, she will turn a nice day into a very horrible one, simply with her presence. With one look, she makes me feel inadequate. It's difficult to work out what goes on in her head. She keeps her personal life very private and we know nothing much about her, despite the fact that we work together day in and day out. I mean, not one of us knows how old Maggie is; we joke that she could be as old as a couple of the books in the library. Maggie could be sixty, seventy, a hundred – nobody would ever know. She has always looked wizened. The one thing we do know though is that she has the most irascible disposition. Even if I did enter the competition and win, I wouldn't be brave enough to ask her for time off.

Suzy and I arrive at the staff room early and notice that Maggie is already helping herself to the custard creams. We grab the last two biscuits on the tiny chipped saucer. Maggie is so tight that she wouldn't dream of using a bigger plate. Sioned walks in, looks at the dish and realises she is too late.

'Anyway, you still haven't told me exactly what happened with Gazza yet,' says Suzy, pouring us both tea.

17

'What on earth has happened? The poor little goldfish, just so sad.'

'Well, Rosie is devastated. I still can't believe anyone would do such a heinous thing… But she thinks that Josh, her now *ex*-boyfriend, well, he—'

'Ahem,' says Maggie, leaning over us. 'Right, ladies and um, you, Trevor. I won't beat about the bush.'

'No, you never do,' mumbles Trevor, our IT manager, and perhaps Maggie's biggest enemy. She shoots him a look that could kill someone less valiant.

'There's no easy way for me to say this. There are going to be cutbacks, and we'll be having to make someone redundant. Now, you can choose voluntary redundancy, or we will have to choose from one of you.'

Her cold, heartless eyes scan around the room looking for victims. A crumb from her custard cream dangles limply from her lip, not that anyone would dare tell her. All eyes around the room focus on the crumb as we try to take in what Maggie is saying.

'Anyone who wants to avail themselves of the voluntary redundancy can let me know by tomorrow morning. Otherwise, it might be a case of last in, first out. Simple as that. Now have a think, ladies and um, Trevor.'

I notice her mouth contorts rather strangely as she says his name. Maggie almost collapsed when Trevor was sent a year ago to assist us with our IT system permanently. She would certainly choose him for redundancy if she had her way but, sadly for her, he is the only one who knows the systems inside out. The truth is that Trevor won't be going anywhere. My job, on the other hand, could be in jeopardy unless some kind soul steps up.

The five of us look around the room, each one eyeing up the other as we try and judge their reactions. Will it be Janine who takes voluntary redundancy? She does moan a lot about some of the books being too heavy to carry since her back started playing up. Then there is Sioned; I know she would love to spend more time with the grandchildren.

'Right, back to work then. You have until nine am tomorrow to let me know.'

We stand around, unsure how to react, when the staff room door flies open. The impact results in a flake of white paint flying aimlessly in the air. It spins around, like an out-of-control helicopter, until finally, it lands near Trevor's foot.

'I am so sorry; it seems Maggie started without me,' says Rebecca, from Human Resources.

'Ooh, it is serious if she is down for the day,' says Trevor.

I hear her whisper something to Maggie. I try to eavesdrop. It sounds something like, 'I told you to wait for me.'

Rebecca then turns to look at all of us with a sympathetic smile.

'Well, it looks as though Maggie has broken the dreadful news. Does anyone have any questions? Well... Anyone?'

'Will there be some kind of remuneration if we choose voluntary redundancy?' asks Sioned.

'Absolutely,' Rebecca replies enthusiastically. She is obviously trying to sell this option to us. 'It all depends on how long you have been here but... Yes... Look, I don't know what Maggie has told you so far, but anyone who wants more details can come and see me in Maggie's office this afternoon. I'll be there to answer any questions you have. This has been a tough decision for everyone involved. I am dreadfully sorry—'

'Will this mean you won't be continuing with the computer system upgrade next year?' interrupts Trevor.

I look straight to Maggie for a reaction. Yes, her eye is definitely twitching.

'Oh, we don't know about anything like that at the moment. It's purely staffing cuts that are taking place for now,' says Rebecca. She gives one of those smiles again, but it just comes across slightly smug. It's all right for her; she isn't losing her job.

'Look, folks, take time to absorb the news and let me know if I can clarify anything for you later. I always think it's better to sit down and make a note of anything you think of in these situations. Take the news in. Deep breaths, a bit of meditation even. Then, when you're calm and collected, we can discuss it privately. I'm going to be hanging around if you want a chat.'

As she turns to leave, Rebecca gives Maggie the most dreadful look. Like a mother who has just seen her child smack another child over the head with his Action Man. It is as if she is saying, 'Just wait until I get you home'.

'Maggie, can I have a word, please? In your office, now,' snarls Rebecca.

'Ooh, drama,' whispers Suzy. 'I'd say Maggie's in the shit.'

'About bloody time Maggie was hauled into HR,' says Trevor, as we leave.

'Yeah, the woman needs some training on how to speak to people. I bet Maggie couldn't care less about any of us,' says Sioned.

'I can't believe someone should step forward to take redundancy,' I say.

'We're all one team. We can't possibly choose between us who leaves, so they're going to have to choose from any one of us,' adds Suzy.

I stay quiet. The team might feel I should be the one to leave. After all, they know I received a payout after Anthony's death. Trevor even helped me open a new bank account for it. What they don't understand is that I enjoy the company. I would never leave the house if I didn't have my job.

'Oh, Martha. I know I moan about Maggie, but I need my job. I don't want redundancy. I've worked here twenty years,' says Suzy.

'I know. It's not fair on any of us,' I reply.

'Let's see what tomorrow brings. Perhaps someone will choose to leave. Maybe there's a secret lottery winner amongst us who has been hoping for an excuse to quit their job.'

'Some chance of that,' smiles Suzy as we leave the room.

A distinguished-looking man, wearing one of those striped scarves that private schoolboys seem to like approaches us.

'Hello, can you tell me where to find *The Non-Objective World* by Kasimir Malevich please?' he asks.

'Oh, for goodness' sake,' whispers Suzy. 'Why are we always interrupted when we're in the middle of something?' She turns to him and smiles.

'Certainly, sir, follow me.' She grins so convincingly that she looks as though she doesn't have a care in the world. However, when you truly know her, you can see the worry that she lives with under that beautiful smile of hers. She will be terrified of losing her position at the library. She has Angus, her autistic son who needs extra support, and her husband Lloyd has already lost his job at the steelworks. Suzy is the sole breadwinner. There are hardly any jobs around here as it is, without this news. Job losses at the library are terrible news for all of us.

# Chapter Three

Following a night of murders, accompanied by mayhem when I spilt cocoa all over my crossword, I feel revitalised. Walking into the library for the announcement of who wants to take redundancy, I know what I must do. I have the life insurance money, so it would be incredibly selfish of me to stay in a job when I have a nest egg in the bank. The money is there for a rainy day and now there is a storm cloud erupting above me.

The mood seems cheerful when I walk into the staff room to tell everyone about my decision. I am amazed to see a whole packet of Jammie Dodgers on the table. What on earth? Surely Maggie isn't cruel enough to push the boat out because she is getting rid of one of us?

'Have you heard the news?' says an excitable Trevor.

'What news? Obviously, something weird is going on,' I say, pointing to the biscuits.

'It's Maggie,' says Trevor, accidentally spitting on me in excitement. 'She's been fired!'

'It's true. Didn't I tell you she was in the shit? I knew it,' adds Suzy.

'Really? Oh, my goodness. I've chosen to take redundancy the same time as Maggie finally gets fired. Just my luck.'

'What are you on about, Martha? Nobody is going anywhere. This means there is an internal promotion.

One of us moves up, and nobody needs to leave their job. We all get to stay!'

'You should apply for the position, Suzy. You've been here long enough. You deserve it,' interrupts Sioned.

It takes me a moment to understand what is happening. I sit down and nibble on a Jammie Dodger as I think about everything. So, there is no redundancy, and instead, a promotion is on offer. What a difference a day makes.

For some reason a small part of me feels disappointed. I suppose I had persuaded myself that I should take some time off. I had even convinced myself that it might help the panic attacks. If I stay home then I may not get them. However, I also know that it would be a dangerous road to take. The less I go out, the more I want to stay at home. So I should be relieved. I mean, realistically, how would I have managed indefinitely without a job? It would take me a long time to find anything else. Employers are looking for youngsters nowadays. They don't recognise the experience people like me have. I should think myself lucky. I should be grateful.

'Suzy, you'll be an amazing manager,' I say. 'Get your application in now. Go on, I'll cover for you while you go and see Rebecca.'

'Oh, really? Would you? You're an angel, Martha.'

Suzy practically skips about for the rest of the day. So do the rest of the team. However, something inside me isn't quite as upbeat as the others. As much as I try to push it aside, I feel a bit sorry for Maggie. I know she was short-tempered – I mean Trevor would go so far as to call her a dragon, which is harsh – but what will she have in her life now? Will she ever find another job? From the little I know about her, she lives alone. She has nobody. Despite the upset she has created in the workplace, I wonder how she will be feeling as she walks into her empty home, knowing she has lost her job. Although we have different personalities, I can't help notice the striking similarities we have. Rosie is heading off into the big wide world, I'm not getting any younger and I also arrive at an empty home every night.

It's something I think about for most of the evening. As I gobble up my twice-weekly treat of Alphabetti spaghetti on toast after work, I can't help but wonder how many other lonely people there must be in the world. It can't be only me and Maggie. There must be others too.

As I contemplate my life and those of the people around me, I swap my usual cocoa for a sherry. I try not to do this often, I would hate for anyone to see me down at the bottle bank recycling more than one empty bottle. Indeed, having a sherry this evening feels hugely extravagant, especially as it is a week night. But the last two days have been rather stressful.

Snuggling under my soft teddy bear blanket on the sofa, I sip at the sherry. Are other lonely people doing the same thing right now? Or are they drinking gin, or wine perhaps? The sherry warms my insides nicely; I feel as though I have a glow around me.

Finally, feeling all warm and snuggly, I decide to rewatch *The Killing of Sheep* episode with the man in the office. Before the programme begins, Gretchen reminds me that there is a chance to enter the competition. All I have to do is send one text message and I could be in Copenhagen with the cast.

*Oh Martha, imagine how wonderful that would be!*

However, as glorious as that sounds, I still think it's safer to remain at home and watch them all on my TV screen. I carefully watch the handsome murderer on TV. I don't think I have ever seen anyone so perfect in my life. I pause the TV to look at him as his hands reach out. Lifting my blanket from me, I walk, as if in a trance, and stop in front of the TV. I press myself right up in front of the telly. Can he feel me? I certainly can't feel him. A couple more glasses of sherry, though, and I might.

I kiss the telly, aiming for the murderer's hand. It reminds me of when I was a teenager and I would kiss the television when George Michael appeared on *Top of the Pops*. I kiss him again. There, perfect aim. It is as though he is watching me, his eyes peering back at me. Yes, it certainly feels as though someone is watching me. It is as though he is here in the room with me.

'Did you enjoy that?' I ask the TV.

'Hellooo!'

I look up and see a tall, dark-haired young man watching me through the window. Has he just witnessed me rub my lips against the telly? Oh, my goodness, it was a moment of madness. I swear I haven't done anything like this since I was fifteen. Will he believe me? Flipping heck. Oh, fiddlesticks with knobs on! I am in a complete panic. My stomach is in knots. I have just been caught kissing the TV. Oh gosh. What on earth am I going to do?

Now the man is moving away from the window towards the front door.

*Ring, ring, ring.* The doorbell chimes incessantly. I don't want to answer. I know I said I was lonely but I don't want a visitor in this state.

I have done an appalling thing, and I was caught. It serves me right, as my Apostolic grandmother would have said.

'Hello, hello?' I hear the man say.

'Hello. Please open the door.'

*Bang, bang, bang;* he's hammering at my letterbox now.

'I've something I need to give you,' he calls out.

If I ignore him long enough, he might go away. I can't answer the door when I have been caught in a compromising position. Also, if I have learned anything from watching my crime dramas, it is that you do not answer the door to strangers. Ever.

I consider the policewoman on *The Killing of Sheep.* Will she find my dead body on the doorstep? Will Gretchen be wearing her leather trousers when she sees me? However, I remember that I am in Wales, not a Scandinavian city, so it would be Pugh the Police who finds me. There will be no gun pulled out of Gretchen's tight leathers after all. The only thing to fly out of Pugh's pocket would probably be a Welsh cake he had forgotten was in there. Perhaps that is a bit mean. Pugh the Police was terrific in finding the culprits when the local farm had their prize sheep stolen; it's just I don't know how he will deal with my murder. I suppose the public are about to find out.

I gingerly open the door. My eyes search for the weapon that he may kill me with.

'Hello. I'm Josh.'

He smiles as if I should know him immediately. Instead, I stare blankly.

'Josh. You know, I dated your daughter for a few weeks…Well, until…'

Ah, that Josh. It's Gazza's suspected killer.

He looks embarrassed. I'm not entirely sure if that is because of my behaviour or his terrible crime. What if I am next on his murderous spree? Can the evening get any worse?

'Josh. What are you doing here?' I ask.

'Look, I know Rosie's really upset with me. I don't blame her, but I didn't hurt Gazza. Please will you let me explain what happened so you can tell her?'

Any embarrassment about my moment with the telly vanishes as Josh starts to explain. It seems he is way more mortified about his situation than mine right now. I still refuse to let him past the doorstep though.

'Okay, I'm listening,' I say.

'Rosie said I strangled Gazza, okay... I swear when she caught me putting my hands around his head, it was because I was trying to check if he was still breathing. I thought he might have a pulse. I saw him floating in the tank, and thought I could resuscitate him before Rosie found him dead. I know how much he meant to her.'

'Well, Gazza cheered her up when she bought him after her dad died. That's why she named him after his favourite footballer,' I explain.

'I know, she told me on our first date. Do you think that's why she overreacted? Because he meant so much?'

'Quite possibly,' I say.

Although I secretly wonder if I have also contributed to her overactive imagination with all my talk of dark Scandi murders recently. It is easier to blame Josh, though.

'Now she won't speak to me and wants to report me to some fish society,' Josh continues. 'I love animals. I do. You're my only hope of getting the truth out there. She won't answer the door to me.' I am wondering how to deal with Josh when he leans around the corner and picks up a small fish tank, pushing it towards me.

'Here. This is Gareth. You know, like Gareth Bale. He's the same breed and everything. Not as the football player... I mean fish... You know what I mean. It's a present to say sorry for everything I didn't do. Anyway, I got Gareth special fish food, Mrs… um, Mrs… Please say you'll take him to give to Rosie.'

'Rosie's going away, though. She doesn't need a replacement goldfish,' I try and explain.

'Please, Mrs… Please. I bought him now. I can't keep him at mine; my mum would kill me. She's allergic.'

'Allergic to goldfish?' I ask incredulously.

'Yeah, she just says that. She doesn't like cleaning fish tanks out. Look, you have to take him. I can't take him home.'

'Okay, okay, I'll look after him while Rosie is away,' I answer reluctantly. He leaves me with no choice.

I carefully place the fish tank in the living room and watch Gareth swim around, oblivious to the fact that his predecessor died in suspicious circumstances.

'Don't worry, Gareth. I'll take care of you,' I say.

It's not Gareth's fault he was caught in a cruel love triangle.

I watch him swim happily about but, as I do, I see this as yet another sign for me not to enter the TV competition.

Perhaps Anthony has sent Gareth to me. Maybe this is his way of telling me, 'Martha, stay at home, look after Gareth and wait for Rosie to return.'

# Chapter Four

The moment I wake up, I remember that my beautiful Rosie is flying to Borneo this evening. The feeling of heart-wrenching emptiness reminds me of just after Anthony died. I would wake up in the morning, turn over, and realise that he was not there. Then I would recall the reason why and remember the police standing at the door, looking all sombre, asking to come in. Now I feel as though I am losing my daughter too. I had only just got used to the fact that she had moved out; now suddenly, she will be thousands of miles away from me. I tell myself she needs to help the orangutans, but the thought still makes me cry. Sorry orangutans, I need her too.

I want to stay under my duvet and hide. If I disappear, maybe Rosie won't go. She will think her mother has gone missing and fail to catch the flight. What an incredibly selfish person I am. Of course, I can't do that. I must do what any mother would do. Smile, wish her well, encourage her to save orangutans and ensure she doesn't miss the coach to the airport.

–

I take a long look at my beautiful daughter at the coach station. How did Anthony and I manage to create such a perfect human?

'You'll be amazing, Rosie,' I say. 'I'm sorry if I was negative before, I just had a bit of a shock. I wouldn't have thought the jungle would be your type of thing nowadays. What with your lashes and hair extensions.'

'I'm sorry too, Mam. I should have told you about my plans sooner. I wasn't thinking how you'd feel. Anyway, you have Gareth to keep you company and Josh said he'd pop by and check you're okay for me,' says Rosie.

'Josh?' I repeat.

'Yeah, after you explained how he came over, I realised that he isn't so bad, after all. We've decided to remain friends.'

'That's good,' I manage.

'But, Mam. I have to tell you something.'

'Oh no, what now?'

I don't like Rosie's tone.

'Well, to be honest, he said he was a bit worried about you. It's a bit awkward… I wasn't going to tell you, but he said to me, "Is your mam all right? I caught her snogging the telly." Why would he say that, Mam? What does he mean?'

Snogging the telly! What a busybody, he doesn't even know me. Why would he exaggerate like that? Maybe he is a monster after all.

'Is that the bus, Rosie? Look, it's coming in.' I point towards the big white bus heading towards the bus depot. I am extraordinarily grateful to National Express for their timekeeping. I had wanted the bus to be delayed so that I could spend every last moment with my lovely girl. However, I don't wish to divulge to Rosie what occurred on that terrible night. I certainly don't want to tell her about the secret loneliness that I suffer in the evenings, which drove me to insanity and made me kiss the telly.

'Mam, what did Josh mean?' repeats Rosie.

'I have no idea, lovely. Maybe you should stay away from him, after all. He seems a bit bonkers, don't you think?'

The passengers start to push forward, rushing with their luggage.

'You don't want to miss the bus, come on,' I say, glad of the diversion.

Rosie picks up her bulging sparkly pink backpack, struggling to lift it onto her back.

'Oh, Mammy. I'm going to miss you. I know you do my head in sometimes, but I will miss you.'

'I'll miss you too, Rosie. And I'm sorry if I "do your head in",' I say. Her remark makes me laugh and temporarily halts the tears that are bubbling away behind my eyes.

'Heathrow, is it?' says the cheerful bus driver, looking at Rosie's scanned ticket on her phone. He pulls at the waistband of his shiny, over-ironed navy nylon trousers as he struggles to keep his tummy within the confines of his belt.

'Aww, her first time away from home is it, love?' he says, noticing my anxious face.

'How did you guess?' I smile.

'If I had a pound for the times I seen that look on a mam's face,' he says sympathetically. 'Been doing this job thirty years, see. I seen it all,'

I am thankful for the driver's kindness. It feels as though I have an ally.

'Right, Mam. I'll call you as soon as I get to the accommodation, okay? I might not be able to ring from the airport as I have to meet the others in the group. It's going to be busy, meeting everyone.'

'No, of course. I understand.'

We hug each other tightly. This will be my last hug from Rosie in a very long time. I don't want to let go.

'Six months,' I mumble.

'What, Mam?'

'Sorry, didn't mean to say that out loud. Won't see you for six whole months,' I say.

'It'll go fast now, Mam,' she answers. Fast for her, maybe, but certainly not for me.

'Right, come on, you two. I got a bus to drive,' says the driver.

Looking around, I realise Rosie is the last passenger to get on. I can't put the moment off any longer. Rosie climbs onto the bus, taking a seat towards the back. I hope she doesn't get travel sick, sitting at the back like that.

We wave at each other until the bus snakes around the corner and goes out of sight. She's gone, and all that is left is a blurry dot in the distance.

Around me, everyone carries on with their lives as though it is a typical day. I want to shout to the passing strangers that this is not an ordinary day whatsoever. When Rosie stepped onto that bus, my life changed and went drastically downhill. I am left all alone, except for a goldfish and the bottle of sherry I am about to treat myself to from Bargain Booze.

–

As soon as I reach home, I unbutton my mackintosh and throw it on the bannister. Quite honestly, this is unheard of for me, but I am not in the mood to place it on the coat hook that it usually hangs from. A mackintosh thrown insouciantly reflects my fragile state of mind. I couldn't even care if it falls on the floor.

The sherry bottle cork makes a little popping noise as I release it. My mouth waters as I think of how that first sip will calm me down. No wonder my grandmother was teetotal. Is this the beginning of a slippery slope involving sherry? Of course, I still worry about the bottle bank, but I have been researching nearby bottle banks. Thus, I have worked out that I can take one empty bottle to the local Co-op bottle bank, and I will drive the other bottle into a neighbouring village to dispose of anonymously.

The sherry tastes so lovely that I pour another. And another. I repeat this until I lose count of how many I have had. *What are you doing, Martha?* Rosie will be at the airport by now. She will be meeting new friends, whilst her mother is becoming a slovenly drunk, ignoring her untidy hallway.

Instead of doing something about it, I quickly dismiss the thought and pour another sherry. As I walk from the kitchen, through the hallway, I spot the figure of a man coming to the front door. He looks the same build as Josh. I knew I shouldn't have had windows in the hallway. If I can see his shadow, then he can surely see mine too. There is no way I am answering the door to him in such an intoxicated state. I quickly grab my mackintosh and lie down on the floor. I pull it over my body to disguise myself. Although my Nordic socks poke out from the bottom, I don't think he will see me. I shuffle about on the floor to hide as much of me as possible. For heaven's sake, why can't my coat be longer? My refilled sherry glass sits beside me. My frazzled brain is tempted to poke a hand out and take a sip, but I daren't in case he sees some movement.

'Hiya!' the man calls chirpily after I ignore the doorbell. I remain quiet so that all I can hear are the heavy breaths I am making.

'Helllllooo. It's Josh,' says his cheery voice. I continue to ignore him.

'Hello, I promised Rosie I'd come and check on you after she left,' he continues.

I desperately want to shout for him to go away, but instead, stay gravely quiet.

'Your car's here, and I just saw your shadow. I know you're there. Are you okay?' This time he shouts louder. 'Hello, where are youuuuu?'

I wait until everything finally goes quiet, and I think he has left. I poke my head out from under the coat to be sure. Alas, I am wrong. Our eyes meet, and I spot him – he is staring straight at me through the letterbox.

'Oh my fucking God, you're on the floor,' he says.

*Language, Timothy!* No need for that. I put my head back down as I try to think of ways to get rid of this awful boy.

'Are you okay? Have you fallen and can't get up?' he asks through the letterbox.

'Umm, yes. I've fallen, but I'm okay.'

I try to wave at him to show my limbs are still working. No need for alarm, young chap.

'Right. Okay. Well, try to stay calm. The same thing happened to my nan, and she was okay,' he says.

*I am calm; it's you who is panicking*, I want to respond.

And what is it with everyone thinking I am an old woman? I really must do something about this. Perhaps I should shave my hair at the sides and give myself a Mohican. That would shock these blasted kids and their blatant ageism.

35

I try and eavesdrop as Josh's voice lowers slightly and I hear him say my address. Why is he reciting my address? What is he up to now?

'Come quickly. An old lady has fallen,' I hear. Who on earth is he talking to? And I am not an old lady, squire.

'I'm going to break down the door now. Don't be alarmed, okay,' says Josh very slowly and very loudly. Does he think I have a hearing impediment, perhaps?

It's no use. I'm going to have to get up off the floor and explain that there is nothing wrong with me, or I may need a replacement door, as well as the conservatory I dream about on my home improvement list.

My knees creak as I get up. I never realised how hard and cold that old tiled flooring was.

I finally open the latch. However, as soon as the door loosens, Josh flies through the door, pushing me to one side with the force behind him. He can't stop himself and lands on the side of the bannister, smashing the side of his temple. He crumples down in a heap at the bottom of the stairs. Oh fiddlesticks! This boy is nothing but trouble.

He lies there, looking as though I have hit him over the head with my sherry bottle as blood spurts down his ghostly white face.

I hear a siren in the distance. It gets closer and closer until I finally see a paramedic pull up outside my open front door. So that was who Josh was giving my address to. Of course. Perhaps if I hadn't so much sherry, I would have realised sooner.

A female paramedic rushes down the path. A male follows closely behind her with the emergency paraphernalia.

'We have a report that an old lady has fallen, is it?' the first paramedic says.

'No, there's been a bit of a misunderstanding,' I begin to explain.

I point behind me to Josh, who is cradling his head in his hands.

'Just as well you called an ambulance. We certainly needed one, Josh.' I say as the paramedic hurries to attend to him.

At least he got help. It makes me realise that if I fell and hit my head nobody would find me for days, perhaps months. I wonder what age you are supposed to be to get one of those fall alarms for around your neck? This may have to be my next impulsive purchase the way I am heading – particularly if I am to continue on this slippery slope with sherry.

# Chapter Five

Suzy is quite excitable when I arrive at work the following morning, since she has been given Maggie's responsibilities already. Although not yet officially announced, the job is practically hers, so she is over the moon.

She can't stop giggling when I tell her about Josh. There was absolutely no need for any of it. He should have left me on the floor and minded his own business. It's only because he wanted brownie points with my lovely daughter that he was hanging around so much.

'Well, that should be the last I see of him, hopefully. I don't think he'll be calling around to see Rosie's mad mother ever again,' I laugh to Suzy, over our lunch break.

'Oh, Martha, what I would have paid to see that. What a carry on. You and that boy are jinxed,' laughs Suzy.

'Jinxed, for sure. Disaster seems to follow him around. I feel sorry for his poor parents. To top it off, now I have a goldfish to look after again. There was even a competition on the TV to win a visit to Copenhagen, but, of course, I can't enter it now because of Gareth. I know it's unlikely I'd ever win, but, you know... I won't be able to go anywhere,' I complain.

I don't admit to Suzy that my fear of travel is really more because of my panic attacks.

'Of course you can go on holiday, Martha,' says Suzy kindly. 'Do you think perhaps you're using Gareth as an excuse not to go anywhere?'

It seems there is no hiding from best friends.

'My goodness, not at all. You don't expect me to leave a poor goldfish all alone for a few weeks, do you? I have to feed him, make sure his water levels are all okay. Gareth is a huge responsibility,' I say.

'I understand what you're saying, Martha. But I'm just trying to explain that you can always find someone to help with Gareth. You don't have to take on all these responsibilities yourself, you know. Sometimes you can just be too... Umm...'

'Too what?' I ask.

'Well, I... I think you see yourself as a bit of a martyr sometimes,' says Suzy.

'A martyr?' I manage to screech. Her comment makes me almost choke on my chicken and mushroom Pot Noodle.

'Oh, my goodness. A martyr?' I repeat, once the stringy substance has cleared from my throat.

'Oh, Martha. I don't mean it nastily. Please don't take it the wrong way. I'm just trying to say that you don't have to do everything yourself. We'd love to help out with Gareth if you ever needed. I know little Angus would be so excited to have a goldfish in the house,' says Suzy.

I pause for a moment while I take on board what she is saying. Are people starting to realise that I am making a lot of excuses to avoid things? A martyr, though! Is that what people call me behind my back when I'm not at work? Do they say dreadful things like 'Where's Martha the Martyr?'?

'Look, all I'm saying is that if you do ever need a break or anything, Gareth would be safe with us,' continues Suzy. 'Please, think about it.'

'I probably won't go anywhere, as I quite fancy investing in a conservatory, but thanks. Besides, my new boss needs me here.' I respond.

'Ah… That's something else I need to discuss with you. As you know, I'm not officially your boss yet, but Rebecca did take me aside to ask why people have so much holiday entitlement remaining. Do you realise you have a lot of holiday time owing to you? You have over a month to take, what with flexitime and all. Why don't you take a break?' says Suzy.

I shrug my shoulders. The braver, old me, knows that a change of scenery is just what I need, but I am not confident enough to go alone. I wish a friend could come with me, but, just like Suzy, they're all home with their families.

I fill the rest of the day by daydreaming about the decision I should make. Should I text the number and enter the competition? I would love to do something to cheer myself up after Rosie leaving, but what? A sensible conservatory is probably the wisest decision.

As soon as I finish work, I look at conservatories online. With so much glass, I may save on heating bills perhaps. Do they act like solar energy? Looking at the prices, I find they are much more expensive than I had imagined. I would certainly need to have some kind of return on it to spend that much. I wonder what value it would add to the house. Do I need planning permission? That would be another cost. Oh gosh, I never knew conservatories were so tricky. There are so many options too. Do I pick a Victorian one? Edwardian? And what on earth is an orangery? They all look nice. How can you possibly choose? I decide to complete an online form with one of the companies who offer a free 'no obligation' quote. It says that someone will ring me within the next forty-eight hours. At least it will be nice to get a phone call and speak to someone, I suppose. I am still waiting to hear from Rosie and starting to worry.

Whilst on the laptop, I recheck Rosie's flights. There were two flights she took, and both have arrived on schedule. It says the second one arrived on time into Tjilik Riwut airport. Where on earth is she? I expect it will be a bit of a drive to her camp, but she must reach there soon.

I am about to log off when adverts for flights pop up. That is the trouble with biccies, or whatever you call them. Companies track everything, according to Trevor. It is so handy having a friend in IT who can explain these things to people like me. He says there is even a dark web. I wonder if conservatories are cheaper on there?

Now I have some kind of robot chat on the screen asking me questions. Can they see my face peering at it? The internet is such a scary place.

'Where would you like to fly?' the robot asks me.

I find myself typing 'Copenhagen' and a departure date for the following weekend, just to get an idea of how much the TV prize must be worth. It comes back with a figure of nineteen pounds each way. That is astonishing! I never thought it would be anything like that. It almost costs that much to get to Cardiff on the train! My goodness, what a bargain. No wonder the TV station are doing a competition to win a holiday if it is that cheap.

Seeing the flight on the screen makes me desperately want to go there. Something comes over me and I search for the paper with the text number for the competition.

It is my last chance to enter as the closing date is tonight at midnight. I take a deep breath and write the short message.

A) Copenhagen.

My heart skips a quick beat as I press send. Then I press send a few more times. After all, the more entries I do, the more chance I have of winning. I put the phone down beside me and realise that the texts probably cost more than the flights. How impulsive of me!

I make a few cups of tea to calm myself down. What if I was to win? Already the thought of going somewhere alone scares me. No, I couldn't possibly go. I shall explain that my boss needs me at work. I made a big mistake. I mean, I am indispensable in the library now that Maggie is no longer there. I don't care what anyone says.

I bite the skin around my nails nervously. *Oh goodness, what have you done, Martha?* I shall make sure I don't answer any phone calls if I don't know the number and hope it isn't the conservatory man.

Just as I start to calm down, the phone jumps to life and I almost give myself a panic attack, until I recognise the tone as 'Dancing Queen'.

Finally, it is my darling Rosie! My heart wants to burst.

'Rosie, Rosie. I'm so happy to hear from you. Are you okay?'

'Mammy, I want to come home,' cries Rosie.

'Oh no, but you've only just got there. Perhaps you're a bit overtired,' I try to reassure her.

'No. I reaaally don't like it. I thought it would be like the celebrity jungle and we would go to a Palazzo Versace, or something. We are *actually* staying in a reserve in the jungle, can you believe that?'

'Well, umm, yes, I can believe that. Why on earth would you think it would be five star accommodation?' I ask.

'Well, I did pay quite a lot for the trip,' says Rosie.

'Yes, but that's possibly because you insisted on adding a stay in Lombok at the end of it. Volunteering was never going to be glamourous. How was the flight, anyway?' I ask, hoping that the answer is more positive.

'Flight was okay. I'd love a Greggs pasty though, Mam. I'm so miserable,' complains Rosie.

'Well, there must be something good, Rosie. People wouldn't go there otherwise,' I say.

'I suppose one of the volunteers is all right, but I can't even use my hair straighteners so he definitely won't be interested in me,' says Rosie.

'Boys aren't interested in your hair, Rosie. Don't be such a poseur,' I say.

I don't know where she gets such vanity from.

'I'm not a poseur, just honest. It's humid, and I look like a troll,' says Rosie.

'Oh dear.'

'And I thought I'd be able to post photos of my trip on Insta,' continues Rosie. 'To be honest, I wanted to become one of those influencers and people would send me free things. But I won't be posting any pics because I forgot my hairspray, Mammy. Can you believe it?'

'Aww, my poor baby.' I say. 'What drama!'

'I know, right, Mam? I thought there might be a shop somewhere selling it, but you can't get my spray in the hut shop thing here. I asked one of the guides when we arrived. You should've seen her face. Then, as if that wasn't enough, she handed me an itinerary for tomorrow's activities. I think she took an instant dislike to me after the hairspray thing. Guess what she wanted me to do?'

'Umm, look after orangutans?' I say sarcastically.

'No, collect the orangutans' poo samples for them to examine,' scoffs Rosie.

'Oh, dear. You're not very good with things like that,' I say, desperately trying to stifle my giggles.

'Exactly, Mammy. That's what I said to her. Luckily, the cute guy, Ben, said I could swap with him as he was helping build a play area for the baby orangutans. Whatever that will entail. But one of the girls was saying you don't even play with them. You just observe. Gutted, Mam.'

'Aww, well, maybe it's for the best. You remember when you dropped your favourite teddy down the toilet. You can be a bit accident-prone,' I say.

'Yes, but I miss you as well. I just want to come home. I'm thinking of asking them tomorrow to book me a flight back,' says Rosie.

'But what about the orangutans that need you?' I say. 'What about the palm oil scandal?'

'One person isn't going to change the world. I realise that now. I can't do this,' says Rosie.

'If everyone thought like that nobody would help anyone, Rosie. And besides, think of the money you spent. Are you sure you can't give it a try? It might get better,' I say, attempting to reassure her.

'Mammy, I want to come home. I'll go to the barbecue they have tonight to welcome us, and then I'll sort my travel tomorrow,' insists Rosie.

'Okay. Well, I look forward to you coming home. At least you tried it, and I am proud of you for attempting to help orangutans, but what a terrible waste of money. Let me know when you have the details for the flight, and I'll pick you up from the coach station. Maybe we can get some money back since you didn't stay.'

'Thanks, Mammy. You're the best. Love you and see you soon.'

'Enjoy tonight, and I'll speak to you tomorrow.' I say.

I put the phone down and wonder if it's possible to recall text messages. I need to be here for Rosie, not trying to win a competition to visit television studios in Copenhagen. What on earth was I thinking?

# Chapter Six

By the time I reach work the next morning, I pray to myself that I don't win the competition. Imagine having to say no to a free holiday! *For helvede*, as they say on *The Killing of Sheep*.

'Hey, what's up? You okay?' asks Suzy, as she watches me gobble my third consecutive digestive biscuit during my first break.

'No, I'm so annoyed at myself. I entered a competition and now I'm scared I'll win. They're announcing the winner tonight,' I say, reaching for my fourth biscuit.

'How on earth can anyone be scared of winning a prize? Unless it's to swim with sharks, or something, and then you just wouldn't enter,' says Suzy.

I explain what I impulsively did last night.

'Well, the chance of winning is very slim, Martha. It does sound like a wonderful prize, though. I'm sure there'll be lots of entrants. But, you know, perhaps you should visit Copenhagen, even if you don't win,' says Suzy.

'Oh no, I couldn't. I would never be brave enough to go away alone,' I finally admit out loud.

I don't admit that I find it hard enough to go to WH Smith on my own and have this strange feeling that I could faint in the queue and nobody would know who I was. I have a recurring vision that the other customers are stepping over me whilst they reach for a highlighter pen, sticky notes, or a packet of strawberry bonbons.

'Hello, earth to Martha,' says Suzy, breaking me out of my dark thoughts.

'Sorry, Suzy. As I was saying, I got totally swept away. It was a very silly idea. Besides, Rosie's coming home so that's much better than any prize or holiday,' I explain.

'She didn't enjoy Borneo, then? That's a shame,' says Suzy.

'No, you know how she is. I knew Rosie wouldn't be able to manage her hair. It will be nice to have her back, though,' I admit.

'Well, perhaps you should take some time off to be with Rosie? I bet you'd love that,' says Suzy.

'That does sound lovely. It would be nice to make the most of having her back. We could go for lunch together. Maybe I'll go to the salon with her. She's always going on at me that I need to get my greys covered,' I say.

'It's a deal, then. I'll tell Rebecca that I've persuaded you to take leave. And, don't tell anyone, but she's announcing my new confirmed promotion tomorrow. Hallelujah!' Suzy says, triumphantly.

'Oh, I'm so happy for you. You deserve it after all your hard work. By the way, has anyone heard anything of Maggie?' I ask.

'She's flown off to Spain for retirement, so Rebecca said. She owned some villa on the Costa Blanca an old aunt left her years ago. Such a dark horse. Who'd have thought she'd shoot off to Spain to retire, hey?' says Suzy.

I am flabbergasted. To think I felt sorry for Maggie. All the time I imagined she would be in the depths of despair, but it turns out she is having a more exciting life than me.

'Well, I can't believe it. I'd never have thought,' I say.

The news of Maggie sunning herself in Spain fills me with jealousy. How can she be brave enough to retire to another country and I can't even face a holiday alone? It hurts to realise that even Maggie is gutsier than me. I haven't always been like this. It's only since Anthony died. When Rosie was small and I'd drop her off at nursery, I would happily go shopping alone. I would buy nice food to make for tea for the three of us and I never once thought I would have a panic attack in a shop. Why on earth would you? What could there possibly be in a shop to be afraid of? Though I did once see a mouse scrabbling around a supermarket.

The news of Maggie being a braver person than me makes me want to beat my demons. So, on the way home from work, I walk into WH Smith and look around. I pick up the first thing I see, which is a pink glittery pen on sale. Ah, perfect. I shall give it to Rosie when she gets back. I am pleased to see that there is a bit of a queue, which means I will have to stand around for a while and can't simply run out of the shop like my brain wants me to.

I wait in the queue and hold my head up high. I am not going to faint and nobody is going to step over me.

'You can do this. You can beat it, Martha,' I say to myself.

'Pardon?' says the man in front, turning around to look at me.

'Nothing,' I smile.

That familiar wave of dizziness starts to take hold of me. It was having someone look at me that started it. My brain begins to threaten me. It tells me to drop the pen back on the shelf and run out. No, I tell myself. I want to buy the pen for Rosie.

Eventually I am served and walk out of the store. I didn't faint and nothing terrible happened.

Martha one, brain nil.

If I can conquer this, then I can be like Maggie. I'll be on my way to Rio next, just as Anthony always promised me. He knew it was my dream to go to the Rio carnival. He told me he would take me there one day. That was when we were first married though; he had stopped saying it more recently.

I am so proud of my achievement that I buy a lovely bunch of flowers while I am out. They were an absolute steal, only a pound for a colourful bunch of daffodils! Back home, I pop them into the crystal vase that my gran bought at an antiques fair in Porthcawl many years ago. I don't use it often, only on birthdays or anniversaries; it is far too precious for everyday life. However, today is a special occasion. My darling Rosie will be coming home soon; this is a moment that is worthy of bringing out the precious vase.

I put the flowers in the centre of the dining table and admire how the sun shines through the crystal, giving off iridescent shades of pink and blue.

Rosie must know I am thinking of her as I hear 'Dancing Queen' in the distance.

I rush in the direction of the ringtone that is coming from the kitchen. I grab the phone with one hand and a chair with the other and sit down to chat with her. How exciting!

'Hello, my gorgeous girl. You okay? All sorted?'

'Yeah, all good. Guess what? Remember I told you about Ben? He's so lush. We had a fab night together,' says Rosie.

'You had a fab night together? What on earth does that mean?' I pull at the button of my cardigan so nervously that I manage to loosen the thread. I don't want to know what that means. 'Look, never mind about Ben. Are you at the airport now? I've taken a month off starting next week so I can pick you up anytime,' I say.

'No, that's why I'm calling. Change of plan,' says Rosie.

'What you mean, change of plan? Has your flight been delayed?'

'Yeah, a bit,' says Rosie.

Disappointed, I stand up from the kitchen chair. I don't feel in the right frame of mind to sit still. 'When will you be back? I took a break from work to be with you.' I say.

I glance at the clock on the windowsill; its Roman numerals tell me that it is only 5:45 pm. Time goes so slowly without Rosie in the country.

'I won't be back next week, Mam,' says Rosie.

'Oh, dear. Well, when then?' I ask.

'I haven't decided. I told Ben I was leaving 'cause I forgot my hairspray. Can you believe he almost left his hair gel at home? His mam had to turn back for it. I had goosebumps when he told me that. It's spooky the connection we have, I tell you.'

'He needs hair gel in the jungle?' I ask.

Anthony would never have used hair gel, although he did once squirt out some of my hair mousse, thinking it was shaving foam. I suppose I should give this boy the benefit of the doubt. Perhaps hair gel is the new mousse.

'He's so funny, Mam. He's taking a gap year. He even has his own YouTube channel. He's totally gorg, and he films himself doing... Oh no, hang on Mam.'

My Rosie is hanging around with a boy with gelled hair and a YouTube channel filming himself doing what? And I thought Josh was trouble!

'Umm, you didn't hear that, did you?' says Rosie to someone in the background. I listen to what sounds like a male voice responding. I strain to hear what he is saying. 'Aww, is it? Brilliant! Yeah, I'll be there now in a minute,' says Rosie to the voice. 'Mam, I have to go. That was Ben.' Rosie breaks into a whisper. 'Hope he didn't hear what I said. Mortified when his head popped 'round then.'

I picture her face. I bet she turned bright red as she usually does when she's caught talking about someone. She always manages to put her foot in it.

'One of the orangutans just had a baby, so everyone's all excited. I have to go. I'll ring when I can, okay,' Rosie continues, a little louder.

'Sure,' I answer flatly.

'What's that voice for? You don't mind me staying, do you, Mam? You'll find something else to do while you're off work, won't you?' asks Rosie.

'I will, darling. I will.'

'What do you mean? You're sounding funny now. You're being passive-aggressive, and I don't like it. Remember when you sent me to that therapist after Dad died? She always said, "passive aggression is a cause of major conflict in families".'

'I'm not passive-aggressive,' I laugh. 'Honestly, I'll be fine. In fact, if you're staying on, I might go on a little holiday to Copenhagen.'

'What do you mean, a holiday to Copenhagen?'

'Well, I entered a competition. To win a holiday. They're naming the winner tonight. It could be me,' I say.

'Why would you win?' asks Rosie.

'Well, someone has to,' I say.

'Umm, okay. But Copenhagen? Isn't it dangerous? Look at all those murders you watch on TV. They're always in that part of the world,' says Rosie.

'I don't think that happens in real life. Denmark is supposed to be the happiest place in the world,' I explain. I don't need Rosie to add any extra anxiety.

'I can't imagine it's the happiest place in the world when everyone on telly is getting murdered,' says Rosie. She breaks off for a moment and it sounds as though she is speaking to someone.

'All right, all right. I'll be there now,' she says. 'Oh, I'm gonna have to put the phone down. Look, you probably won't win, but just be careful. I don't want anything happening to you... Like it did to Dad.'

It might have been two years, but the scars we both carry from the sudden death of Anthony are as prominent now as the day it happened. It has made us both terrified of losing one another and no matter how hard we try, it is never far from our minds. Rosie still misses her dad terribly. She isn't helped by the fact that I have overcompensated by spoiling her.

'Oh, but some advice before I go. Why don't you stick to watching *Coronation Street* or *Emmerdale*? Perhaps there's a competition to win a bus tour to the Yorkshire Dales? That might be safer for you.'

Her advice makes me smile.

'Oh, no, got to go, Mam. Ben's still waiting, and he looks in a bit of a rush. I'll send photos of the baby, okay? Love you lots,' says Rosie.

'Send me photos of Ben while you're at it. Love you lots, Rosie.'

From the photos Rosie previously sent me, I imagine her rushing out of the hut she shares with four other girls. There are no windows, it's all open, so I do hope she uses her mosquito net tonight. All sorts of bugs could creep in. I forgot to remind her to ensure she is safely tucked in, away from all the beastly creatures that could bite her on the bottom. I pick my phone back up to message her and remind her that she reacts terribly to insect bites, but something makes me stop. I can almost hear Anthony's voice. He always had more faith in her than I did. I suppose I'm a born worrier.

'She's a big girl now, Martha. She'll be fine.'

Smiling to myself, I remember Anthony saying those words when she started secondary school. I worried about her so much on her first day. Now I am doing it again, and she is a grown woman. Parents never stop fretting about their children.

An hour later, as I'm sitting in the armchair watching *Pointless*, I finally get the photos Rosie promised. The first one that downloads is of a tiny baby orangutan.

'This is Oreo,' announces Rosie in the message.

I couldn't be prouder if it were my own grandchild! What a beautiful baby. Then, a few photos of the girls that Rosie shares a room with download. They're starting to get a tan and look as though they are all getting along. And then I spot him. Dreaded Ben. His hair is preposterous. He certainly must use some hair gel to keep it that upright in such a humid environment. My goodness. His lashes are very dark. Is he wearing mascara? I worry my innocent daughter is being led astray by some kind of YouTube mobster. This is much worse than I feared.

For comfort, I look over at Gareth, who is swimming about in his tank without a care in the world. Life must be so much easier being a goldfish.

Pouring myself a sherry to steady my nerves, I message Rosie.

*He looks very unusual.* I type.

*Unusual? He looks like the rest of the species*, replies Rosie.

*Not Oreo, Ben.* I message back.

*He's not unusual. A bit quirky, perhaps, but that's a good thing. Look, here's a link to his YouTube channel. You'll see what I mean.*

Apprehensively, I click on the link. The only time I ever went on YouTube before was when I saw a handy steam cleaner advertised on the shopping channel, and it said, 'As seen on YouTube', although I never did see it on there.

I do, however, find Ben via the link. It says he has 27,000 subscribers. How does he know so many people? The video starts, and I see that unmistakable spiky mop of hair and notice that he is definitely wearing mascara. However, I have to admit that I jumped to dreadful conclusions. Beneath the mascara is a pair of kind, olive-green eyes. They almost remind me of Anthony's when he was younger. He is not some type of rocker as I imagined; instead, his channel is all about animals, and he is explaining how he has just saved some sort of mammal in the jungle. Ben, it seems, dreams of being a vet. Ben serves as a reminder to myself that I must stop jumping to terrible conclusions.

'Oh, Gareth, what a relief. He's a nice boy,' I say.

I message Rosie to tell her that he seems lovely and perhaps he is just what she needs. I imagine that even Anthony would have approved of him, although he always said he would shoot any boys who came near her. I believe he was only joking, though.

It is wonderful to see Rosie so happy. If only I could find such happiness too. It is another reminder that I don't want to spend the rest of my life grieving, lonely and afraid. The time has come to focus on myself and stop worrying about everyone and everything else.

I begin my new era of self-care by pouring myself another sherry. Its warmth tingles in my chest. I am ready to watch tonight's episode of *The Killing of Sheep*.

'Stay tuned for the winner of our competition. Gretchen will be announcing the winner after the show,' says the TV presenter between commercials.

It's going to be me, I know it. I can feel it. They might want me to travel immediately. They didn't say when the trip takes place. Maybe I should buy some new clothes. *Oh, you devil, Martha, you are getting carried away!*

I am almost trembling with excitement as I look up clothes on eBay. There are so many bargains to be had, and I am helping save more rubbish from ending up in some landfill somewhere. People are so wasteful.

The first thing that comes up is a lovely black elasticated skirt for three pounds. I wish I were a size twenty; how disappointing. I filter the search a little so that only the size sixteens are shown. Finally, one skirt catches my eye as it is just one pound fifty. What a great deal! It ticks all the boxes, as it's from Primark and polyester; however, it is bright green. Would I ever be brave enough to wear such a vivid jade colour? I remind myself that this is a new Martha. Recklessly, I enter a bid of up to four pounds. Whilst I'm on there, I go a little mad and snap up a pack of three T-shirts and a flesh-coloured T-shirt bra for underneath. Better to be safe than sorry, as mother used to say.

With three minutes left until the end of the auction, I see I am still the only bidder for the skirt. Oh, I do hope one of those mean people doesn't come and bid at the last minute. I can barely look. I close my eyes, open them, finish the last sip of sherry and wait. Forty-eight seconds remaining, thirty-nine seconds… Oh, the tension!

Amazingly, there were no other bids. It must be my lucky day.

'Yay!' I shout to Gareth. 'I got the skirt!'

Knowing that I am about to win the trip, I return to watching the remainder of *The Killing of Sheep*. I watch the credits carefully when the programme finishes, looking for the handsome murderer's name to come up.

Jesper (Morder) – Kristian Johansen

So that's his name: Kristian. I can't wait to meet him when I win.

As Gretchen comes on screen I can hardly cope. I focus on my breathing before I hyperventilate.

'And the winner is…'

Oh my goodness, I can't look. It's Martha Jenkins, isn't it?

'Julie James, from Scotland,' says Gretchen.

'What?' I scream at the TV. 'You can't be serious?' I can't believe the disappointment I feel.

Why is it that when you can't have something, you want it more than ever? Now I really want to go to Denmark. So, I find myself doing something completely out of character. I search for those cheap flights again and book them for the first day of my holiday time next week.

The airline offers me a choice of accommodation and so I also find myself confirming my first night's stay in a two star cheapy hotel in Copenhagen. Hotels seem to be easy enough to get, so I only book the first night and then I can see what I want to do after that. I'd hate to book a month stay and then discover the hotel was full of cockroaches, or even bed bugs! With Rosie no longer coming back, and a break from work having been forced upon me, there isn't much to keep me here. Except for Gareth.

Oh no, poor Gareth. I quickly message Suzy to ask if she and Angus could look after him.

Unfortunately, though, I wake up the next morning completely sober and realise what I have done. I sit bolt upright in bed in a panic. I grab my phone and look at it. I immediately see a message from Suzy. *Oh Martha, what carnage did you create last night?*

I peek at the message. Oh no, I don't want to read it.

We're so excited to have Gareth. We'd love to look after him. So happy you're off to Denmark. Sorry you didn't win the competition though. See you in work to arrange. Xx

Oh, my goodness. The sherry made me forget my responsibilities. I can't possibly go. Gareth could drown, anything could happen. I'll just take the break from work and stay at home instead, pottering around the garden. Surely I can find some excuse not to go?

# Chapter Seven

The sun shines down on me as I enter the library for my last day at work. I remind myself that I am only taking a break from work as suggested by Suzy, but I feel as though I am quitting my job today. The truth is that since Anthony's death, I haven't stopped working. I have been too afraid to stop in case I fall apart.

What if I start thinking about the nasty arguments that were becoming more frequent before he died? I don't want to remember the hurtful things he said when he was in one of his bad moods. Neither do I want to remember his death; the police and the shock on Rosie's face when she was told. I need to stay busy.

'Good morning, Martha,' says Trevor, happily biting on a Garibaldi. I am immediately disappointed that whoever was in charge of today's biscuits has chosen these. I've never liked them. Of all the biscuits they could have picked on this traumatic day.

'Beautiful day for it. Can't believe you're leaving this weather behind. Suzy says you're off to Denmark. Sure you want to jet off?' jokes Trevor.

The truth is that every bit of confidence has vanished since last night. Bidding on a bright green skirt, what on earth was I thinking? That's not me at all. Now that I am back at work, reality has hit me. I feel as though I will crumble when I walk out of these doors later today.

'Maybe you're right; I don't think I should go. It's too nice here. I could do some gardening. The weeds are dreadful 'round the back and—'

'I was only joking, Martha,' says Trevor, putting a hand on my shoulder. 'You bloody go and enjoy yourself, now. You'll have a brilliant time.'

'Will I?'

'Course you will,' interrupts Sioned. 'Urgh. Who the hell bought the Garibaldi's?'

I notice Trevor put his head down in shame.

'You all set to jet off then,' says Suzy.

It all feels overwhelming. Everyone is so excited for me, but all I feel is the beginning of a panic attack.

I concentrate on my breathing. How can I admit that the sherry made me do it and that I am now terrified? I think of Maggie. She would go. I scrunch my eyes together and imagine Denmark. Would it be as I pictured? What if I bumped into Kristian? I try to convince myself that the trip would be worth it if I got to see the sights of Denmark and tracked him down.

'You all right?' asks Sioned. 'Something wrong with your eyes?'

'You okay, Martha?' says Trevor.

'Sorry, yeah, just some dust.' I open my eyes to see everyone watching me with a concerned look on their faces. I am desperate to escape.

'Look, I've got to go, lot on today, it being my last day...' I say. A small tear prickles away at my eye and escapes down my cheek.

I quickly shuffle out of the staff room and don't look back. I head in the direction of the children's section and notice a school party already assembling at the doorway. Suzy must have arranged a visit for this morning, which is a shame as I don't know that I am in the mood for a gang of children asking questions. Perhaps Sioned can take over instead. I just about manage a smile at the teacher in charge and think of ways I can escape the noise of the children chattering away. I feel the start of a tension headache.

I hear my name being called and look back to see Suzy following behind me.

'Hey, stop. I was thinking, do you want to tidy up the adult biographies? You look like you need a break away from the kids today,' she says.

'Thank you ever so much. I'd appreciate that,' I say.

Grateful, I head over to the adults' section, which only has a young lad studying in there. It seems very quiet for a Friday, but I am glad of the peace and quiet. I pull up a chair and start working my way through the books alphabetically, even though I find it hard to focus. I can't even work out if Dylan Thomas should come before Alan Carr, and why did I plonk one of David Walliams' children's books in beside Monty Don? *Ooh, Martha, you are in a tizz!*

I try to pull myself together and concentrate a little when Mrs Morris spots me. She comes in three times a week, on a Monday, Wednesday and Friday. I know it is more for the company than the books. On many occasions, I have tried to discuss how she enjoyed the books she took out, but she can never answer me. You can also see by her thick glasses that her eyesight isn't up to much nowadays. So, unless she has a magnifying glass at home, there wouldn't be the faintest possibility that she would be able to read the books. I am so glad that I have the opportunity of saying goodbye to her before I leave.

'Hello, bach. How are you today? Suzy said I'd find you here,' says Mrs Morris. She puts down her shopping trolley and pulls out the empty chair beside me. 'Ah, that's better. Ooh, my legs,' she says, grabbing at a bit of elasticated stocking. 'So, you all right, bach?'

'Yes, I'm okay. Suzy sent me to the naughty corner,' I smile.

'The naughty corner? What you mean, love?'

'I'm a bit stressed today. I needed a quiet space.'

'Aww, what's wrong, lovely? What you stressy about?'

'It's silly, I know. I should be excited, but I'm supposed to be taking a holiday, you see. Haven't taken any holiday time since, well, Anthony.'

'Aww, you'll be fine, dear. Where you off to? Some-where nice?'

'I don't know. I want to stay at home, but I stupidly booked flights to Denmark. Not sure what I'll do.'

'Ooh, what a predicament. Well, I know what I would do,' says Mrs Morris.

'What?' I ask.

Mrs Morris is always wise. Whatever she says I will do.

'Well, bloody go, innit? You're only young once, my dear.'

'Oh, I thought you might say stay here,' I say.

'Why would I say that?'

'Well, it means going away on my own and I'm a bit, well, apprehensive,' I say.

'Aww, don't be silly. I'd come with you in a heartbeat but, you know, at my age… Anyway, you wouldn't want me as a liability traipsing behind you.'

'Oh, I'd love for you to come with me. Do you want to come, Mrs Morris?'

'No, bach. Only joking. I don't think I could even sit on a plane with my varicose veins playing up. You go and enjoy yourself. You might even meet a nice man. You're not going to pull with me behind you.'

Mrs Morris giggles so hard that for one scary moment, her false teeth become dislodged. The student looks up over his glasses in disdain at being interrupted by all the laughter. I have frightful visions of Mrs Morris's dentures smacking him straight in the face. I manage to calm her down a little so that we don't have any calamities and her teeth, fortunately, pop back into place.

'I will miss you, mind,' says Mrs Morris. 'Sioned doesn't give me as much time as you. She's always making excuses to get away from me.'

'I'm sure that's not true,' I reassure her.

'No. I can tell she doesn't want to spend time chatting to an old bat like me.'

'Goodness, Mrs Morris. Please don't say things like that. I love chatting with you. I'm sure you've got it all wrong, and you're definitely not an old bat.'

'Bless you, kiddo, but you get that feeling. Anyway, love, I'll be here waiting for all your stories when you get back. I'm not going anywhere… Well, hopefully not.'

Now I feel guilty for leaving Mrs Morris with nobody to chat to. What if something were to happen to her before I get back? I put the Jeremy Clarkson biography that I am holding down on the desk and get up from my seat. I reach out and give Mrs Morris a big hug – although hugging someone whilst they're still seated proves exceptionally tricky, and so I practically squash her tiny frame into the chair.

'Sorry,' I say. I hope I haven't broken any of her frail, tiny bones with my clumsiness.

Mrs Morris looks at me, slightly startled. She then straightens her pale blue jacket and smiles. Fortunately, nothing seems broken.

'Well, blooming heck, I haven't had a hug since my Gerald was alive. Even then, we didn't have much of that; didn't want to encourage him. No time for hanky-panky stuff in the later years, *uch*!' She makes a disgusted face and we both laugh. I had never imagined Mrs Morris doing anything with her Gerald before. I try not to think about it.

Hanky-panky… There will certainly be none of that for me either, now that Anthony is gone. It doesn't bother me. Although imagine if I bumped into hunky Kristian and he ripped his shirt off and offered me hanky-panky? What in heavens would I do?

I touch my cheek, feeling the warmth of my face and realise the thought of Kristian has made me a little hot.

'Oh, dear, have I made you blush?' says Mrs Morris.

'No, Mrs Morris. Nothing you've said, don't you worry,' I say.

'Are you sure? I shouldn't have mentioned hanky-panky, should I?'

'No, don't be so silly. It's me. I thought of something, that's all.'

'A man?' grins Mrs Morris.

'You wouldn't believe me if I told you,' I smile. How on earth could I ever tell lovely Mrs Morris I secretly quite fancy a murderer on the telly? 'I think we'd better change the subject.' I say.

I frantically think of something that will take her mind off probing me any further.

'How do you feel about taking this book out today?' I say, without looking down at the Hugh Hefner biography that is next to tackle on the pile in front of me.

'That's perfect,' she says, looking at the cover.

I check out the Hugh Hefner book for Mrs Morris, and she leaves the library happy in the knowledge that I haven't been embarrassed by her candid confession. However, she has made me wonder if I will ever have another partner. Right now, that doesn't seem likely. It would be lovely to have company to go to the theatre with, to take me for dinner, but perhaps I should focus on the positives of being alone. I mean, I have nobody snoring in bed or asking me for hanky-panky when all I want is to read the latest Scandi noir thriller that I found in the book sale. Despite the fact that I am still on the lookout for an elderly fall alarm, there might be some benefits to living alone after all. This is something that I consider for the remainder of the day.

Just before my shift ends, Trevor calls me into the staff room.

'I've got ten minutes on duty yet,' I tell him.

However, he insists that I go with him and rushes me along. We open the door to see Sioned holding something.

'Surprise!' says Sioned, holding out a big plate of cream cakes.

'I felt guilty about the Garibaldis,' explains Trevor. 'I thought perhaps I'd upset you this morning by not getting your favourite custard creams in. So I upgraded and got us all cream cakes. I don't blame you; Sioned wasn't pleased with me either.'

'Oh, thank you… But really, it wasn't the biscuits. Just a bit anxious about going away, that's all.' I say.

'Well, have a cream doughnut, anyway. Food always makes worries go away,' says Trevor.

'Thank you,' I say, grabbing the doughnut. 'Oh, I'm going to miss you all so much.'

I think I'm going to cry again.

'Hey, come on. It's only a holiday. You haven't been fired,' says Suzy. 'And I'll be seeing you later to pick up Gareth. Angus can't wait to have him over with us.'

'I guess you're right,' I smile.

Angus would be so disappointed if I don't go away. I don't have much choice now. My irrational moment means I am in too deep to cancel.

We enjoy our cream cakes and chat about Scandinavia. Apparently, Sioned's aunty once went to Stockholm and came home with a pair of red clogs. She wore them in her kitchen and fell into the Welsh dresser, and smashed all her china. I decide that I will steer away from such purchases.

'Hey, sorry to interrupt, ladies,' says Trevor, looking at his watch. 'Going to have to head off. Got an upgrade on the system to do before I leave tonight. I'll never get home at this rate.'

I say goodbye to Trevor, then Sioned and Suzy, until finally I am left alone in the staff room. I look around at the familiar interior: the big comfy red sofa; the tatty armchair in the corner that we always save for Trevor and the mugs by the sink. You can tell everyone's personalities from those mugs. Sioned has a big fluffy cat on her cup, Trevor has 'Best Dad' and a medal, and Suzy's says, 'I wish I were a Unicorn.' Mine's the boring plain white one. Perhaps I will treat myself to a Copenhagen mug whilst I am away, I think to myself, as I close the staff room door and finally make my way home.

At eight pm, an eager Suzy and Angus turn up at the front door, ready to pick up Gareth.

'I'm so excited,' squeals Angus when he spots Gareth. 'I've never had a goldfish before.'

'That's great, Angus. I hope you'll take good care of him whilst I'm away.'

'I promise, promise, promise. Scout's honour. I love him so much,' says Angus.

'Oh, he will. He hasn't stopped talking about Gareth. We're going to put him in your bedroom, aren't we?'

'Yes, Mum. I'm going to watch him *all* night.'

Suzy glances at me nervously. 'I told you; if you don't go to sleep, then I'll have to take him from your room, so don't forget that,' she says.

'Yes,' I add. 'I think he can tell when people are sleeping. He's like a magic goldfish. You have to go to sleep, or he can't sleep.'

Suzy mouths 'thank you' at me and picks up Gareth's tank. Even though little Gareth was an unwanted present, I will miss him. He's been very pleasant company. I can't hug Suzy because of the big tank in the way, but I touch her arm and tell her how much I look forward to being back at work with her again soon.

With Gareth gone, I take my mind off things by making a start on the packing. I find the small case that I used to take on our family holidays and half-heartedly throw in a couple of Pot Noodles to start with. I have heard the food is expensive in Scandinavia. I also throw in a heap of undies to last me a couple of weeks, socks and some comfortable shoes. I expect there will be a lot of walking involved if I want to see the sights of Denmark for a whole month.

Finally, everything is more or less packed, except for the most important thing – my passport. I search the drawers. Where could it be? Perhaps it is a sign that I am not meant to go. I fling everything about until I come across an old pair of Anthony's underpants and a T-shirt that I didn't know were in there. They stop me in my tracks. They must have got mixed up in the laundry at some point. They should be in *his* drawer. I study the T-shirt for a moment and then press it against my chest. His smell is long gone from it now, and there is only the faint aroma of pine from being stuffed at the back of the drawer for too long. I gently place it in Anthony's drawer, along with the rest of the things that I still can't bear to clear out. His Mr Men socks are still rolled up in neat balls at the front, as if waiting for him to put them on. I pick up one of the balls and unroll it. Mr Perfect. Why couldn't I pick out the Mr Grumpy socks so that I would think of him in one of his bad moods? His socks feel like a message from the gods. 'Remember, Mr Perfect.'

Once again it feels like a sign that I should stay home where I belong.

# Chapter Eight

When Anthony died, the grief counsellor told Rosie and me to take baby steps. We couldn't recover from the shock in one day, we were to take things step by step. So, I decide to take the trip to the airport step by step; still waiting for the slightest inconvenience to make me turn around. If the flight is delayed then I will go home, I tell myself. I hope it is cancelled and then I can tell everyone at work that I tried, but sadly my flight wasn't going anywhere. Maybe there will be a freak Scandinavian snow storm in the middle of May, I pray. However, I can clearly see my flight on the departure board and it looks as though it is on time. Drat.

In the airport lounge I sip at my tea. If this were to spill over me and I were to need a change of clothing then I would most definitely go home. But it doesn't. There are no inconveniences and the next thing I know, I am boarding the punctual flight.

Oh, come on, fate, flights are never this punctual. Something has to step in to make me not go and have a jolly good excuse. Perhaps there will be a problem with the engines and we won't be going anywhere.

I take my seat on the flight. What if the seat won't recline? Is that a safety issue? I would tell the crew and then they might not let me use this seat. There will be no other spare seats and they will have to remove me from the flight.

I recline my seat and test it out. It works and the child behind me slams the back of it so hard that I fear I might get whiplash. Cheeky little thing. He doesn't need as much room as me and my strong thighs. I would never have allowed Rosie to behave like that. I decide not to confront the family, though, as I would hate to have an air rage incident with a small child. Imagine if they restrained him! If anyone is being dragged off this flight, I want it to be me.

The doors of the plane close and the noise of the engines fill the cabin. It seems there is nothing wrong with the plane. It's time to accept that I am going to Copenhagen.

A wave of claustrophobia springs upon me, but I choose to fight it. Those doors are closed. I can't exactly jump out now; we must already be ten thousand feet up in the air. This is not going to help anyone, I tell myself. As I accept my fate, I begin to calm down. I must make the most of this wonderful opportunity.

For the first time since Anthony died, I am doing something for myself. I picture Maggie on a sunbed in Spain and remind myself that it is my turn to be as gutsy as she is.

I decide to take out the map of Denmark that I quickly ordered before I left. I may as well make the most of this trip and see the sights, now that I am on my way. I rummage through Anthony's Tottenham Hotspur back-pack that I've used to carry my hand luggage with my all-important passport and iPad. I smile as I remember how much he loved this backpack. He would take it everywhere, even if it was only a trip along the windy roads of Brecon. He was a man of habit, my Anthony. He always needed his copy of *Accountancy Weekly* and a tube of mints before he would leave the driveway.

I search around the bag for the map, but I am horrified when I pull out Anthony's lucky underpants that I put in there at the last minute. I'm not really sure why I brought them; it seems silly now. I guess I was afraid of the unknown and needed something familiar with me. I do hope the man sitting next to me in bright red trousers and a polo shirt hasn't noticed.

As I desperately tuck them back in, I see that the edge of a yellow sticky note has got stuck to the waistband. It's rather crumpled. It must have been in the rucksack all along and I didn't notice. I open it up, and smooth it out on the tray table in front of me. It's Anthony's writing. I read it carefully.

*I'm so sorry we argued, I love you with all my heart. Always yours, A x*

A gasping noise comes from deep in the back of my throat. Oh, Anthony. When did he write this? So, he didn't mean to be nasty. Where was he even going to stick this?

I look up when I hear an insistent voice.

'Anything? Can I get you anything?' says one of the cabin crew.

I was going to have tea, but I have had quite the shock. I try to speak. It comes out as a squeak at first, but I clear my throat and manage to ask for a sherry.

'Sorry, we don't have any sherry,' says the young lady.

I catch her looking at the male steward, and she rolls her eyes; he puts his head down to avoid anyone noticing his sniggering face. Quite why they are mocking me, I don't know. Have they not tasted sherry? It's not only for people with a blue rinse, you know. I decide that I won't tell her about the big red lipstick stain that she has on her teeth.

'We have gin, vodka...' she says after she has composed herself. This is as bad as when I had my supermarket delivery substitution, and they gave me Cornflakes instead of my usual Weetabix. Those spirits really are no substitute for a sherry, but right now I would take just about anything.

'I'll try a gin and tonic then, please.' I say. 'Yes, gin and some crisps. Thank you.' I think I need some emergency carbs.

The young lady hands me my gin and tonic, along with my change.

'Goodness, is that the price?' I say out loud, as I notice what is left of my twenty-pound note. The lady ignores me, rolls her eyes again and continues responding to the requests of the other neighbouring passengers.

I look down at the note once more. *Oh, Anthony.* I take a huge sip of the gin. I don't want to start crying in front of all these passengers. I gulp back the tears and put the note safely away.

The man beside me closes his eyes and sits back, pressing his head against the headrest. I hope that kid behind doesn't start whacking his seat, as Mr Tomato Trousers is looking rather green. I do hope he is okay.

I look out at the clouds for company. They remind me of Rosie. She swore the clouds were giant cotton wool balls the last time we were on a flight. She asked if the captain could open the window for her to feel them. I study the clouds and realise what she meant. They do look rather soft and hygge-like. It seems sad that we didn't make the most of our lives and hadn't been away for a while. Anthony always seemed to be at work. I suppose he was trying to impress his bosses for the promotion that he never succeeded in getting. It turned out that it didn't even matter in the long run. He worried for no reason.

I am still daydreaming about the time Anthony, Rosie and I were on our last flight to Majorca when Mr Tomato Trousers turns to me.

'I don't feel very well.'

'Oh dear, would you like me to ask for some water for you?'

'Would you?' he says weakly.

I press the call bell, but there is no response. I can see that the cabin crew are huddled in the galley chatting after finishing the service. As I try to wave and get their attention, the sniggering steward pulls the blue curtain around them and then laughter bellows out from the galley. I press the call button again, but still, the cabin crew ignore it.

'I'll go up and ask for you,' I say, trying to be helpful. I'm sure there's nothing worse than being ill on a flight, and I could do with an excuse to stretch my legs. Quite honestly, I am glad of the drama of a sick passenger to stop me thinking about Anthony. I knew I might get emotional with all this spare time on my hands.

I squeeze myself out of the seat, my bosom pressing against Mr Tomato Trousers' left cheek as I make my way past. The lady on the aisle seat, who hasn't said a word since we sat down, immediately jumps up as I begin to reach her.

Pulling at the blue curtain around the galley, I spot the eye-rolling stewardess. Only this time, she is not rolling her eyes but stuffing a massive baguette into her mouth.

'Yeah, we're coming to clear in the rubbish now,' she says, as bits of lettuce and mayonnaise splatter her chin.

'It's not that. There is a sick passenger beside me. He needs some water,' I explain.

Finally, she puts her baguette down and hands me a bottle of mineral water.

'That will be two pound fifty,' she says.

Begrudgingly I hand her the five-pound note that I had in my trouser pocket for emergencies. My goodness, what a rip off!

'Two pound fifty. I presume it comes from the very highest Himalayan mountains for that price,' I say to Mr Tomato Trousers, handing him the bottle of mineral water.

'You're a lifesaver, thank you. I'm so dehydrated,' he says.

He takes glug after glug of water, and the colour that had vanished from his face starts to return. Since he's looking a bit better, I repeat the price.

'Two pound fifty, can you believe it?' I say.

'I think I'm going to be sick,' he says.

I notice that he doesn't have a sick bag in his seat pocket, so I grab one from mine before he makes a mess everywhere.

'Here, in case you need it,' I say, handing it to him.

He holds his hand out then closes his eyes and pretends to go to sleep. I know he isn't sleeping though as every now and then he opens an eye to see if I am looking at him. He obviously didn't want to reimburse me for the bottle of water.

With not much longer until we are due to land, I attempt to pull out my map again. This time I have more success. I spread it out in front of me, and look at all the places I will be able to visit. I remember reading a magazine interview that said that some of the cast lived in a place called Esbjerg, so I use the pen I brought along for my crossword puzzle and circle 'Esbjerg'. I don't have time to mark out the other places I want to visit, such as Karen Blixen's house, as the cabin crew announce that the flight is about to land, and it's time to stow our things away.

I tighten my seatbelt as the plane bobs about a little. Looking at the North Sea below eases my nerves from the increasing turbulence. I remind myself that land isn't too far away now. The sea surrounding the airport is scattered with giant white wind turbines that look like super-duper modern windmills. I want to turn to Mr Tomato Trousers and say something but think better of it as he's still fake sleeping.

'Ooh, ooh, look,' I squeal to myself as a long bridge that appears as though it runs from Denmark to Sweden presents itself. I wonder if it is the very bridge that is on my other favourite TV programme? I take a shot of it on my phone in case. What an imposing bridge. It looks just as I had imagined.

I don't get the opportunity to bid goodbye to Mr Tomato Trousers as he rushes off the plane with his hand luggage the moment the seatbelt sign goes off. He looked a lot better once we landed. However, I saw a flash of his trousers racing through the green channel, but some customs officers surrounded him and led him away. He then looked rather ashen again. I wonder what he had done? Was he part of an international drugs ring? On an Interpol wanted list? To think, I was sat next to him all that time.

Whatever his offence, I do miss his company as at least he spoke English, unlike most of the people I have met so far. I know I shouldn't be surprised but all the food signs in the airport are in Danish, and I struggle to understand anything. I thought I had some basic grasp of the language after all the TV programmes I had watched, but the truth is I picked up nothing.

I realise from my previous extensive research that I need to find a train into the city, but I can't work out the ticket machine as it is all in Danish. I'm sure there must be a way to translate this into English. I do wish Trevor was here to help.

I retrieve my second-hand pocket English-Danish dictionary from my rucksack, hoping that it can help translate a few words for me. I press a few buttons, but it is no use. The system just spits out a list of towns I have never heard of. I spot some kind of tourist information person and head over to him. At least he looks like some kind of official with his badge and navy uniform. He seems pretty friendly and smiles as I summon him. I glance at each word in my dictionary that is needed to explain my predicament.

'Hello, *jeg er tosset*, from UK,' I say.

The man looks at me curiously. 'You're from UK?' he says.

'Yes, that's right. Oh my, you speak English.'

'Yes, but why are you telling me you are crazy from UK?' he says. The man proceeds to make a snorting sound as he bursts out laughing.

'Is that what I said? Oh dear, I am sorry. I meant to say I am a tourist.'

Once he stops giggling away, I explain that I want to go to my hotel in the city centre. He understands immediately and presses a few buttons on the ticket machine, and tells me which platform I need. This is so much easier than trying to read the instructions on the screen.

By the time I arrive at the train station in the centre of Copenhagen I gain a little more confidence. I feel so confident, in fact, that I attempt to stop a very tall young man who drops something on the exit floor. I pick up the strange small silver canister from the pavement. I have never seen anything quite like this.

'Excuse me,' I shout. But he doesn't turn around immediately.

'Excuse me.' I tap him on his shoulder and point to the strange canister.

'You dropped this, sir.'

The young lad doesn't look too happy and snatches it from me without saying anything. Not even a thank you!

I watch as he walks a few metres ahead and throws it on the ground again. Oh, my goodness, what a litterbug. I want to shout for him to get back and pick it up, but perhaps that isn't the best idea in a strange country.

Walking in the direction of the hotel, I notice more of these silver canisters on my way. Odd how they are littered everywhere. I pick one of them up for evidence. I feel like Gretchen, as I consider how I will investigate further and get to the bottom of these strange capsule-like things. Perhaps there is some secret mission going on, and young-sters are dropping them for others to collect later. Maybe Mr Tomato Trousers is the supplier, which is why he was detained at the airport. It suddenly feels quite scary being in a big city like this alone. What if I am surrounded by criminals? These people could be anyone. I miss the safety and security of home where everyone knows someone's uncle or cousin. Nobody is ever a stranger and nothing terrible really happens there. I feel incredibly uneasy as I make my way to the hotel. I look over my shoulder and am a little paranoid. Instinctively, I hold my handbag a little tighter and try to stop my imagination from running riot.

But then I turn the corner and in front of me is a larger-than-life statue of Hans Christian Andersen. I look tiny in front of him as I stand and admire it. He sits, stretched out with his long legs, a book on his lap and a cane in his hand. He looks over towards Tivoli Gardens and it is as though he is gazing over the city, keeping everyone safe. At that moment, the anxiety I feel about being in a big city vanishes from within me. This is a place filled with fairy tales; not darkness, I tell myself. This is what I came here for. My real-life fairy tale.

# Chapter Nine

Impatiently, I wait for the hotel receptionist to finish serving the lady in front of me. It is surprising what you observe when you have to stand in line waiting. Firstly, I notice the bits of wood that chip off from the dark mahogany reception desk and the chewed red pen beside a notepad with the hotel logo on it. Next, I turn to the guest who is keeping me waiting and eye up the casual trousers and comfortable boots she is wearing. She is also carrying a large backpack, with a flask hanging off it, and so I decide she must be on some kind of trek; that is until she asks where Tivoli Gardens is. Has she not seen it? It's not that far away. Perhaps she needs the flask for her hot water as she is planning on bingeing on Pot Noodles, just as I am. As the Scouts say, you should always be prepared – especially when you are in an expensive city and can't even afford a glass of water.

The hotel guest asks for directions for half of Copenhagen whilst I loiter behind her with a silver canister in my hand. I want to get to the bottom of this mystery. I've never seen one of these in my town. What does it do? What if it explodes? There is a sense of urgency here.

*Come on, come on,* I want to shout.

My patience is starting to run thin now. We could have an explosion here, and this lady is asking where Ripley's is!

The tension is so high that I could use dreadful language for the first time in my life.

'And this… Where will I find the Museum of Copenhagen?' asks the lady as she points to the map in front of her. An uncontrollable gasp comes out of my mouth, and the guest turns to look at me. I quickly look away as I have never been the confrontational type; it is so much easier being passive-aggressive.

The receptionist continues with her directions, and I notice what perfect English she has. I attempt to calm myself down by being grateful that at least I will be able to explain everything to her.

Finally, the tourist is given all the information she needs to start exploring, and it is my turn to be served.

'*Hej, velkommen*,' says the friendly receptionist.

'Hello, I'm checking in…'

'Fantastic. If you can fill this card in for me.'

'Yes, of course. But before I do, I have something urgent. Can I ask you a question?'

'Sure,' she smiles.

'You see this.' I hold my hand out to show her the cannister.

The receptionist looks at me and grins. 'Okay, what about this?'

'I wondered if you could explain to me what it is? I'm with the police in Wales, you see, and I wanted to investigate it.'

As soon as the words escape, I realise that I have said the most stupid thing ever. Why would I even say I am with the police? What is wrong with me? I just wanted to sound important.

'You're a policewoman? Why then don't you know what this is? Every teenager is doing this now,' says the receptionist.

'Not where I'm from, they're not. What is it? It's not drugs, is it?' I ask, putting it down on the desk, suddenly worried I will become intoxicated and start hallucinating.

The receptionist takes the canister from the top and carelessly throws it into the paper basket behind her.

'It's laughing gas. Do you know? Makes you speak like Donald Duck,' she laughs.

'It's nothing to do with some huge criminal gang or anything?' I ask.

'No, I think you would have known this for a police-woman,' laughs the receptionist.

I feel ridiculous and complete my form in silence. I suppose there is a reason I am not Gretchen Rasmussen. I remind myself that I am merely a librarian with an overactive imagination, and head to my room with my tail between my legs.

–

After a long day of travelling, I am eager to get to bed. However, what surprises me after having brushed my teeth, put on my long comfortable nightshirt and climbed into bed, is that the loneliness I thought I would escape from has followed me to Denmark. How could that possibly happen?

I came away to escape my life, but the truth is that I eluded nothing, and for a moment, I feel sorrier for myself than ever, as I realise I don't even have Gareth to talk to. What a shame you can't take your goldfish on the plane with you.

Perhaps I should be grateful for the hotel background noise that makes me realise I am not alone in this world. Thankfully, I don't understand the words coming from the room next door, for I fear they might be rather rude, as the couple enjoy their noisy evening of passion. Of course, I could do without the passion, but how nice it must be to have someone to put your cold feet on. Even now, my feet are cold, despite the room being at a comfortable temperature. So, I seek out the comfort of my Nordic socks. I pull them tightly up my shins, and they comfort me until I finally fall asleep.

At 2:22 am, I wake up to the sound of a fire alarm. A blue flashing light illuminates the room. It takes me a moment to realise where I am until I remember I am in a hotel and on the eighth floor. I quickly run out of the door to the exit and get down as many flights of stairs as I can. Thank goodness I am wearing my socks.

Streams of people come running down the stairs in their dressing gowns until we all tumble out onto the street.

'Is there a fire?' I ask. It might seem an obvious question, but there are always false alarms.

'Yes, on the first floor,' says the receptionist who was on duty earlier.

'Room 803, yes?' she says, ticking off a list in front of her.

All around me, people stand about on the street and then two fire engines screech in front of the hotel. Now I understand why Hans Christian Andersen is thought to have carried a rope around with him when he was travelling, in case he was in a hotel fire. I think I might do the same after this.

Beside me, a young couple starts kissing. Don't they realise we are in the midst of a severe emergency? I would put money on it they are the ones in the room next door – they are all over each other! Goodness, even on our honeymoon, Anthony and I didn't behave like that. Although, secretly, I would have liked Anthony to have been a bit more passionate. Of course, I never told him that. I think back and realise that we should have communicated with each other a lot more. Instead, I don't know that either of us really told each other what we were thinking. The sticky note is a prime example. Why did he have to write that down instead of simply telling me? My marriage was just like that of my parents. No communication and everything always brushed under the carpet until it was too much and there was an eruption. Anthony never opened up to me. Perhaps I should say what I think in future and throw caution to the wind a little more.

However, before I can think about anything else, I sense an imminent panic attack. Oh no, I thought I might have left these back at home.

My head becomes dizzy, and my heart is beating so fast it feels as though it will explode. I lean against the wall and take deep breaths. Please let nobody notice anything is wrong. Why would I suddenly get a panic attack at the thought of Anthony and me and our relationship?

'Are you okay?' asks the receptionist.

'I'm fine,' I respond, between deep breaths.

'We shouldn't be too much longer. I think we'll be back inside in five minutes. Just a small oven fire,' she adds.

Fortunately, focusing on the receptionist calms my heart rate, and I distract myself by watching the firemen run back and forth to the two fire engines. It is then that it truly dawns on me that there could have been a serious fire here tonight. God forbid I could have died, and what would I have achieved in my life? Of course, my beautiful daughter is my most important achievement. But what else do I have to show for these forty-nine years on the planet? I haven't made a difference in anyone's lives, and the only thing I do for charity is donating or buying stuff at jumble sales. I am horrified at myself. I have been so wrapped up in making sure Anthony and Rosie were okay that I haven't done anything much for anyone in the outside world. I am just one speck on this giant planet who means nothing to anyone except for Rosie. I would soon be forgotten if I was in a fire. My photo would be in the papers for a week, and then I would end up in a recycling bin somewhere.

'Come, come. You can come back in now,' says the receptionist.

The guests around me wander back in like zombies in dressing gowns whilst I tag behind.

A whole eight floors' worth of guests await the two small lifts, all eager to return to their rooms. I stand and wait patiently as I observe the other guests. I look at the lady in the pink slippers and white waffle dressing gown. What did she contribute to the planet? The man wearing stripy socks and no shoes, has he achieved anything? Did either of these make their mark? Or is it only me who has never made a difference to this world? We could all have died tonight and how would each one of us have been remembered? This is something people don't think about when they shout at the barista because their latte is cold, or at a poor unsuspecting member of the public because they are having a bad day. But they should. Because this is how you will be remembered – as someone who gave a stranger a really bad day. We all need to be remembered for something.

# Chapter Ten

The receptionist isn't surprised when I check out earlier than planned.

'We had quite a few guests check out early after last night's fire,' she says apologetically.

'It's fine. I just thought I should get on with what I came to Denmark for. It's not the hotel's fault,' I say, making an excuse.

I resolve to find another hotel in Copenhagen that hopefully won't wake me up with a fire alarm in the middle of the night.

'Ah, what did you come to Denmark for?' she asks.

'To see the sights. And to see where *The Killing of Sheep* is filmed.' I say.

'Ah, yes, that's big in Britain too, huh? Everyone talks about it. But you won't find anyone filming at the studios. Some of the scenes are filmed far away.'

'Oh, I didn't realise. I thought it all happened right here in Copenhagen,' I say.

'*Nej*, many scenes are filmed in Esbjerg and around. I think maybe just the scenes in the police station are filmed at the studios. They film more in the country.'

How silly of me, it is obviously countryside in most of the scenes. How could I think it was filmed in a big city?

'Do you know where Esbjerg is?' says the receptionist.

'Yes, I saw it on a map. I think a lot of the cast come from there,' I say, thinking of the handsome Kristian.

'That's right. Well, if you decide to go to Esbjerg, you can take a train and stop in Odense on the way,' she says, reaching for a map and some leaflets. 'I'm from Odense, so I always tell people to visit. It's where you find Hans Christian Andersen's house.' She draws a ring around Odense on the map and hands me a leaflet about Hans Christian Andersen's house.

'Thank you, you've been most helpful,' I say.

I decide to leave Copenhagen after all and book a hotel room in Esbjerg that the receptionist recommends for this evening. How exciting to do something on the spur of the moment. I only hope it doesn't set off a panic attack when I least expect it.

On my walk to the train station, I see a colossal tower shooting up from Tivoli Gardens. It is some kind of ride full of people screaming. Why would anyone want to go on a ride that makes them cry out in fear? I know I said I wanted to be a bit more reckless, but that isn't quite what I would have in mind for fun. I am tempted to explore Tivoli, but I decide to come back another time as I have my luggage with me. For now, I want to head out of the city and explore. I am so excited about the thought of visiting Han Christina Andersen's house.

This time, at the train station, I understand the system a little better and find the translation button into English. It isn't as difficult as I first thought and I feel quite pleased with myself as I manage to purchase a return ticket from Copenhagen to Esbjerg, stopping off at Odense. I have discovered that Odense is almost exactly halfway to Esbjerg so it will break my journey up a little.

I am one of the first to get on the train and I grab a window seat to enjoy the sights of Denmark. The carriage is soon packed with passengers and some stand up in the aisles. I wonder where they are all going.

We stop at various stations, all of which have completely unpronounceable names. As we depart another town, I smile to myself as I see windmills, pretty cottages, and lots of greenery whizz by. The countryside is absolutely stunning and already I am so pleased that I left the city to discover this. Being in the countryside makes me feel more like I am in Wales, although it is all so flat compared to the hills and valleys back home. I can understand why people seem to cycle everywhere here. Whenever we pull up at a station, I watch the passengers head towards their bikes that are chained up rather than any parked car. I suppose it must be a very healthy lifestyle here, what with the glorious fresh air and the cycling.

An hour and a half later we reach Odense. I step off the train and head towards Hans Christian Andersen's house, which is now a full museum according to the leaflet that the receptionist kindly gave me. I am not surprised that she told me to visit. It is such a pretty town with cobbled streets and is all very olde-worlde. How charming!

The museum is unmissable, with its tall glass windows and wooden structure. It looks so different to Hans Christian Andersen's former humble yellow cottage that sits beside it. I am mesmerized when I enter the museum and see a huge holographic Hans Christian Andersen and the wonderful displays bringing the stories he told to life. As I look around at the exhibits, I see a copy of his will. Elsewhere, there is a trunk with his rope in it. I think about the fire once again. So, it is true that he carried a rope in case of fires. At least Hans Christian Andersen left a lasting legacy, unlike me.

A shop on the grounds sells books with an official stamp from the house. I can't resist picking up *The Ugly Duckling*. How I can relate, although I am never going to become a swan.

After a couple of hours in Odense, I take the train to Esbjerg for my hotel accommodation. Onboard, I flick through my new book. I look at the passenger who sits opposite me. He is a young lad who is wearing headphones that are bigger than his small head. I want to tell him about my book; about what I have seen today. I want to share it with someone. However, I realise that he would probably prefer to listen to the rock music that is escaping from those oversized headphones.

After sending Rosie and Suzie photos I took of Odense, I pull out my iPad and type up some notes. I want to remember all these wonderful details. I don't ever want them to slip from my mind. It is then that I think of how people have travel blogs; what if I created a travel blog as my legacy? But then I realise that those normally involve adventures, like trekking to Everest or journeying along the Silk Road; not reading fairy tales on a train with a guy opposite drinking a can of Danish lager.

With an hour and a half to get to Esbjerg, I read up on how to start a blog. Lots of people do blogs, it can't be that hard, surely? The site I am on offers templates, so all I have to do is press one click and type in what I want to say. Even I can manage that. I play about with blog ideas. What blog could I do? It is then that it hits me. I could write a blog about my experience as a widow. A widow who was scared of living after losing her husband, but is slowly finding her feet.

I decide to call the blog 'Losing Yourself'. I did consider other names such as 'Diary of a Widow' or 'In Loving Memory', but I realise that not only did I lose Anthony, but I also lost myself when he died. I forgot who I was whilst I battled with my grief, so this name feels right somehow. I only hope people don't think it is about getting lost in Woolworths as a child or something.

I begin to fill in my first blog entry. Gosh, this is difficult. Do you introduce yourself? What are you supposed to say to strangers? Will anyone even see this? So I start with the obvious.

> Hello,
> I'm starting this blog because I hope it will help someone. I was recently in a hotel fire, and it made me realise that I wanted to do something for others. Unfortunately, I know about grief only too well, so I hope by reaching out with this blog, I might help someone feel better after losing a loved one...

I explain my story about Anthony and how he was killed in an accident. I don't go into the finer details, but I write how we had been together since I was seventeen. I tell the readers how I had not known any other life but the one with him, and how I suddenly had to lead a life without him. I omit all the bits about how loneliness made me do some irrational things over the past two years, or the dreadful argument that led him to lose his life as he drove in such a temper.

Finally, I sign off.

Please message me anytime you want to talk. You
can also leave comments, but please remember to
be kind.
Always here for you.
MX

I press enter, and the blog is live. Then I think about
deleting it. Should I have pressed that button? I have
second thoughts about talking to strangers on the internet
like this.

As I consider what to do, an announcement comes over
the tannoy that we have arrived in Esbjerg. Unfortunately,
I have to pack my laptop away, so it will have to stay online
for now.

It is time to try and find the film locations. I wonder
how close we are to Kristian's house or how big the town
is. I am confident everyone will know him and the TV
programme since it is such a big thing.

I hail a taxi to the hotel and decide this might be the
right moment to find out where Kristian and the other
celebrities live. I remember when Sioned went to Los
Angeles, she went on a tour of celebrity houses, so the
taxi driver should know the houses that they all live in.

I tell the driver the name of the hotel that I booked this
morning but, before he drives off, I show him a photo of
Kristian that I keep on my phone. I really don't mean to
sound like a stalker, but he is very cute. As Mrs Morris
would say, 'He's a bit of eye candy.'

'Do you know this man?' I ask.

'No, I never saw him. Should I?'

'He's a very famous actor. He's from here,' I explain.

'Don't think he famous. My kids watch TV all day. I
never see him before.'

'He's on a big Danish TV programme. You know, *Drabet på får*, it's called.' I pray he understands my pronunciation.

'Okay, I know it, but I don't know him,' says the taxi driver.

He might be a big celeb to me, but I guess he only had a small part in the show now I think about it.

'This lady in *Drabet på få*, Gretchen, she very sexy lady. Now I like to know where she lives,' laughs the taxi driver.

'Oh, she doesn't live in Esbjerg?' I ask. I thought she would be here.

'I don't know. But there is some filming. I know outside in the next town they closed the roads one day to film chase with cars. It was inconvenient for me as a taxi driver.'

I rest my head against the seat. 'Just take me to the hotel, please.' I say.

We drive past some cosy-looking pubs and a cobbled town centre until eventually the taxi driver turns a corner and pulls up outside a hotel that looks cheap but decent enough for the night. Quite what I will do here if I can't find all these filming locations I do not know.

Perhaps Rosie was right; I should have gone to the Yorkshire Dales, or Manchester to see *Coronation Street* being filmed, not somewhere I didn't know.

*Oh dear, Martha. What have you done now?*

I try to console myself with the fact that I can easily get back to Copenhagen. I shall return tomorrow if I don't find anything exciting here.

When I am settled in the hotel, I log on to the blog to see how many views it has had. I decide that if nobody has seen it, then I will leave it on there. If hundreds have seen it, I will delete it immediately as I don't want that many people knowing my business. Perhaps nobody will find it, in which case I will use it as my own diary. I begin to think that sharing my story of grief was another of my silly, impulsive ideas.

A counter on the page informs me if anyone has seen the blog, and I breathe a sigh of relief when I discover that it only has one view. I figure that will be mine, and so I continue with my next blog post. On the upside, I suppose it will be interesting to one day look back on these posts and realise how far along I have come.

I start typing.

> It has been two years since Anthony departed this world.

I can't quite find the strength to write 'died.' This sounds as though he gently departed and not the gruesome scene that occurred.

I continue…

> As I write this, I am practically on the other side of the world. I foolishly went to Denmark all alone to see the sights and the filming locations of my favourite TV show. Tomorrow I am going to try and find them, but if I don't then it might be a wasted journey. That's what loneliness does to people. It drives them bonkers and makes them do extraordinary things. I always find it odd that people can find themselves so incredibly lonely when the world's population is so vast. Isn't it strange? Are you lonely too? Let's unite all the lonely people under one blog.

I smile to myself as I shut my iPad off for the night. Putting my thoughts out there makes me feel so much less alone.

The following morning, I check to see if anybody has read my blog and then wander around the streets of Esbjerg. It is a lovely old town, with beautiful shops and restaurants. There is even a large McDonald's in the centre, which is nice to see. I think it's always good to spot a familiar sight when you're travelling. I have never been an adventurous traveller, always sticking to fried egg and chips in Spain, that type of thing. I am almost tempted to treat myself to a fillet of fish, but then remember that I have plenty of Pot Noodles back in the room.

During my wander around, I spot the sea in the distance. I have always loved the sound of waves lapping up against the shore, so I head in that direction. It takes me fifteen minutes to reach the area but it's not the beach, as I thought it would be. Instead, it is more of an industrial port, with big shipping containers and a small ferry terminal perched on the edge of the North Sea. I am curious about whether this is one of the filming locations, although it doesn't look particularly familiar.

I watch a ferry come in, and the passengers disembark. Foot passengers and people with bikes wait to board for its next departure. A young lady pushes her bicycle into the terminal building, and I can't resist stopping her.

'Excuse me, where does the ferry go?' I ask.

'Fanø. The island over there,' she says, pointing in the distance.

Excitement washes over me. What an adventure it would be to go to an island! I adore anything to do with islands, apart from that silly *Love Island* that Rosie talks about, of course.

'Do they have electricity and toilets on the island? Is it far?' I ask. I'd hate to have to use a leaf in place of toilet paper or anything.

'Yes, it has electricity and toilets too,' she laughs. 'There are also shops. It's just ten minutes or so on the ferry.'

The young lady continues heading inside the terminal, and I see a notice displaying the ticket prices. I hand over my kroner and purchase a ticket on the spur of the moment.

I am lucky to catch the ferry before it leaves on its next sailing and run straight up the steps to get a good view from the top deck. It's a beautiful warm day, and the sun is reflecting on the water. How glorious. This is the life. Never mind finding filming locations.

I send Rosie some photos of the boat and the view ahead.

*Cool xx*, she writes back.

She seems busier than ever with Ben and the orangutans at the moment. I have noticed her messages are becoming a lot less frequent than when she first went to Borneo. I expect that is a good sign, though, as she only seems to want me nowadays whenever there is a crisis.

The ferry crossing passes so quickly that I am the last one off the boat as I am still distracted by the beautiful scenery. The sea stretches out for miles in front of me. It looks so calm and peaceful. Across from the sea are colourful buildings that would no doubt be a welcoming sight to fishermen after time at sea. I am mesmerised. I notice that the ferry is already starting to load people for the return journey and a man dashes past me as I stand in the way. Finally, I get myself together and follow the other passengers who have disembarked towards what looks like the direction of the town centre. Even though I have never been here before in my life, it is as though I belong here. If I believed in reincarnation, I would say I was from here in a past life. Something about it feels so familiar, and the atmosphere is incredibly relaxing.

The sea laps against some rocks and it is the only sound I can hear. The sun shines above me and there is not a cloud in the sky. I look over at the sun glistening on the water and then it's like a mirage. I can't believe what I see. For a moment I think it could be Hans Christian Andersen's Little Mermaid, but I remove my glasses, give them a wipe and look again. It is a seal! I notice another pop along and one more. A whole family of seals are basking in the sun right in front of me. My goodness! What is this wonderful place? Oh my, I have never seen anything quite like it!

I almost stumble on the cobbled pavement that runs along the seafront as I admire the seals. I take a photo for Rosie and Ben, I'm sure they will love them. I walk further inland and see a row of the most beautiful thatched cottages. White picket fences surround them and each one has a garden packed full with pink flowers. People ride along the cobbled streets on bicycles with baskets on the front. It is as though I have stepped into a magical world that got stuck in a time warp.

I pass a traditional butcher with all sorts of meats and condiments in the window and an estate agent. How wonderful it must be to live here and buy your food in the local shops. I can't resist stopping and peering into the estate agent's window. Anthony always liked to look in estate agents' windows; he forever fantasised about properties we could never afford.

The houses advertised have thatched roofs and are mostly cute little cottages. They are adorable!

I have to prise myself away, as I am keen to see what else the island has in store. It is then that I see a shop renting out bicycles. Although I have not ridden a bike since Anthony and I shared a tandem in Majorca, I find myself tempted into hiring a red bicycle with a wicker basket, just like the ones the locals are riding. I pay a deposit and agree to take it for two hours. The man in the rental shop helps adjust my seat and hands the bike over. I wobble as I start off and almost knock a poor lady and her dog over.

*Oh, Martha, Anthony would laugh at you now!* If he saw me, he would probably say, 'Get off. You look bloody ridiculous!'

The memory of him sometimes being mean to me comes back into my mind. I can see him in Majorca when he insisted he had to be in charge of our tandem because I'd be 'stupid and get us both killed'. I knew I wasn't stupid but shrugged it off as I didn't want to 'cause a scene', as Anthony would say. Something inside me stirs. How dare he call me stupid? I notice my pedaling has increased, and I am going faster and faster on the bike as I recall that moment.

I fear I am on the verge of another panic attack but manage to make it stop. Feeling the wind in my hair, I realise that I am a free agent. Is that so terrible after all? But then a voice in my head reminds me yet again that I am the reason the man is dead. Perhaps if he hadn't been in such a terrible mood with me, he would be here today.

My pedaling slows as I meet some pedestrians crossing the road, which gives me time to recollect myself. I notice a pancake shop a few doors down the street as I stop and wait. My tummy rumbles, right on cue. There are queues outside so it must be popular. I can't resist parking my bike up as the smell of pancakes hits my nostrils. I notice there are menus in around fifteen different languages and I am pleased to find the English translation. My mouth waters as I read all the different types of pancakes on offer. I opt for the marshmallow and ice-cream pancake, which delights the inner child in me. Mother would never have allowed me to eat something like this. I manage to find a space on a wooden bench outside as inside is already full. I don't mind though, it is nice to take in the fresh air in the garden area. I make my order and am served quite quickly. I guess they need to get people in and out as it is such a popular spot.

The waitress puts my snack down in front of me.

'Goodness, this looks nice,' I say.

'Enjoy,' she smiles. She looks as though she is only too familiar with seeing the expressions of customers when they see these monster creations. I take a big spoonful of the whipped cream on top of the pancake. Oh, my goodness. This was certainly one of my better life choices.

Full up from my pancake, I decide I have had enough of cycling for one day and head back to the bike shop to return my bicycle in time. I would hate to have to pay for an extra hour because of tardy timekeeping.

With the bike dropped off, I make my way towards the ferry terminal. I am incredibly sad that I have to leave this paradise island. However, I stop in my tracks when I notice a tourist place offering holiday lets. I can't resist popping in to see if they have anything available.

A friendly man named Olaf welcomes me and tells me to take a seat. I swivel about on the chair as he explains that most of the holiday lets are booked from year to year, but he will check his computer to see what is available.

'Ah, I have one cancellation that might be good for you. It's quite far out. On the other side of the island, but it's a nice cottage. It's a little cheaper because of its location. Here…'

I look at the picture on his computer and fall in love with it immediately. It is a thatched cottage with a little white door and a white picket fence around it, just like the ones I have seen here. It is perfect. I check the price is within budget and, amazingly, it is cheaper than booking a hotel by the night.

As I have to pay a weekly rate, I decide to take it for four weeks, taking me up to the remainder of the holiday. I figure that I can use the island as a base for exploring, since it works out so much cheaper than any hotel room. I am astonished it is such a bargain.

'I'll take it,' I say.

'Okay, you want me to take you over there now?' asks Olaf.

'Well, I have some unfinished business in Esbjerg yet. I still have my things in the hotel. Can I come later tonight?'

'No problem. The last ferry is around 11:30 pm, but I finish around nine this evening. Can you get back by then?'

I tell him I can get back in time and bid him goodbye. We arrange to meet at the ferry terminal at 8:45 pm.

Heading back into what now feels like city life, I am so excited. I almost skip off the ferry as we get back into Esbjerg, then I head on one last walk about town before the shops close.

As I wander about, I keep an eye out for any familiar actors from *The Killing of Sheep*, particularly Kristian; you never know, he might be around somewhere. I look in all the shop windows, searching for those beautiful eyes peeping out from somewhere, but fail to see him. Finally, in the hope that he could be doing his food shop on a weekday afternoon, I go into the local supermarket in a last-ditch attempt to find him. First, I look around the alcohol department, then the magazines. What would a man like Kristian read, I wonder? Then I remember I saw online that he has children, so perhaps he would be in the frozen section, stocking up on meals.

That is the moment I see him. I recognise his hair. I have studied him enough times to know every part of his body. It's him. I know it. Instinctively, I start shaking. How can a grown woman start shaking at the sight of a man? My stomach is full of butterflies. I have to say something, and so I tap him on the shoulder.

'Excuse me,' I say.

He turns around and looks at me with hazel eyes. Oh, my goodness, Kristian has blue eyes. It's not him. I don't know what to say. So, I squeeze in behind him and pick up a frozen leg of lamb and say, 'Just trying to get this. Pardon me.' And I walk away clutching a leg of lamb and head to the till.

# Chapter Eleven

Olaf pulls up outside a little white wooden gate with lawns that lead to the beguiling cottage. It is even more glorious in reality. It reminds me of the pictures on the jigsaws my gran used to do of pretty country cottages.

Even though it is dark and I can't see everything clearly, I am delighted to have booked it for a whole month. This is what I needed and so much better than busy hotels in Copenhagen and Esbjerg.

'Okay, I leave you to it. Here's the key and the office number. We'll be in the office from seven thirty tomorrow morning if you need anything,' says Olaf.

'Great. Thanks for all your help... Oh, and here, I bought you a present. Well, it's for your family,' I say.

Olaf opens the carrier bag to see a leg of lamb that is quickly defrosting. Well, I had to do something with it.

'Umm, thanks. I guess.'

He quickly drives away, and I notice how dark it is here without the help of his car lights. It dawns on me that there is no lighting for miles around. The light falling from the full moon is the only thing that guides me up the garden path. Fortunately, it is enough for me to fumble about, and I manage to open the wooden front door. I scrabble around on the wall inside and feel for the light switch. I press for the lights to come on, but nothing happens. Oh, my goodness, there is no electricity! I said there would be no electricity on the island. That woman lied.

I feel the start of a panic attack coming on; the familiar dizziness takes hold and a feeling of sickness gnaws away at my stomach. I must take control of this before it takes control of me. Finally, I make out the outline of a chair and sit down in the darkness.

*You have never been scared of the dark before, Martha. What on earth is wrong with you?* An owl hoots outside as if confirming that this is the spookiest place I have ever visited. For a moment, I begin to think that the hotel was better after all. I try to steady my breathing and tell myself to think rationally. What would Anthony have done? Maybe there is a fuse box somewhere and something has blown. That is what Anthony would think if he were here now. Anthony would be logical. Surely there is electricity. I manage to use what little phone battery I have left and press on the torch. Finally, I discover a fuse box near the kitchen. I push hard on the circuit breaker, and a light in the nearby bathroom appears.

*You did it, Martha!* I am proud of myself for managing a panic attack in such a crisis.

With power finally available, I snoop around the rooms. Oh my, it is just perfect! There are teeny little floral curtains in every room like you would find in a doll's house. In fact, this could be a real-life doll's house. There are little white wooden chairs, and a small dining table with a plastic cover with another floral pattern reminiscent of something from a cottage Snow White would live in. A candlestick lays in the middle with a small candle. I am not surprised they need that if the electricity keeps going out. I make a note to buy some matches tomorrow when the shops open.

In the lounge, a weather barometer on the wall indicates that tomorrow's weather will be changeable. I must remember to take my mackintosh with me when I go shopping.

I venture upstairs, climbing the staircase with its open slats, carefully navigating them. I would hate to have an accident and slip. Nobody would find me here for weeks.

I reach the top of the landing, where I spot a bookcase full of books with Danish titles. One of the books is by Virginia Woolf, but it is a Danish translation. *Bolgerne*, it says.

There are so many books that my hand twitches forward, wanting to sort them into alphabetical order, but that would be a busman's holiday, so I resist.

Walking into the bedroom, I am surprised how basic it is, although sufficient. At least it has a bed, yet more floral curtains and a small wardrobe. I search in the closet for sheets for the unmade bed. All I have is a hard mattress and one uncovered pillow. I enter the other bedroom in the house, but still, I don't find any bed linen. There are no towels anywhere either. I wish Olaf had informed me where to find things.

I put my mackintosh over me to sleep, to combat the chill in the cottage that makes it feel as though it is haunted, but the travelling soon catches up with me, and I drift into a deep sleep.

It feels like I have only been asleep for an hour when a noise awakens me. *Tap, tap, tap.* Rubbing at my eyes, it takes me a moment to fathom out where I am. *Tap, tap, tap* it goes again. I open one eye to see the sunlight peeping in through the bedroom window beside me. I realise that it is already daylight and the tapping noise appears to be coming from the wardrobe. I am almost too scared to open my other eye, and it desperately wants to remain closed. I don't want to know if there is a murderer in the wardrobe. I should have known houses in Denmark had murderers after all those dramas I have been watching. What was I thinking?

*Tap, tap, tap.* I lift my mackintosh from over me and gingerly step towards the wardrobe; as I get nearer, the noise stops. Even though I know it is futile, I put my backpack in front of the closet to prevent anyone from jumping out from it. At least it will give me a bit of time to run if someone stumbles over it on the way out of the wardrobe. I leave the bedroom, closing the door behind me. I quickly forget there could be someone hiding in the wardrobe, though, as something else is happening in the garden. As I come down the stairs, I see something move outside. A shadow lurks around the side of a giant tree that I hadn't noticed last night. Does the murderer have an accomplice?

# Chapter Twelve

I lock myself in the bathroom for five minutes while I think about what I should do next. What would Gretchen do? She would probably have a gun on her, but I don't have that liberty. So, I do what any average British person would do. I make a good old-fashioned cup of tea. Luckily, I brought my proper strong Welsh teabags with me. Nobody is going to mess with someone with a boiling drink in their hand, surely? I calmly boil the kettle and get ready for attack. I check the view from the kitchen window and see the shadow is no longer by the tree, but there is rustling outside. Someone is out there for sure.

I walk around to the other window and spot a furry little bunny rabbit eating some grass. How wonderful! I do hope the intruder doesn't spot it. Despite the barometer's pessimistic prediction, the sun is shining down on the bunny, like some kind of divine occurrence. I leave the bunny munching away, oblivious to any danger, to check the other window. The rustling noise is getting closer and closer. And then… We come face to face! How on earth does Gretchen remain so calm in the face of danger?

'Flipping heck!' I shout.

I startle the intruder in the garden and stumble back onto the coffee table, spilling the hot tea all over me. I jump about and scream, trying to get my nightshirt off as it scalds my skin. Then, standing in just my knickers, I see two big eyes staring directly at me.

What is it? My word! Is it some kind of elk? We don't see these in our gardens in Llanelli. I have no idea what it is. I suppose it does look a lot like Bambi, so it must be a deer.

Goodness, I wasn't expecting a deer in my front garden when I woke up. As I begin to calm down, I realise that what I have just witnessed is yet again magical. It truly is like *Snow White*'s house here, apart from the mysterious intruder in the wardrobe.

I grab a dressing gown I left on the sofa and cover myself up. Now that I am confident there is no intruder outside, I walk out into the garden to see if I can catch a closer sight of the deer.

Unfortunately, the deer and bunny rabbit hurry away as soon as they see me, making me feel guilty for encroaching on their habitat. Eventually, the bunny disappears, and I watch as the deer walks off into the woods nearby. The only sound left is that of the birds. There is nobody around for miles. Nobody will ever hear my screams if there is a murderer in the wardrobe, I remind myself.

Sitting down at the table and chairs by the front door, I notice a summer house in the garden. It looks like a mini version of the cottage. I haven't the confidence to investigate it yet though; who knows what or who could be lurking inside?

Instead, I pick up the phone to call Olaf as I need to get to the bottom of why there are no sheets and towels, plus he might be able to assist me with the slight problem of a murderer in the wardrobe.

'Hi Olaf, I can't find the towels and sheets. Can you tell me where they are, please?' I ask.

'There aren't any. You have to pay a deposit, and then we bring you some,' he explains.

'Okay, that's strange, but... I obviously need them.' Why on earth would they not think I need sheets and towels? No wonder the cottage was cheap if you have to pay a deposit for a towel. My goodness, I wish he would have told me when I booked. Did he think I carried around a duvet in my backpack?

'No problem, I bring them around for you now... If you can give me your card details,' says Olaf helpfully.

When Olaf arrives ten minutes later, I ask if he can put the items in the wardrobe upstairs for me. I should have warned him, but I thought I might sound rather strange telling him there was an evil man in my closet that, technically, I haven't physically seen. So I pretend to busy myself in the kitchen until I hear the knock of the wardrobe door closing and Olaf running back downstairs.

'Okay, everything you need is in the wardrobe. Enjoy your stay,' says Olaf, cheerful as ever.

I look at his crisp black shirt and jeans; there are no signs of a struggle.

'Was everything okay up there?' I ask.

'Umm, yes, how do you mean?'

'Oh, just that I heard a funny noise.'

'I didn't hear anything,' he says.

'No, not now, earlier. Oh, never mind. As long as there are no skeletons in the cupboard.' I laugh.

Olaf looks at me, bewildered.

'Sorry, I mean... Oh, bother. Ignore me.'

I don't particularly want Olaf to leave. I want him to stay and have tea with me, but he rushes towards the door.

'Is there a lot of wildlife here?' I ask, trying to keep him here longer.

'Yes, the island has lots of deer, rabbits, birds,' says Olaf, reaching for the door handle.

'I had a deer in the garden earlier. Gave me quite the fright,' I explain.

'Ah, I should have warned you that you might find visitors in the garden,' he laughs. 'Now, have a good day,' he says, hurrying to leave.

Olaf bids me goodbye, and so I decide to get ready for my first day of exploration. I missed much of it on the journey last night, so it will be good to see it in the daylight.

I hurry to get dressed and decide not to bother washing my hair, instead scraping it back into what Rosie would describe as a messy bun. Finally, I put on my Nordic socks and walking shoes and head off towards the clouds ahead; it seems the barometer was right after all.

The dirt path outside winds around. I had no idea the cottage was so far away from everything else; no wonder Olaf said it was a good deal. It must be a good ten-minute walk before I see another cottage.

'*God morgen*,' says someone, smiling at me over another of those white picket fences that seem popular here.

'*God morgen*,' I say. What a pleasant man!

I carry on my walk and see an enormous Danish flagpole in one of the gardens ahead of me. The Danes certainly seem very patriotic. I can't imagine a giant flagpole in my garden in Wales with a big dragon on it.

Next, I pass an elderly couple who also bid hello to me and then return to chatting with each other. Everyone I pass seems to be happy and smiling. It is like I have landed in some extraordinarily happy universe where people are friendly, and Bambi is in the garden waiting for you to get up in the morning.

I soon find the happiness contagious and start smiling to myself, something I don't think I have done since I pushed Rosie around in her pram. Rosie would probably say I look like a madwoman, but I genuinely feel happy and want to smile at people.

I greet a man walking his dog, who is coming towards me, and he smiles back. I say hello to the dog and think yet again how wonderful this place is. Even the dog is happy and wags his tail at me. I begin to wonder if they have put something in the water.

By the time I reach the shops, my stomach reminds me that I skipped breakfast. I was in such a tizz after everything that I forgot to eat one of the Pot Noodles still in my luggage. The travel, sea air and skipping dinner after my pancake means I am ravenous, and so I decide to find a restaurant before I venture any further.

I spot an impressive thatched property in front of me, which has a metal sign hanging outside saying *Kro*, so it doesn't look like an ordinary house. I peer into the windows, and what I see looks like something from a Hans Christian Andersen storybook. Little tables are set with candles and jugs of hand-cut flowers, and an old-fashioned lantern hangs from the wooden beams. It looks glorious. I search in my dictionary to see what *Kro* means.

Ah, it's a pub. *Oh, Martha, you shouldn't enter a pub at this time of day!* Anthony would be horrified. However, I think of him and all the things he never managed to do. Life's far too short not to visit a pub for lunch every now and then. So, I find myself opening the door and sitting down at one of the tables by the window. Some excellent pub grub would be very lovely right now.

A tall waitress with long dark hair greets me in Danish. She says something like, '*Hej*, blah, de blah, de blah. Yah?'

'Umm, I only speak English, sorry,' I explain.

'Ah, okay. Here's the menu. If you need any help, just let me know.'

I look at the menu and see the word *Baksuld*. What in heavens does that mean? There are also funny dishes such as pickled herrings; *ych a fi* as Mrs Morris would say. I don't fancy anything like that.

The bell at the entrance announces that someone is coming in. I put my glasses on to see who it is and notice a very handsome man enter the pub. I self-consciously smooth back my hair that has gone frizzy and is flying away in every direction after the combination of drizzle and north-easterly breeze on my walk over here. Why, oh why did I not wash my hair this morning? Oh goodness, I can't look at him. He is far too handsome. Ooh, I think I am getting a bit flustered. I don't know where to look. I turn my focus to his feet and look at the sturdy brown boots he is wearing. Golly, he has big feet. I am sure Mrs Morris once casually said that meant something quite rude. I look at the menu again to take my mind off Mrs Morris and her lewd comments.

When I look back up, the man is sitting at the table facing me. Oh dear, does he have to sit there looking straight at me? The waitress seems to know him, and they chat in Danish for a while before she returns to take my order.

'The house omelette, please,' I say.

At least I know what that is, and it was the only thing I could understand on the menu. It comes with bacon, chives and crispy bread. Oh yummy.

'I'm sorry, that's for two people. You don't have anyone else joining you, do you?' she asks.

'Oh, dear. No, I don't. Oh, I fancied the omelette,' I complain.

I look at the menu again and realise there is nothing else on it that I could eat.

'I don't particularly want anything else,' I say. 'I'll just pay for my orange juice then.'

'Hey, you want me to share your omelette with you?' says the man across from me.

I stare at him, not knowing what to say. My cheeks redden. The shade gets deeper and deeper as he sits there staring at me, waiting for an answer.

'I don't know,' I say eventually.

'They're delicious. It's their speciality. It's just a problem when you're dining alone. I told Dana before they should make them for one person,' he smiles.

I can't help but notice his beautiful white teeth. Goodness, he is as perfect as Kristian.

'Umm, well, I was going to say that I didn't want any tomato in it. Would you be okay not having tomato?' I say.

'Sure, sounds good,' says the man. 'One house omelette, no tomato please, Dana,' he says, turning to the waitress.

He stands up and walks towards my table.

'*Hej*, I'm Lars. Do you mind if I sit here? I can't reach the omelette from over there,' he grins cheekily.

'Umm, no. Umm, sit. Yes.'

Oh gosh. I have suddenly become quite discombobulated.

'So, your name is?' asks Lars.

'Sorry, yes. Umm…'

'Your name is umm?' he laughs.

'No. My name is Martha, not umm,' I say, quite matter-of-factly. Oh goodness me.

He rocks back in his chair, and I study his face as he laughs. His smile reaches his eyes. It is a genuine, kind-looking smile. His eyes are an icy grey yet seem so warm. He has the build of a fireman and looks like he would save a kitten from a burning building, and all the women would swoon as he hurried out covered in soot. He seems pretty self-assured as he rocks on his chair, which makes him all the more attractive. *Oh my, Martha!* His presence makes me quite nervous, and now I am expected to eat in front of him. I have suddenly lost my appetite.

'So, I guess you're not from around here,' says Lars, trying to make conversation.

'No, it's my first day. I'm from Wales and stumbled upon the island when I…'

I stop and decide not to explain that I was silly enough to come in search of filming locations in nearby Esbjerg.

'I hope you like what you see?' says Lars.

I love what I see, I think to myself.

'Oh, absolutely. It's gorgeous. Are you from the island? Were you born here?' I ask.

'No, I'm from Skads. It's a bit away from here. But I do business here. That's how I met Dana.'

The waitress that I now know is called Dana puts down a pint of Carlsberg in front of him and squeezes his shoulder. She smiles at him, and I feel an immediate pang of jealousy. She is very attractive. I guess the two of them do suit each other.

'Oh, that's your wife,' I say, failing to hide the disappointment in my voice.

'No, no. I supply food from my bakery here, all the staff know me. So, I guess you could say I'm a regular here,' says Lars.

My heart gives a little leap as he looks at me. I don't even know what to say to him, but the best I can come out with is…

'So are these your rolls?' I say, gesturing to the bread rolls in the basket on the table.

'They are. Try one. Tell me if you like them,' says Lars.

I look at the poppyseed roll in front of me. They look impossible to not break a tooth on. They are so hard. What if the crown I have on my upper left molar pops out and I choke on it right in front of him? As he watches in anticipation, I can no longer avoid taking a bite.

'Sure,' I say and take a tiny bite, fighting with the roll. I fear I look like a nanny goat chewing on some grass. 'Lovely,' I say, once I've finally managed to swallow it without choking.

'It's my dad's recipe,' he smiles. 'It was a family business… Well, before he died.'

'Oh, I'm sorry. My husband died. It's so sad when our loved ones leave us. I just started a blog for bereaved people. Only, in some ways I am hoping nobody reads it…' I start, realising that I am rambling, and he won't make sense of anything I am saying.

I am relieved when Dana arrives with our food.

'*Hej*, one house omelette. Enjoy,' she says, putting down a cast iron skillet with a large omelette fitting snugly inside it.

'This looks good. It's always the right choice, even without tomatoes,' smiles Lars.

I smile back and start to cut out a chunk for myself. It looks delicious.

'How do you say in English… "Tuck in", is that right?' asks Lars.

'Yes, that's right,' I agree.

He puts his head down as he cuts up his omelette, and I can't help but stare at the top of his golden-blond hair. He is so adorable. I am not surprised Dana keeps glancing over at him. He might not have noticed, but I can see from the way she looks at him that she likes him.

I am wondering how I can discreetly find out if he is with anyone when his phone rings and he speaks to someone in Danish.

'Ah, sorry. I'm going to have to let you finish the rest of this. I have to leave. It's urgent,' he says, pointing to his phone.

'Oh, was it your wife? You needed at home?' I mentally thank my brain for thinking so quickly.

'No, no,' he says, holding out his finger, where there is a faint pale line but no ring. I notice that it is the right hand and not his left, so I am none the wiser. 'Just work. Oven has broken at the bakery. Have to sort it out,' says Lars.

He grabs some Danish kroner from his pocket and throws it down on the table.

'That should cover my half. See you around, hey? Hope you enjoy your stay in Fanø.'

'Oh, I will, Lars. I think I will.' I smile.

# Chapter Thirteen

At eight am, I am again woken up with a tapping noise. *Tap, tap, tap.* It's coming from the wardrobe again. Has someone been hiding in there whilst I slept?

The tapping is freaking me out. Someone is definitely inside the closet. I know that Gretchen would confront the noise in the wardrobe, but I have to finally admit that I don't have anywhere near her courage. Perhaps it is one of the reasons that I admire her so much. She has all the qualities that I lack.

I jump from my bed and run downstairs, where it is peaceful. There is no deer in the garden like yesterday, but I see the bunny tucking into the lawn again. I make tea and decide to dress quickly. As cosy as the cottage is, I am desperate to escape. I am not at all comfortable with the strange noise from the wardrobe.

As I walk to the safety of the shops, I spot a bicycle rental place in a small shed at the side of the road. There seem to be many rental places dotted around the island; no wonder there are so many people on bikes. I venture inside the shed, noticing a shiny blue bicycle with a white wicker basket on the front.

'It's six-speed,' the man hiring the bikes tells me proudly.

I touch the smooth handlebars and the sleek metal. For a bicycle, it is undoubtedly impressive. I walk around admiring the bike. It gives me the same feeling as when I picked up my Renault Duster from the showroom.

'Can I hire it for a month?' I ask.

'Sure,' the man tells me.

I eagerly pay the deposit, along with the rental fee, in advance, and shoot off on my new wheels. As I cycle away, the wind blows through my hair, and I feel the freedom that my bicycle brings.

I follow the coast, riding for miles, and decide to see where the road leads me. Sometimes life needs no plans.

I don't even feel the muscles in my legs working over-time as I pass woodland and then a more built-up area, which must be the next town along. A bus hurries past and whooshes against me. It doesn't unnerve me though; my method of transport is perfect, and although there are a few clouds ahead threatening to erupt, even the weather is ideal. It's not too hot and not too cold. Like Goldilocks and her porridge, everything is just right.

However, as I get nearer to the town, the cycling becomes a little more complicated.

Throngs of people are milling about the cobbled streets. It is becoming harder to balance as I struggle to maintain my speed, and I find myself stopping and starting as people cross the street. I am surprised at quite how busy the town is for mid-morning. What is also strange is that the people are dressed up in old-fashioned clothes. They have long skirts and are wearing scarves tied around their heads. Some of the ladies are vibrant; some are wearing black. A little blonde girl dressed in one of the colourful costumes stands before me; she happily waves around the basket she is carrying, and I have to swerve. After almost colliding with her, I decide it might be easier to push my bicycle, as I have noticed many Danes do.

All around me, people carry Danish flags and wave them about. What on earth is going on? It is as though this is the equivalent of our town's carnival day. The crowds begin to part either side of the cobbled street to make way for something or someone to come through. I hear music. It sounds like a violin. People gather to each side of the road, happily chattering away. Yes, it is most certainly a carnival or parade of some kind.

I strain my neck to discover what is happening further ahead and see men and women walking through the centre of the road, playing folk music with violins. The women are dressed in the same costumes that everyone around me is wearing. A tall man walks in front of them in black tails and a big top hat. He reminds me of a funeral director, but I think he is part of the parade.

People are singing and clapping, and couples start dancing together. How magical. I begin to wonder if I am still alive or if something has happened and I have travelled back to the past. But then I realise that I am in the present as I see someone in front of me. I blink my eyes a few times to make sure I am not mistaken.

It's Lars.

I didn't expect to bump into him this soon. Of course, I secretly hoped I would, but it comes as a surprise when I spot him nonchalantly entering a small supermarket. I know it is him right away because, as extra confirmation, he is carrying a plastic basket full of loaves. Unlike when I had my phantom sighting of Kristian, I positively know that it is Lars as I park my bike up and stroll in and attempt to get his attention.

However, when I see him, he is chatting to one of the supermarket workers. It makes me feel insanely jealous. She is beautiful with dark skin, brown eyes that twinkle as she talks to him, and the sleekest dark bobbed hair. Does everyone have to be so flipping perfect in this place?

Even though it is a mild day, she has little pixie boots on and sways from side to side in them as she talks. She dazzles him with her smile, and Lars smiles back at her. It is as though every woman just falls captive to Lars' boy-next-door demeanour. What chance do I have? *He is not going to be interested in you, Martha. Silly, silly, woman.*

I can't compete with these gorgeous women who so obviously adore him. So I turn around and attempt to escape before he sees me. But who am I kidding? He wouldn't even remember me. I slip through the exit unnoticed, and then I hear someone speaking English.

'Omelette lady! Omelette lady!'

Could he be talking to me? Surely not. Anyway, my name is Martha, not Omelette lady, for heaven's sake.

I take a sneaky peek behind me and see him smiling at me with empty bread baskets in his hands, having finished his delivery.

'Ah, I told you I would see you around. Fanø isn't such a big place,' he says.

'Oh, hello. I didn't see you there,' I lie.

I try to be friendly, but his female fan club has deterred me slightly.

'So, what are you having for lunch today? I don't have time to share an omelette with you, sorry. I have more deliveries to do. It's a busy day today,' he says.

As I focus on Lars' handsome face, I point to the crowds around us.

'I can see it's a busy day. Something going on?' I manage.

'Yes, It's *Fannikerdagen*,'

'*Fannikerdagen?*' I repeat. I cringe, noticing that it sounds nothing like the way Lars pronounced it.

'Yes, it's a special day to remember the island's history. It's a fun day with music and food. People volunteer to organise it… You came to the island at the right time,' explains Lars.

'Looks like I did,' I say, as I notice a folk band who have started playing nearby.

'I have to go now. More deliveries,' he shrugs. 'But, if you're around later, maybe I could show you something?'

'Um, like what?' I ask. I do hope he is not some kind of weirdo.

'One of my favourite places in Fanø. Would you let me show you?' he asks.

I find myself agreeing, as I am certainly in no rush to get back to the cottage and the mysterious banging wardrobe.

'That's very kind of you. Okay, thank you.' I say.

Lars looks at me for a moment, and I feel myself blush. *Oh, Martha, you are almost fifty years old and blushing at the local baker like a teenager!*

I hang around the town for most of the day, still refusing to go home. Really, I should head back to the cottage, get changed, and smartened up for my date. But then I realise it isn't a date. He said he would show me something, not take me to a fancy restaurant. *Ooh, Martha, you do get carried away!*

I spend the remaining few hours in the town, listening to the music and joining in with the atmosphere. Then, I treat myself to a delicious hot dog that a young girl serves me from one of the food stalls. It is the perfect afternoon and before I know it, I have to get back on my bicycle to meet Lars halfway across the island.

I see the bakery van as I reach the woods where Lars asked me to meet him.

He jumps out as soon as he sees my bicycle approach.

'*Hej.*'

'Hi,' I say, putting my bike safely on the grass verge.

I notice that Lars is still in his casual work jeans and those brown boots he wears. I am relieved that even though it is early evening, he hasn't gone home to smarten up either.

'So, where are you taking me?' I ask.

'Into these woods,' he says.

'The woods?' I look at the dense forest in the darkness in front of me. It doesn't look the type of place that would be safe for a woman to go with a stranger that she has just met.

*Oh golly, Martha, you only have yourself to blame for going off with a stranger like this.* He might look cute, but he is obviously a psychopath like you have seen on the telly. For some reason, I foolishly follow him. I want to stop myself, but I am mesmerised by him. It is as though he is the Pied Piper as I walk behind him, following his lead. We get deeper and deeper into the woods, and I become more nervous. I look back behind me; my bicycle is too far to run to now.

'Here, sit down and be very quiet,' says Lars.

I do as I am told. But then I feel something prickly underneath me and realise I am sitting on a thorn, so have to wriggle about.

'Ouch,' I squeal.

'Shh, you have to be quiet. Don't move an inch,' says Lars.

I attempt to make myself comfortable and stay as quiet as I can. I feel fidgety.

'Look up,' says Lars calmly and quietly. Again, I follow his instructions.

'There,' he says. He points to the sky which is perfectly clear except for the stars shining down on us. His face and hands are animated with excitement.

'The white-tailed eagle. Its wings are over two metres, and...'

I look at the bird flying overhead with a white tail and its bright yellow beak. It is quite a remarkable bird of prey.

'You know, in the eighteen hundreds, this bird was hunted. People thought that these eagles stole animals on farms. There were even stories that they stole babies. Can you imagine?' says Lars.

I have visions of the eagle swooping down and grabbing me by the hair. The eagle suddenly feels a bit too close for comfort.

'But then, people realised they weren't stealing babies. This bird reminds me that not everything is as it seems. You can't assume anything unless you see it with your own eyes,' says Lars.

No, I suppose you're right there, I think. I don't say I was worried he was going to murder me in the woods, not take me birdwatching.

As the bird flies away, Lars gets up to leave.

'In the nineties, the eagles were re-colonised, and if we are lucky, we see one like we did tonight. I come out here often to find one. It is my happy place,' says Lars.

'Well, I'd say most of the island is a happy place, if you ask me. You don't have to go far to find happiness here,' I say.

I can't help notice a hint of sadness in Lars' eyes when I say this.

'It is happy here, but there can be sadness too. Like anywhere,' he says.

I want to ask him what he means, but feel it might be a bit impertinent of me. I hardly know him. We walk back in silence until I see the glint of my bicycle's handlebar shining in the moonlight.

'Thank you. I've enjoyed this evening,' says Lars.

'Me too. Very educational.' I say.

'Do you think you would like to go for a drink sometime? It's nice talking to you. It's not so often I get to use my English,' smiles Lars.

Does he mean to go out for a drink as a date or simply to have a drink with a female acquaintance so that he can speak English? If it was a date, I don't even know how old he is. He could be much younger than me. Anthony was a year older than me, and that was about perfect. Why am I even thinking about how old he is? He hasn't exactly asked me to marry him!

'Sure,' I say. 'It would be nice to have some company. I'm still finding my feet.'

'Your feet are there,' he says, pointing down at my grey trainers.

'It's an English expression. Sorry.' I smile.

'I know,' he shrugs. 'My sense of humour. Ignore me.'

'Oh, ha ha.' I manage.

It is somewhat awkward as we stand and say goodbye. Am I supposed to kiss him on the cheek, shake his hand and thank him for taking me birdwatching?

'Okay, well. How about we have a drink tomorrow? I mean, you're on holiday. It's not like you're here forever,' says Lars.

Something about that makes me feel sad. Perhaps that is the sadness Lars touched on, when you have to venture from the island?

'Sure, let's have a drink tomorrow,' I say. 'Can I ask you to do me a small favour?' I figure since he didn't kill me in the woods whilst he had the chance, I can trust him a little.

'Of course, what is it?' he says.

'Would you mind accompanying me home? Can you check my cottage for me? This might sound a bit strange, but I think someone or something is living in my bedroom wardrobe.'

Lars laughs at my comment, even though it is a serious concern for me.

'You know this is a very safe place, yeah? I'll check, but I'm sure you have nothing to worry about,' says Lars.

I put my bicycle into the back of his van and explain where I am staying. I don't need to give him directions; he seems to know the island like the back of his hand.

I am glad of his company as we pull up in the dark. We enter the cottage, and I turn the lights on whilst he runs upstairs to check my room.

'No, nothing there,' he says moments later. 'Perhaps it is the wind you can hear?'

'No. It's not like the wind. It's a knocking noise,' I say.

I tap on the front door and attempt to explain the noise I hear, but Lars doesn't think it is anything unusual.

'Nothing to worry about, I'm sure. Really. Look, I'd better head back. See you at six pm tomorrow. Is that okay? I have an early start in the bakery on Monday, so can't stay out late.'

I arrange to meet him at the bar since it is pretty easy to get to on my bicycle, and Lars heads off.

Even though Lars assures me that all is safe upstairs, I delay going to bed for as long as possible. I decide to procrastinate by logging on to the blog and seeing how many people have viewed it today. I am pleased that there are no more viewers, so I start to confess more of my feelings.

I have had the most incredible evening. Who knew birdwatching could be so much fun? But whilst I am enjoying myself, I am reminded that my husband is dead and can't enjoy himself. I am so ashamed. I know people always say, 'He would want you to be happy', or 'It's what he would have wanted,' when someone starts to move on after the death of their partner, but is that true? Do you really think your husband would be happy knowing his life is over, and you are sleeping with another man, for example? Of course, nothing quite like this has happened to me. I only went birdwatching! But I feel so awfully guilty. What do you think, dear readers? When can you move on? Is two years too soon?

I shut my laptop away for the night and finally head to bed. But when I walk into the bedroom, I see something horrific.

I was in such a rush this morning that I left my big knickers hanging off the edge of the bed. Lars would have certainly seen them. You can't exactly miss them.

There and then, I decide that I will most definitely not be going for that drink tomorrow. So instead, I shall hide for the rest of my life and hope I never see him again.

# Chapter Fourteen

*Tap, tap, tap.* I rub my eyes. Ouch, it feels like the middle of the night. I check the phone beside me, which shows it's 6:30 am. The murderer in the wardrobe is starting early today. I wrap the pillow around my head to try and block out the noise, but still it continues, *tap, tap, tap.* It is a worrying din that won't go away. However, this morning, instead of running away, I decide it is time to find out what is going on. Perhaps it is the fact that I am half asleep and not thinking clearly, maybe I am just annoyed at being woken so early on my holiday. I pick up the wooden chair in the corner of the bedroom, ready to smash the intruder over the head. Holding the chair with one leg, I gingerly creep towards the wardrobe door. The noise gets louder as I approach.

I open the door, screaming at the wardrobe: 'There, take that!' I assume that's what Gretchen would say, although in Danish, obviously.

My eyes are closed, too scared to look at what is behind the door. I didn't feel a bang with the chair as though I had hit anyone though, so I open my eyes slowly. I look around and see nothing. An empty room and an empty wardrobe. How could that possibly be? The noise was coming from there moments ago. *Oh, Martha, what is going on?*

Staring in disbelief at the empty wardrobe, I hear the noise again: *tap, tap, tap.*

Now it feels like someone is behind the wardrobe, but that isn't possible as it is flush to the wall. What on earth…? I decide to go downstairs and bravely take a look from outside. The tapping seems to be coming from the wall itself. What if someone was buried in these walls, and this is their ghost banging for help? A shiver runs through me at the thought. I run around the back of the house to take a look and see if I can find any hint of bricks that may have been replaced or any signs of a struggle in the back garden, but there is nothing to signify anything horrible.

I look up to where the noise is coming from and see a pretty woodpecker with green and red feathers pecking away at a wooden frame that has come loose from the back upstairs window. I laugh at myself as I realise that it is he who is responsible for my early morning wake-up calls and not a murderer.

Safe in the knowledge that there is nothing sinister in the bedroom, just my silly imagination yet again and the work of Mother Nature, I crawl back to bed for an hour.

However, as I lay there, I start to worry about the date I am supposed to be on later tonight. I don't have a phone number for Lars, so I will just have to stand him up. He has plenty of women desperate for his attention anyhow, so he will probably enjoy himself and soon get chatting to someone. I don't feel particularly guilty for letting him down. He will be okay.

Sunday is quiet on the island, so I relax and sit in the garden before taking the bicycle out on its daily ride. By the time I get back, I realise it is already four pm. I should be starting to think about getting ready by now if I had kept my word about meeting Lars. But, instead, I read the Scandi noir thriller I picked up at the airport and haven't yet started.

A few hours later, after I finish my tea, I am so engrossed in my book that I don't notice a knock on the door. I am beginning to get so used to the wildlife around here that, at first, I consider it is yet another wild animal. However, when there is a bang on the living room window beside me, I am startled. I look up to see Lars staring straight at me. Oh, my goodness, I thought he would realise that he had been stood up and not come around and find me.

Why, oh why, did I show him where I was staying last night? I think back to that embarrassing time when that pesky boy, Josh, came round uninvited and I had to try and hide in the hall. If I'd had more warning, I could have slunk down in my chair and hidden, but now I have nowhere to escape. I simply look back at him and reluctantly get up from my comfy reading chair.

'Hello,' I say, opening the door to him.

'It's seven o'clock, where were you? I was worried something had happened to you, and you'd fallen off your bike,' says Lars.

'Oh, is that the time? I'm sorry, I didn't realise. I guess I was engrossed in my book. Oh, dear,' I say.

Lars looks at me, seeming quite disappointed, which makes me feel dreadful. I didn't think I was important enough to miss. Since when has someone missed me when I haven't shown up to something? I have never been that type of popular person.

I think of his words, '*I was worried something had happened to you…*' Really? He worried about this random stranger that he shared an omelette with. I can't imagine any good-looking chap with women falling at his feet thinking like that. Perhaps he has some kind of ulterior motive. I know it definitely wouldn't be of the hanky panky sort after he saw my knickers, so I can't fathom out what he wants from me.

'Sorry for not making it. I really am. Look, I don't know how to say this, but you're a very handsome man. You should go for a drink with the lady from the supermarket, or Dana. I don't think you want to waste your time being nice to me. I'm not exactly your type,' I say.

'How do you know what my type is? I enjoyed meeting you. I like to meet people from different places. Here, everyone knows my history,' says Lars.

'Everyone knows your history?' I repeat.

'Never mind. Look, how about a drink tomorrow? I have to get back to the mainland and catch the ferry now. Shall we meet at the pub at the same time tomorrow? Would you come and I can tell you a secret?' he asks.

I am intrigued. His history and his secret. What can he possibly mean? The Gretchen investigator in me wants to learn more. Does he have some kind of sordid past? I have a yearning to find out, and so I agree to another meeting. Only this time, I promise to turn up.

## Chapter Fifteen

Lars is already sitting at the bar when I walk into the pub. His short, spiky blond hair and stocky build stand out as he chats to the bar staff. I knew he wouldn't be alone for long. As he tilts his head to look at a newspaper that the lady behind the bar is showing him, I notice his hair is slightly thinning on top, something I didn't notice before. I wonder how old he is. It is difficult to put an age on him. Somehow, I feel he is younger than me, but there are also signs that we could be the same sort of age too. I look at the giveaways, such as the frown line between his eyes and the way the lines around them crinkle when he smiles. They all add to his appeal. I can see that the lady is enjoying his attention and can't help but feel as though I am interrupting something as I approach them.

'*Hej*, here she is. You came this time,' teases Lars.

'I did,' I say.

I am not sure how to greet him and once again am confused about Danish customs. Am I supposed to shake his hand, hug him, or give him two kisses as on the continent? What do people do when they greet each other in Denmark? Fortunately, Lars doesn't seem to mind that I am not familiar with any local customs.

'What can I get you to drink?' asks Lars.

'Do you have Harvey's Bristol Cream, by any chance?' I say to the barmaid.

'What?' she says. I can see that she has no idea what I am talking about, which is a shame as I always ordered one when I went for dinner with Anthony. I look at Lars' cold beer and feel a sense of adventure. I have never drunk from a pint glass before.

'I'll have a pint of Carlsberg, please,' I say.

*Oh, Martha, a whole pint!*

Lars leads me to a quiet corner of the pub, where we grab a table. I wrap both my hands around the pint glass, unused to holding such a big drink.

Lars lifts his glass, leans towards me and says, '*Skol.*'

I have heard it enough times to understand what it means, and so I try to teach him the Welsh equivalent in return.

'*Iechyd da,*' I say.

'What does that mean? "Yukky daaa",' he laughs.

I giggle at his pronunciation and find myself at ease in his company.

'You have to pronounce it LLUH,' I say, almost spitting everywhere.

'Oh, but have you tried to say "*Rød grød med fløde?*"' he asks.

We laugh so much at this that it makes me realise how long it has been since someone made me smile. Lars is so easy to get along with. Maybe this is why he garners so much attention when he is out.

We chat about his family. He tells me he has a sister, Agnete, who is older than him. I refrain from asking how old they both are. Imagine if he was much younger than me and a toyboy; I would be so disappointed. Mrs Morris would find it funny, though. She is always going on about toyboys, but I expect there aren't many men left who are older than her at her age.

Lars then tells me about his brother-in-law, Ludwig, and how he likes to grow vegetables in his garden. How they play chess together every Tuesday night and that he has been great company since his wife perished.

'Perished?' I say. What a strange choice of word.

'Yes, we don't talk about her. She perished,' he says.

'Like perished in a fire?' I ask.

'Just perished,' Lars insists. What does he mean? Was she killed somehow?

'I'm sorry, I don't like to talk about it. I promised I'd tell you some things about me, but... I don't feel ready yet. It's a sore subject, as they say,' says Lars.

'No, absolutely. That's fine. I understand. I found it hard to talk about my husband for a long time. Now that I've started writing about the grief, it's like an outlet that helps. Perhaps you should write about it? Get it down on paper and let it all out,' I say.

'Ah, I like to block out bad things and not remember them,' says Lars.

'Oh, me too,' I say, amazed. I thought it was only me that hated facing up to things.

'Anyway, I'm not much of a writer. I'm creative in different ways. I like baking and making kites. You know, we have a big kite festival here. I like to make my own every year. This year I am making a kite like an eagle,' says Lars.

His eyes light up, and I smile as he ebulliently describes his kite. He is so attractive that I can't imagine him spending hours building something like that in his shed. He looks more the type of person who would ride a motorbike with some woman clinging onto him. She would swing her head back, her long hair flowing, they would be laughing, and then they would pull up outside a cool party somewhere.

'So, do you?' Lars asks.

'Do I what?' I say.

'You were miles away. I don't think you heard anything I said,' says Lars.

'Oh, no, I didn't. I'm so sorry.' I daren't tell him I was imagining him on a motorbike with an attractive woman.

'Do you like your beer?' he says.

'Oh, yes, very refreshing. I might have found a new drink. At least it's easier to explain than sherry when I go out in Denmark,' I smile.

Lars orders us another, along with what he calls a 'special drink', whatever that is. He tells me I will like it and, as I am so adventurous tonight, I agree.

'Now, it's time for a little one,' he says with a big grin. He lifts the small shot glass to his lips, downing the drink in one. I look on cautiously.

'I don't normally drink shots,' I say.

'It's nice. I promise. It's aquavit.'

I take a sip. The clear substance stings my throat, and immediately makes me feel quite merry.

'Ooh, I could get quite used to this,' I laugh.

Lars looks at me for a moment longer than friends do, and I feel as though there is something between us. *But, oh, Martha, you must be mistaken!* I decide it must be the aquavit and that he can no longer focus his eyeballs properly.

We carry on drinking and chat about Rosie and how she is getting along in Borneo. I tell Lars about the baby orangutans. I tell him about the library and all my wonderful colleagues and the regulars who come in, including Mrs Morris. He tells me again about his dad, and how close they were. How he took over his dad's bakery, and how his father taught Lars everything from when he was a small boy. He tells me how they used to make *kringle* together, which he explains is a kind of pretzel. But I notice that he only mentions his close family. He doesn't say anything about any friends. I wonder what they would be like. Do they sit there birdwatching and making kites too?

Lars is trying to explain about some special flour he uses at the bakery when Bon Jovi starts blaring out from speakers in the corner of the room. I hadn't noticed there was a jukebox to the side of me. My startled expression must make Lars think I want to dance to the music that has surprised me. He waves his arms around and looks as though he is bursting for the toilet, but I think he is trying to dance.

'You want to dance?' shouts Lars, pointing to a small section reserved as a dance area. I would never usually agree to dance in public, but the combination of aquavit and Carlsberg are loosening me up. The last time I danced was possibly my wedding day. Anthony hated dancing of any kind. We only danced at the wedding because he was forced to do the first dance with me.

This feels so different. Lars and I laugh as he swings me around by my waist. Something tingles through my spine as I feel so close to another human being. I had almost forgotten what it feels like to be held this close. I don't want him to let go.

However, finally, he peels himself away to put some new songs on the jukebox.

'What songs do you like?' he says, leaning on my shoulder. It is as though I am seventeen again.

We look through the list of songs that range from the seventies to the current day.

'Ooh, Tiffany. I love that one,' I say.

'Okay, but if you have that, then I must choose one too,' laughs Lars.

He won't show me what he has put on but says it is a song we can dance to.

'It's a slow one,' he promises, with a naughty glint in his eye.

We dance to Tiffany, and I find myself bopping about all over the place. This is so much fun. In fact, I almost twist an ankle as I jump about.

'Careful,' says Lars, catching my arm.

As he steadies me, we look at each other, and there is definitely chemistry between us. The song trails off, and he leans in and kisses me lightly on the lips. *Oh, Martha, he kissed you!* I can hardly look up after we kiss; I feel so self-conscious.

'You're lovely, Omelette lady, you know that?' says Lars.

'Oh, I don't think so, ha. Um,' I manage.

Why is it that I find it so difficult to accept a compliment?

Lars kisses me tenderly once again, and my body feels as though it is on fire. *Oh goodness, Martha!*

'This is my song for you,' says Lars.

I listen carefully as the song starts, but as my ears tune in, I feel sick.

'Don't you just love David Bowie?' says Lars.

I listen, horrified to hear 'Absolute Beginners'. It feels like a sign from Anthony.

'That's our song, Martha and don't ever forget it.'

I can hear Anthony saying those words the first time I went over to his place for dinner. He played that on his cassette deck over and over, and from that day forward, it was 'our' song. This feels like another sign that I should remember him and not be making any sort of life for myself. We would still be together if he hadn't zoomed off in a bad mood that evening. It's all my fault.

'No, I'm not a fan of this song, sorry,' I say.

Tears start to fill my eyes, and I know I must leave. My heart is racing, and a panic attack is taking over my body. I need to get outside and escape. What was I thinking? I will never move on from Anthony or these blasted panic attacks.

'Hey, what's wrong?' says Lars, as I open the pub door to leave.

'I'm sorry, Lars. It's no good. I just want to be alone. It's not you; it's me. I'm the one with the problem. You haven't done anything wrong,' I say.

'I don't understand. I thought you were having fun. Is it David Bowie? I can put Tiffany back on.'

My heart is beating far too fast to speak. If I don't focus on my breathing, I will collapse.

I look around at the dark sky, which seems as black as my heart feels right now. I will never move on, and nor should I. Anthony is dead, whilst I walk about able to do whatever I want.

I have what I deserve. When I married Anthony, I made a vow that it was forever and even after his death, he is still very much my husband.

## Chapter Sixteen

I toss and turn for most of the night. Then, in a dream, I see Anthony's face followed by Lars looking at me. Finally, they are standing side by side, both staring at me. I wake up with a jump. Anthony is now even haunting my dreams.

I feel the sudden need to open the laptop and share my feelings. Typing furiously on my blog is instantly cathartic.

> I feel like I am going mad. I see Anthony everywhere
> I look. I hear his voice in my head. It is as though I am
> afraid of his ghost. What on earth is wrong with me?
> I think it might be guilt. I feel so guilty about the night
> he was killed. It is all my fault. When will this stop?
> Perhaps I don't deserve any happiness.

I sign off from the blog. Still, nobody is reading it, so it is now my confessional. Ironically, this was supposed to help other people, but now it is helping me.

Feeling better after my confession on the blog, I start getting my bike ready for today's trip out when Rosie calls me on WhatsApp. I am thrilled to hear from her; she is exactly the person I need to speak to right now.

'Hello, how lovely to hear from you. How's it going? How's Ben?' I say.

'All good, Mam. Just got a break from cleaning duty, so thought I'd give you a ring. I know I don't call much, but it's so busy here.'

'That's okay, I understand. Cleaning duty, though? You've changed your ways.' I laugh.

'Yeah, I've learnt so much about orangutans now that even their toilet habits don't put me off. Can you believe it?' laughs Rosie. 'In fact, they are such beautiful creatures, and I'm so good with everything here that Ben is encouraging me to train as a vet.'

'Oh, my goodness, that would be fantastic. But you're not very good with blood, don't forget. I don't want to put you off; just trying to be realistic,' I say.

'Being here has changed me, Mam. Honestly, I didn't even care that my hair extensions got ruined in a tropical rainstorm the other day. Ben says I'm beautiful no matter what. Even he is using less hair gel nowadays. Anyway, that's my goss. What's happening there?'

I think about my blog and wonder if I should tell Rosie. She might be proud that I am now using modern words such as blog, so I pluck up the courage to tell her.

'Well, you're going to be impressed when I tell you what I've been doing,' I start.

'Ooh, tell me more then,' says Rosie.

How I've missed our chats. It's so lovely to hear from her again.

'I've started a blog. It's about grief and—'

'A blog?' laughs Rosie. 'A blog!'

I feel my cheeks start to redden.

'Have I said it wrong or something?'

'Oh, Mam. You are clueless sometimes. Nobody is doing blogs nowadays. It's all about TikTok,' says Rosie.

'TikTok, what on earth is that?' I ask.

'Oh, I'll send you a video now and you can have a look. Well, I never expected my mother to want to be an internet sensation,' laughs Rosie.

'I don't want to be an internet sensation. I just wanted to help people. Make a difference. That's all.' I say.

As I say it out loud, I remember how the only person I have helped is myself. Therefore, I realise that I must make an effort to stop using it for my own benefit.

'Well, if you want to do TikTok, then I'll tell Ben to get in touch with you. He's brilliant at that sort of stuff. It'll be nice to introduce the two of you anyway,' says Rosie.

I don't think I will be joining TikTok, whatever it is, anytime soon, but it will be nice to meet Ben finally, even if it is only a virtual meeting.

'Anyway, listen, I've got to go. I'm sorting lunch out for everyone today. I'm making a salad,' says Rosie.

'That's great. You're no longer craving the Greggs pasties then?' I ask.

'No, everything is so fresh out here; I'm beginning to enjoy it. I'm even eating seafood nowadays,' says Rosie.

'My goodness, you have changed then.' I smile.

I think how this Borneo trip has been just what she needed to get her life together. Rosie's new healthy influence rubs off on me, so I decide it might be time for me to say no to the Pot Noodles and even the Alphabetti spaghetti. It's time for me to sample proper local food finally. I will start with the meatballs, which I heard Lars call *frikadeller*.

Later, I cycle down to the butcher to get some bits and pieces. I run in and out of the shops quickly in case I bump into Lars. Luckily, we never swapped phone numbers, so he can't phone me.

In the early evening, I am heating the oil for the *frikadeller* when I see a face around the kitchen window.

'Oh, my goodness, you startled me,' I shout.

'Just let me in. I need to speak to you.'

I take the pan from the ring and open the back door to Lars.

'There's nothing for me to say,' I tell him.

'I just want to know what I did wrong,' says Lars. 'I don't want to hassle you. I really don't. I just want to know if I said something. One minute we were dancing, and the next, you looked like you'd seen a ghost and ran off.'

'Yes, I did see a ghost, kind of,' I say.

'What do you mean?'

'Look, never mind. I told you. It's not you. It's me,' I say.

'But we were getting on well. I thought you liked me as much as I liked you,' says Lars, looking puzzled.

For a moment, I feel sorry for him. He is a kind man and doesn't deserve such strange treatment from me.

'It's difficult, Lars. You know my husband died, and nothing feels right any more. You're a lovely person, but I keep making excuses for everything. I don't know what I want,' I try to explain.

'Well, at least let me help you with your *frikadeller*,' says Lars, looking at the frying pan as they begin to burn. 'Us Danes are the best at cooking them,' he teases.

'Okay, well, you can help if you want,' I agree.

Half an hour later, we sit down to eat *frikadeller*, red cabbage, and *kartofler*, which are just boiled potatoes but sound so much more glamorous in Danish.

Lars provides some beers, and we chat all night like old friends. Yet again, I am reminded of how easy he is to get along with.

Just before midnight, Lars announces that he had forgotten he had driven here. How anyone can forget they drove is beyond me, and it does strike me as a bit of an excuse.

'Uh-oh, I got carried away. I have the van outside,' says Lars.

'Oh no, you can't possibly drive in this state,' I say.

He must have had at least three beers.

'Can I stay in the summer house in the garden? Would you mind? I guess I had such a nice time I didn't think about getting home. Uh, I also missed the last ferry,' he says, looking at his watch.

It feels strange allowing someone I don't particularly know to stay over, but it is also lovely to have someone here with me, so I find myself agreeing.

'Okay. Sure, you can stay, but not in the summer house. It could get cold out there in the middle of the night,' I say.

Lars looks at me with wide eyes.

'Oh no, I couldn't... No... I am not hinting for anything like that to happen,' says Lars.

I blush as I realise that he has got the wrong impression.

'No, silly, I don't mean like that. I mean, there are two bedrooms. You can sleep in the spare one if you don't mind that there are no sheets on the bed.'

'I sleep anywhere. It's absolutely fine,' smiles Lars.

'Okay, well, as long as you don't mind,' I say.

I lead him up to the spare room, next to my bedroom. He pulls my arm back gently as I go to walk away in the direction of my room.

'Can I at least get a kiss good night?' asks Lars.

Shyly, I walk back to him. I kiss him on the lips, and he holds me tight. He runs his hand through my hair and around the back of my neck.

'I really like you. Do you know that?' says Lars.

'Well, I suppose you do keep turning up. Um, yeah. I guess,' I smile.

Oh goodness, this is so difficult.

'Now, get some sleep. We have both had too much to drink.' I say.

I head to my bedroom before Lars has any ideas and close my door. I put my rucksack against the door in case he gets carried away, even though he tends to behave like a gentleman. I climb into bed and clutch a pillow happily to my chest. It feels so good to find someone who wants to spend time with me.

I am lying there thinking how absolutely perfect Lars is when I hear a loud snore and then a cough to cover it up.

I chuckle to myself, which is so much nicer than the crying or loneliness that I mostly feel when I go to bed. I snuggle under the covers knowing that a very handsome man is laying in the room next to me. As I drift off to sleep, I smile and decide that perhaps I don't want to push him away for the rest of the holiday after all and fall into the most wonderful blissful sleep.

—

In the morning, I wake up to a knock on the bedroom door. I can see the light peeping in through the thin curtain.

'*Hej*, can I come in?' asks Lars.

'Umm, just a minute.' I say.

I jump up, move the backpack, stroke down my hair and pull up the duvet to cover every inch of me.

'Okay, come in.' I say.

Lars' blue T-shirt that he wore last night is creased and looks like he slept in it. Perhaps he was cold with no blankets on the bed. His hair looks a bit ruffled, and I almost wonder if I should offer him my hairbrush.

He holds out a tray in front of him. 'Tea and some toast for the Omelette lady,' he smiles.

I sit upright to balance the tray on my lap. Looking down at the wooden tray, I notice a small flower that I have seen growing in the garden, carefully placed to one side of my mug.

'Oh, Lars. This is so kind of you after the way I have treated you. Why are you so nice to me?' I ask.

'Because I see a sadness in your eyes that I once had. Like someone who had their heart broken,' he says.

I sip at my tea and wonder how to respond. It must be to do with what he won't tell me about his 'perished' wife.

'You enjoy your breakfast. I've got to deliver some orders. Will you see me again?' asks Lars.

'I'd like that, Lars and I'm sorry I've been so strange. You don't deserve it.' I say.

'I'm so happy to hear you'll see me again. I have to go to Bornholm for a few days to visit family. Perhaps I can pick you up next weekend. How about Saturday, seven pm? We could take the ferry over to Esbjerg and go for dinner?'

'I'd love that.' I say.

Lars lets himself out as I nibble on my toast. I get my laptop from my rucksack and update my blog from bed.

> It's a new day, and today I feel so different. I have met someone nice. He makes me feel special, he makes me feel attractive, and he is gorgeous!

*Oh, Martha, should you say that last bit.*

> I'm happy! I never thought I would ever say those words, but I am smiling after two years of misery. If I

can do this, so can you… If anyone is even reading this, my wish is that this gives you hope. One day someone might come along and sweep you off your feet. I know it takes time, but you will know when you are ready to move on, and despite all the reservations, I feel as though I could move on, but it doesn't stop the guilt. It doesn't mean that I don't care for my deceased husband, but part of me died when he did, and I don't want to live like this any longer. I want to live. But I also feel guilty about living. What a mess I am!

I press 'enter' and look at the words in front of me that are now there for all to read. Then, I close my laptop, smiling to myself.

'I want to live,' I repeat to myself.

However, as I say the words, there is a chill in the air, and something makes me feel uneasy once again.

'Anthony?' I call out.

I realise it is time to stop talking about the ghosts of my past when I see that the front door has swung open. Lars mustn't have closed it properly.

'Martha, stop this nonsense now,' I scold myself. There is no such thing as ghosts.

# Chapter Seventeen

The sun is shining, it is the most beautiful day, the bunny is keeping the grass in the garden down, and I am meeting the lovely Lars again this evening. I am surprised at how excited I am to see him again. It has been quiet without him all week, and all I have done whilst he was away is spend my days on the bicycle and walking around the beaches. I have found hidden coves, spotted lots of new birds and seen Dana in the pub whenever I passed. I wanted to ask her about Lars and what she knew about him, but I am not sure I want to know if there is anything untoward. I want to enjoy this moment.

Unlike when I have seen Lars previously, it takes me hours to get ready when we finally have our next date. I throw almost every T-shirt I have onto the bed. They are all so dull. I take out the Primark skirt that I bought on eBay and try it on. It just about fits, and at least it is brighter than anything else I have in my wardrobe. I resolve that I will spend some of my savings as soon as possible and have a revamp of my wardrobe. Something inside me has shifted; I want to be seen and not hide in the background.

'Oh, Martha, are you sure?' I say out loud.

'Yes,' I reply, annoyed at myself. 'And I may even stop talking to you one day.'

The habit of talking to myself started not long after Anthony died. It is hard to stop once you start.

At seven pm on the dot, Lars pulls up outside. It is the first time I have been looking out for him and waiting for him to arrive. My tummy starts doing somersaults as he walks up the path. He looks so muscular in his tight white T-shirt and khaki trousers.

*Ooh, Martha, he's a bit of all right, as Mrs Morris would say!*

'*Hej*, you look nice,' says Lars when I open the door to him. It is the first time he has ever commented on my appearance.

'Thank you, so do you.' I smile.

*Are you flirting, Martha Jenkins?*

Lars drives carefully to the ferry. Unlike when Rosie drives me places, I don't even have to hold onto the dashboard as we go over bumps in the road.

Finally, we drive off the ferry and arrive in Esbjerg. Lars doesn't take me straight to the restaurant but on a slight detour.

'This is where my grandparents lived,' he says. The three-storey white house that Lars points out is quite spectacular.

'Wow, it's beautiful,' I say.

'Just like some people, it looks beautiful, but it has a difficult past,' says Lars.

'What do you mean?' I ask.

Lars sighs and starts to explain. 'One night when my father was small, there was a knock on the door. It was the Nazis.'

'Oh, my goodness. That's terrible. What happened?' I ask.

It was so different in Wales in World War Two for my parents as many were sent there for safety. I remember my mother telling me she had a Mickey Mouse gas mask, but that is all I remember.

'My father and his brother just stood there in their pyjamas ready for bed with their teddy bears in their arms, and then the Nazis took over the house. My family had to move into one room. Just like that, one knock on the door and their house was taken over,' explains Lars.

'Oh, Lars. That is so awful.'

'I guess it's nothing compared to what others experienced. My family were some of the lucky ones,' says Lars.

My heart aches as we sit there in silence. It makes me realise that, although I think I have problems, they are nothing compared to what others live with during their lifetime. There I am complaining about my boring wardrobe, and then things like this have happened to people in the world. I promise not to complain about anything so superficial again.

By the time we arrive at the restaurant, the mood has lightened. It is buzzing with crowds, and everyone is enjoying themselves. Music is pumping out from the bar, and Lars informs the staff that we have a reservation in the restaurant section. As we reach the table, Lars pulls my seat out for me at the dining table. What a polite man! I don't remember anyone doing that for me before.

Unfortunately, though, as if in slow motion, I misjudge the chair and slide down onto the floor. I pick myself up quickly before anyone notices, but it is too late as several people are now stifling their laughter.

'Are you okay, Omelette lady?' says Lars.

He looks slightly fazed, and I am not sure if his expression is one of hilarity or concern.

'I'm okay, I'm okay. No big deal,' I say, trying to brush off my embarrassment. *But stop calling me 'Omelette Lady'*, I feel like snapping.

*Oh, Martha, that's so mean.* It wasn't Lars' fault I embarrassed myself.

I attempt to compose myself by hiding behind the menu in front of me, pretending to study it as I slowly calm down.

Eventually, I am ready to order and decide on the pasta as that is a safe bet – I am still not prepared to try the rollmop herrings.

'So, tell me more about your grandparents,' I say to Lars as we wait for our food. 'What stories they must have had.'

'I don't remember much as they died before I was born. It was only stories I got from my dad. Now I'm older, I want to know more. When you're young, and your parents tell you stories, you don't listen so much. Now I wish I had,' says Lars.

'I know what you mean. You have an older sister, though. Maybe she can tell you some things that you don't know.' I suggest.

'Yeah – in fact, she started to put together a family tree. It was interesting. But now she's busy with work and so she didn't quite finish. But we were just a family who had a farm and then started the bakery, that's about it, I think. Nothing exciting.'

'Well, I still think you have a fascinating family. Do you have children?' I ask.

'No, my wife… She didn't want them.'

'Oh, I'm sorry. I always wanted more than one child, but my husband didn't. It's difficult when you're not on the same page, so to speak. Anyway, *Iechyd da*,' I say, holding up my glass of wine to his cola.

Wow, that was a deep conversation for our first 'proper' date.

'*Skol*, and *yukki daaa*,' laughs Lars.

The meal looks lovely when it is finally placed in front of us. I didn't know pasta could look so nice. Even the spinach seems appealing. Lars certainly chose a nice restaurant for us to come to.

I make myself eat all the food types on my plate, and am struggling to get to grips with the spinach, when I see someone who looks familiar looking over at the table. Then he turns and starts to walk towards us. I don't believe this. Surely it can't be! Lars also seems to recognise the man and he gets up from the table and starts talking in Danish to him.

I stare at them both chatting like old friends and can't believe what I am seeing. It is definitely him.

'This is my friend Kristian; we were in school together. Kristian, this is Martha,' says Lars.

I feel as though I might have another of my panic attacks. Lars was in school with Kristian?

'Hello,' I manage. I notice my hands are shaking. Why do they do that when you meet a celebrity? I try to remind myself that he is only human, like all of us.

'Good to meet you,' says Kristian.

His voice sounds different speaking in English.

He returns to speaking Danish to Lars and then finally says, '*Farvel*'. The odd thing is that, standing next to Lars, Kristian doesn't look as good as I thought he would. Lars looks handsomer and much more approachable. Kristian seems polite, but a bit aloof. I suppose he is a small celeb, after all.

'Oh my goodness, you know Kristian.' I say to Lars.

'Yeah, sure, he was one of my best friends at school. He was always in the school plays. Now he's an actor. Just small parts, but he has a big audition coming up soon. You seem as though you know him?' says Lars.

I take a big glug of wine. How could I ever tell Lars that Kristian and the TV programme he stars in are part of the reason I ended up here? It seems ridiculous now.

'Oh, I may have seen him on TV, that's all,' I say, and then pretend to choke on my last piece of spinach to get out of any further questions.

# Chapter Eighteen

During my stay, Lars and I have the most fantastic time together. We cycle, swim on the beach and watch the sun go down on the horizon. Lars and I both love the nature that the island offers, and every day I discover how much more we have in common. We have chatted about climate change, politics, and all sorts of discussions that could typically create tension. However, not once do we have a cross word. Okay, it does irritate me when he calls me 'Omelette lady', but I think he means it as a term of endearment. I haven't brought it up, though, as I will leave the cottage in a few days, which means that it is almost time to go home. How quickly one month goes when you're having the time of your life.

We are having a picnic on the beach when I remind Lars that I leave in two days' time.

'You don't have to leave,' says Lars. He picks at the corner of our blue, checked woven picnic blanket and waits for my response.

'Suzy is expecting me back at work. I need to get back to Gareth and relieve Angus of his goldfish-sitting duty,' I explain.

'What about us?' says Lars.

Until now, I wasn't sure what was happening between us. We are not officially in a relationship; nothing has happened between us. No hanky-panky, if you know what I mean. Finally, however, it looks as though it is time for 'the talk'.

'Well, there is no *us*, is there?' I start. 'I've loved your company, and we've had an amazing time, but that's where it ends. We're from two different worlds. You have your job. I have mine in Wales.'

'You could find something here. I could help. You have your blog. Maybe it could make money? Or, I could employ you at the bakery. Look,' says Lars, taking a bite out of the Welsh cakes I made this morning for our picnic. 'These are delicious. I'm sure I could sell them… I know; how about I pay you to make Welsh cakes?'

'I love your enthusiasm, but they need me at the library. I need to get back, as much as I don't want to leave you or Fanø.' I say.

'Well, why don't you call Suzy? Ask her if you can have some extra time off. Even a week or two? It would be nice to spend some more time with you. We can get to know each other even better.' Lars grabs hold of my hand, and I feel as though my whole body is going to explode. Before Lars, the last person who held my hand was the undertaker at Anthony's funeral, and I didn't want to let go then, either.

'So, what do you think? Can I convince you to at least stay another week?' asks Lars.

He leans over and kisses me on the lips, still holding my hand. His kiss is gentle and delicate. He tastes of Welsh cake.

'Well, that is very tempting, now you put it that way,' I say awkwardly.

I realise that I don't know how to flirt. Some women seem to be naturals at it. I am most certainly not one of them. I never flirted with Anthony. He would have asked me if I had a stiff neck had I cocked my neck and coquettishly looked into his eyes. So, I put my head down and don't know where to look.

'It's okay. You can take your time to think about it,' says Lars, lifting my chin so that I look at him. 'I just thought we could have a special week together. I just want a little longer with you. I could take you to meet my family and friends.'

The thought of meeting Lars' friends makes me shudder. I don't want to see Kristian again. Even though nobody here knows I had a secret mid-life crush on him, my embarrassment hasn't dissipated.

'Why would you want to introduce me to your family? I'm leaving; we don't have a future.' I say.

'You haven't told Rosie about me?' says Lars.

'No, umm, should I?' I ask.

'I thought you would have said something. I told my sister all about the lovely Omelette lady that I met,' smiles Lars.

'I would have to know someone very well to tell Rosie. It would break her heart to find out I had...' I go to say, 'met someone,' but have I? I don't know what we have between us.

'I understand. It's different for you. I know that. But I want to get to know you more. Know every inch of you. I could so easily fall in love with you, Omelette lady.' Lars leans over to kiss me once again. It feels so good, but I am also scared. Even though it must have been over ten years since the last time we had any proper relations, the only person I have ever been with in my life is Anthony. I don't know what it feels like to be with anyone else.

'I'll check with Suzy to see if I can take another week off. I'm sure she won't be happy as she needs me there, but I'll ask. Look…'

I pull my phone out to message Suzy. She will probably say no, I expect.

I am biting on a delicious sweet *spandauer* that Lars made in return for my Welsh cakes when Suzy messages.

> Martha, that's amazing. Of course, you can have an extra week off. Honestly, no rush at all. You have a fabulous time. We're all sending our love. Mrs Morris is asking if you met a hunky man yet.

Mrs Morris's remark makes me laugh. If only they knew.

'What did she say?' asks Lars.

'It's not a problem. I can stay another week, but only if the cottage is available. I'll have to check on that first.'

'What are we waiting for? Let's go to the office and get that extra week booked in,' says Lars.

'If it's available,' I remind him.

—

Olaf is at his usual desk at the front of the office when I walk in.

'Hi,' he says. 'Hope everything's okay at the cottage?'

'Absolutely. In fact, so good I would like to add an extra week on if I can.'

'Ah, I'm sorry. It's full next week. We have no properties available for the next six weeks. We have a couple of events coming up and…'

His voice trails in the background. I don't hear what he says. What he means is that I have to go home and leave the beautiful cottage, along with Lars and this heavenly island. It is time to go back to the real world.

Lars is waiting in his van outside when I break the news.

'Would it be too soon for you to come and stay with me in Skads?' he asks.

'Yes, it would. We're only putting off the inevitable anyway. I may as well get it over with and head home,' I say.

'But you wanted to see so many places and—'

'I know. I'll come back one day. Then I will visit Tivoli, travel on the bridge to Sweden. Perhaps I can bring Rosie with me. Who knows?'

Lars doesn't say anything on the drive back to the cottage, so we sit in silence, both deep in thought. However, the reality is that I have commitments in Wales, whether Lars likes it or not. It is my home, and Rosie will be back in a few months expecting me to be there. I can't stay here forever.

'I'm sorry, Lars, but I can't possibly stay. We've had a wonderful time, but we both have different lives,' I say.

'Could I arrange a lunch with my family, like a leaving lunch, Please? I'd love you to meet them, and I'm sure my brother-in-law would like to practice his two words of English on you,' says Lars.

'Sure, that would be nice. Just perhaps keep it small and no friends like Kristian or anyone if that's okay,' I say.

'Whatever you want, your wish is my command, Omelette lady,' says Lars.

Something between us has changed. The fact that we can both see the inevitable is coming gives us this urgent closeness I never believed I would have with anyone again. When we arrive at the cottage, Lars holds me tight.

'I don't want to let go. Can I keep you here forever?' he says.

'We haven't known each other long enough,' I say. I curse myself for being so sensible. 'Besides, Gareth will be pleased to see me and Mrs Morris and...'

'I can't come to Wales because of the business, but please promise me you'll come back. As soon as you can, okay?' says Lars.

'I will, I promise. But, in the meantime, let's just enjoy the time we have,' I say.

'And how do you suggest we do that?' asks Lars, with a smirk on his face.

There is no mistaking what he means. Unspoken words have passed between us. Lars takes me by the hand and leads me up the stairs.

# Chapter Nineteen

I am not sure why Mrs Morris is so opposed to hanky-panky – she has obviously never met anyone like Lars. My whole body is still tingling this morning. I am overcome with emotion and seem to be having some kind of flush, and I am pretty confident it is not a menopausal one. Every muscle is more relaxed than it has ever been in my life. I curl my toes happily and stretch them out, feeling pleased with myself. I have died and gone to heaven. Although that thought immediately leaves me racked with guilt once again. Someone did die, and it should never have happened.

I look over at Lars for reassurance as he lies beside me. I touch the muscular arm that is dangling out of the duvet. I find it odd that we have two separate single duvets on the bed, and it suddenly bothers me. I want to snuggle under the duvet with him. It didn't matter when I was sleeping on my own, but Lars tells me they do this in Denmark so that your partner in bed doesn't steal the duvet from the other. I suppose it could save some marriages from divorce. Anthony was terrible for stealing the duvet. I think about how he would pull it off me in the night, but then the guilt starts again. He is no longer able to do that. I decide to confide in my blog whilst Lars sleeps peacefully.

Last night I had the most amazing sex, and today I am wracked with guilt. I am enjoying myself far too much for a widow. I shouldn't be behaving like this. I should be dressed in black and crying, not having sex with a handsome Danish blond man I have only known for four weeks. Is this the latest silly thing that loneliness has driven me to? But, if I am honest, I truly enjoyed every second. What a selfish person I am.

I check the blog counter on the top and notice there are forty-eight views today. Oh, my goodness, it must finally be reaching people. I shall delete that blog entry. It's far too personal if people are actually reading it, and so are the other entries. The inbox shows two messages. Oh, dear. I click on the first message nervously.

Hi, I just found your blog. I was searching on the internet for help after my wife passed on. I would love to chat with you about it. I don't have anyone else I can confide in. My children are grown up and living all over the world. I have a spaniel who listens to me cry myself to sleep, but that's all I have in my life. Would you chat with me, please? It would be such a help, Tom.

The message brings tears to my eyes. I immediately delete the latest blog post. I can't possibly tell people I am having a nice time when they are so miserable. I respond to Tom by telling him that I am here for him and happy to chat anytime he wants. I begin to wonder whether Suzy would mind if I started up a grief support group in the library after reading this. I will certainly put this idea forward at the next staff meeting.

I move on to the following message.

Hello, I love your blog posts. I was searching on the internet for help following a bereavement when your blog popped up. It helps knowing someone out there has gone through the same things I did. It is so hard when you love someone so much, and then in an instant, they're gone. Anyway, I feel silly writing to a stranger like this, but I just wanted to thank you for making me realise I am not alone. My partner died in a terrible accident. Every day I just wish I'd had the chance to tell him how much I loved him one last time.
Izzy X.

'Oh goodness, Martha! You weren't alone. So many feel like you did!' I say to myself.

'Huh, what you say?' says Lars sleepily.

'Nothing,' I say, deciding now would not be the right time to tell him I talk to myself. 'You're awake, finally. You had a nice lie-in.'

'I used up a lot of energy last night,' he smiles. He makes me so at ease that I am surprised that I don't find his comment a little cringey the morning after. I simply think how I wish for it to happen all over again.

Lars pulls me close, and we squeeze together under the single duvet.

'I really could fall in love with you, Omelette lady,' he says, in between kissing my neck.

Both the revelation and the kissing take me by surprise. Plus, I didn't know there were so many nerve endings in my neck until now. The goosebumps rise from the tips of my toes to the top of my head. Finally, I can take no more, and I jump on top of him – something I would never have dreamed of doing to Anthony, who would have screamed for me to get off.

When we are finished, Lars gets up and walks about. I love that he is so comfortable in his skin. I can't help comparing him to Anthony, who would have rushed to put his underpants on before I even caught a glimpse of his bony bottom.

'I'll be back with your breakfast, Omelette lady,' says Lars.

Then, confidently, he walks downstairs, makes breakfast naked and brings me up tea, scrambled egg, and some of those wonderful Danish sausages from the local butcher.

'You're spoiling me,' I grin. How awful it will be to have to make my own breakfast again before rushing into work.

As Lars has to get back to Esbjerg and then over to the bakery, I decide to take the ferry with him. I leave my bike behind and jump in his van across to the mainland. I am meeting Lars' family tomorrow for a farewell lunch and want to make my best impression. So, I decide I will spend some of Anthony's life insurance money on myself. Yet again, this thought makes me feel dreadful. But, until now, I have been extra cautious. Would he be annoyed with me for spending money on some new clothes – the first brand new ones I have bought in twenty years? *Yes, Martha, if Anthony knew it was to meet another man's family, he would be blooming livid*, I remind myself.

I push the voice aside and open the door to a smart-looking boutique in Esbjerg.

Walking into a store of this calibre makes me feel self-conscious.

*Ooh, Martha. You don't belong in a store like this. Look, that assistant is laughing at you!*

'Just shut up,' I snap to myself.

'*Hej, kan jeg hjælpe dig?*' says the assistant.

'I'm just looking, thank you.' I say.

I pretend to study a suede miniskirt and walk out; a bout of social anxiety overwhelming me.

As I walk the streets of Esbjerg, I am so angry with myself. *This is a new you. You are having the best sex of your life, you are helping people on the blog, and you are worthy of lovely shops.*

I hold my head up high and bravely walk into the next store I see selling women's wear. The window is filled with expensive-looking outfits. I am particularly drawn to a vibrant silk blouse with a co-ordinating scarf. It looks so effortlessly put together.

'*Hej*,' smiles the shop assistant.

'Hello,' I say.

'Ah, you speak English,' says the immaculate lady.

'Yes, I'm on holiday.'

'Welcome. We have a small discount for tourists. If you see anything you like, I can check the price.'

'Thank you,' I say.

The lady smiles warmly, making me feel more at ease than in the last shop.

I look at the kaleidoscope of colourful silk blouses hanging on the rail. There is a beautiful blue blouse first, then purple, which leads to a shade of pink. They all blend perfectly, and it is like looking at a rainbow.

'Would you like to try one? We call this colour "acai berry". It would look very nice with your skin tone,' says the lady, picking out one of the blouses.

'Okay, I guess.' I don't dare look at the price tag.

'You have something to wear it with? These go nicely.' She picks up a pair of black leather-look trousers. They remind me of the type of thing Gretchen would wear. My goodness, I wonder if she shops here!

'Oh, I don't think they'd look good on me,' I say.

I touch the trousers, about to explain that this fabric would make me look like a leather sofa, but the material is so soft and luxurious.

'Try them. You'd be surprised. They're our best seller. Very flattering.'

I find myself agreeing.

'How about shoes?' she asks, looking down at my usual grey sturdy trainers.

'Well, I probably do need a new pair of shoes,' I say.

'Here, you try these on, and I'll bring you some. What size are you?' says the lady, handing me the items.

I tell her my size and head into the fitting room. I pick up the trousers thinking how futile this is; these trousers will never fit. I put one ankle in, almost toppling over and then another and pull them up.

*Ooh, Martha, have you lost weight? They fit!*

It must be all the cycling and walking I have been doing.

I button up the blouse, which fits well too.

'Here, try these shoes,' says a voice from around the fitting room curtain.

The sales assistant hands me a pair of suede pumps that are luckily not too high. I step into them and look into the mirror.

'Wow, perfect,' says the lady.

I look at my reflection and have to agree. It's a lovely outfit, although I'm not quite sure that it belongs on me. I ruffle my hand through my hair. It now looks neglected compared to the rest of my outfit.

'I can give you a discount if you take them all?' says the sales assistant hopefully.

I look at the outfit again. How can I possibly walk away from these beautiful clothes?

'I guess if you can give me a discount, I'll think about it,' I say.

As the lady works out the discounts on her calculator, I admire her sleek brown hair. It's so glossy and so unlike mine, with my flyaway bits everywhere.

'I like your hair,' I say.

'Thank you. Mikkel's salon is the best. I have his card if you'd like.'

'Okay, that would be good.'

'They just opened a new salon, so you may get an appointment with one of the junior staff if you're lucky. Mikkel himself is booked up for months. But they're all great, and the junior staff are cheaper. Tell them I sent you. My name is Louisa. Now, do you want these?'

Louisa shows me the calculator displaying the total sum that the outfit will set me back. Oh goodness, even Rosie would be shocked at spending that much on clothes!

'As you've been so helpful, why not? Thank you,' I say.

*Oh, Martha, that's so naughty!*

Despite a considerable dent in my purse, I leave the store feeling on top of the world. A new haircut is exactly what I need next.

I follow the directions Louisa gave me and arrive at a trendy-looking salon with graffiti on the walls. Oh, dear. It doesn't look very welcoming.

A young girl with huge chunky boots greets me. I notice that one of the boot's soles is tightly wrapped with elastic bands connecting it to the rest of the shoe, and I can't work out whether her heel has snapped or if it is a fashion statement.

'*Hej. Velkommen.*'

'Oh, do you speak English?'

'Yes, of course.'

I explain that Louisa sent me, and she fits me in right away. She places a fuchsia pink gown around me and starts chopping. I am too scared to watch, so keep my eyes lowered. I have never liked looking at myself in the mirror at any hair salon. They are like those distorted mirrors you find in the funfair. Am I truly that hideous?

The stylist has insisted that I put a plum colour through my hair, which she promises will take years off me. I don't know why young people are so obsessed with making people look younger. Cosmetic and skincare companies all do the same. What is wrong with looking your age? Older people are human too.

By the time we finish, and I look into the mirror, I am barely recognisable. Anthony would be horrified. I certainly don't look like the woman he married, that's for sure. He never liked any changes. I once cut a fringe in and he looked as though he might faint.

I study the reflection staring back at me. *Oh my goodness, Martha. It doesn't even look like you!* The woman staring back is smart, confident, and not the woman who walked in here at all. I realise that the woman who walked in here has gone and so has Anthony.

Neither of them exist any longer.

# Chapter Twenty

The following day, I decide not to tell anyone it is my fiftieth birthday. Of course, Rosie rang me first thing and asked Ben to sing 'Happy Birthday'. I have had texts from Suzy and Trevor as they saw it was my birthday on Facebook, but I haven't advertised the fact and certainly haven't told Lars. However, I subconsciously make an extra effort on my appearance, although perhaps more so because I am meeting Lars' family for the first time.

I put on a little make-up and get dressed in my new outfit. Lars hasn't seen my new hair yet, so I hope he isn't too shocked when he comes around to collect me.

'Holy *meatballs*! You look… Wow, turn around,' says Lars when I open the front door to greet him.

'Oh, I just did something new to my hair. It's a bit too much, isn't it?' I apologise.

'No, no… You look fantastic. Oh, Omelette lady, I am not letting you leave. Who needs lunch? Let's stay here,' says Lars, teasing me. He pulls me to him and starts kissing me.

'Watch out. My lipstick will smudge,' I say.

'Hmm, perhaps I prefer you without the make-up,' he laughs.

I have never been one to take a brush or lipstick out with me in my handbag. I'm more a wet wipes and handy pack of tissues type of person, but my new haircut has made me take a little more pride in my appearance. So, I grab my brush and even a lipstick I bought after the hair salon yesterday and head to Skads to meet Lars' family. I only hope I can make a good impression on them. Somehow this feels so important. What if they hate me?

Forty minutes later, we pull up outside a small bungalow.

The bungalow has one of those ubiquitous Danish flags on a flagpole at the front and a vegetable patch to the side of the property. I can see what Lars meant when he told me Ludwig enjoyed growing vegetables. I have never seen cabbages so big. He must feed them steroids. I wipe my sweaty palms on my shiny new trousers, leaving a trail of moisture on my upper thighs. My trousers look as though a slug escaped from Ludwig's vegetable patch and attacked me.

Ludwig, I soon discover, looks like a happy little buddha you can buy in the market with his cheeky face and a chubby belly. He is a man of no words and just smiles and nods his head at everything we say.

'Ludwig didn't study English in school as we did, isn't that right, Ludwig?' says Lars.

Ludwig smiles and nods his head like one of those nodding dogs, oblivious to every word we have said.

'Thank you,' he says.

'Oh, yes, he knows that much, don't you, Ludwig?' smiles Agnete.

'*Ja*, thank you,' he replies.

Once the introductions are out of the way, the three of them stand around chatting in Danish for a moment, which makes me wish I understood the language. In fairness, Ludwig's English is probably better than my Danish. I am pretty ashamed of my lack of linguistic skills. The comprehensive school I attended only taught us a bit of French, and I failed that.

I cast my eyes around the neat little bungalow. It is typically Scandinavian, with minimalist wooden furniture and a dining table with six light wood chairs gathered around it. Agnete instructs us to the sit at the table. I sit down on a thin blue cushion, which scarcely protects my bottom from the hard surface of the chair.

The dining table is already set for lunch. The table is decorated with Danish flags and a wooden salad bowl filled with colourful vegetables. Plain white serving plates display *frikadeller* and other hot dishes. It is quite the spread that Agnete has put on. She pours some white wine, and we talk about Wales, how she has never been to the UK, and the general pleasantries you would expect when meeting someone for the first time.

'So, let's eat,' says Agnete pointing to the feast laid out. 'Lars tells me you like *frikadeller*, so I made them this morning, especially.'

'I love them,' I say. I only hope my waistband on these shiny new trousers doesn't pop with all this food.

'Salad?' offers Agnete.

'Yes, I should probably fill up on that,' I smile. I notice how fresh it all looks. 'Is this from your garden, Ludwig?' I ask.

'*Ja*, thank you,' he says, smiling and bobbing his head.

'More wine?' says Agnete. I look at her glass and notice it is already empty. Goodness, she drinks fast.

'No, I'm fine, thank you.' I say. I would hate to get drunk and make a spectacle of myself at Agnete's dining table. What if I started twerking or something in my fancy new trousers?

We have almost finished lunch and I am putting the last *frikadeller* in my mouth when Agnete looks at me seriously.

'So, you have good sex, *ja*?' she says, without any warning.

I am horrified. Has she had that much wine already?

'*Ja*, thank you,' says Ludwig.

Lars looks at me and laughs. 'My sister is a sex therapist; this is the first question she asks everyone. It's nothing unusual. You're lucky we got this far into our lunch,' he explains.

I am not sure if I am more shocked that a stranger is asking about my sex life – which, incidentally, is fantastic – or that Agnete is a sex therapist. I thought that was an occupation I only read about in magazines like *Cosmopolitan*, and they were fictional people who were agony aunts in the world of hanky-panky.

I study Agnete with her long grey hair neatly tied into a plait that almost reaches her bottom. Although now I think about it, she does look like someone who would sit cross-legged on the floor and teach that tantric stuff I once read about in the library while no one was watching. No wonder Ludwig smiles so much.

'It's okay, you don't have to say anything,' says Lars. 'It's just a habit of hers. She can't help herself. I guess it's a habit in the same way you always talk to yourself.'

I stare at him in horror. I had hoped he hadn't noticed. I sip at the wine and hold my glass like a comfort blanket, suddenly feeling uncomfortable.

'Ah, sorry. I mustn't say this. Perhaps it's not appropriate. You're my brother's girlfriend. I apologise. Just something I ask every day in my job. I forget I'm not at work sometimes,' says Agnete.

'It's okay,' I smile.

Her brother's girlfriend? Is that what he told her?

'Good. Now that's over with… Are you ready for some strawberries?' asks Agnete whilst pouring herself yet more wine.

'*Ja*, thank you,' says Ludwig and we all burst out laughing.

Once we finish the lovely fresh strawberries from the garden, Agnete tells me she has a surprise and goes into the kitchen to get something. After the first revelation of the day, I am a bit concerned that she might return with some kind of battery-operated toy in her hand, so I am very relieved when she returns with a bright red accordion. Agnete puts the strap over her shoulder and sits down on a stool in front of the TV. She then starts to sing and pumps away at the accordion, its bellows rising up and down. She sings in Danish, and Ludwig and Lars join in. The song is unfamiliar to me, but it is nice to observe the happy atmosphere that Agnete has created with her accordion.

'It's an old Danish folk song,' explains Lars, as he stops singing in between choruses.

My eyes flicker to everyone in the room. How wonderful to have such a close family. Rosie and I have never had this. I was an only child, and there had been a row between Anthony and his sister Lauren many years before we met, and they never made up. I never found out what it was about. He would never speak about her, so Rosie grew up without aunts or uncles or even grandparents, as they had all passed on by the time she was a year old. Even after Anthony's parents died, he still never spoke to his sister. She didn't even bother coming to either her parents' funeral or Anthony's. I always wondered what the feud was about. But, as Anthony always said, you can't choose your family.

'You want to join with the singing?' says Lars.

'Oh, I don't know any of the words,' I laugh.

'Ah, don't worry, let me show you how to play accordion instead,' says Agnete.

'It looks difficult,' I say nervously.

'It's not so hard,' she reassures me.

I take the accordion from Agnete. It is heavier than I imagined.

'You open and close it like this,' she says, showing me the basics.

I pull the bellows of the accordion outwards.

'Now you have to move the bellows and press the button at the same time,' explains Agnete.

'Wow, this is quite therapeutic,' I say, moving it back and forth.

Unfortunately, though, the noise of the accordion is anything but therapeutic. It makes a terrible racket, and we all laugh together. It certainly doesn't sound the way it does when Agnete plays it. I quickly hand it back to her after protesting that I don't think I would ever get the hang of it.

Once again, she plays it effortlessly and sings another folk song, and this time Lars pulls me up to dance to the music.

I giggle as I attempt to dance to the tunes of the accordion, and all the feelings of apprehension about meeting a new family disappear. The accordion has brought us all together, the warmth in this home makes me feel as though I have known them all my life. They truly are a lovely family, and I am utterly blessed to meet them.

By the time we head off later in the evening, I can't help but think how I will miss these people, even though I have only just met them.

All the way back to Fanø, I am sad as I realise I am leaving this behind tomorrow morning. Lars holds my hand for much of the journey back to the cottage, and he appears to feel just as miserable as I do about me leaving.

'Come on, let's not waste a moment we have together,' he says, as he leads me up the stairs of the cottage and into my bedroom.

He undresses quickly and kisses me with urgency. It is different to the times before when he was gentle yet passionate. This time neither of us can control ourselves, and I discard my new clothes on the floor. Lars stands on the leg of my new trousers as he leans into me, and I don't even care. If that were Anthony, I would have shouted at him to be careful of my trousers.

After the most terrific sex of my life, I start crying. I have no control over it. It is as though some kind of emotional floodgate has opened, and I can't stop it.

'Oh, Lars, I don't want to leave Denmark,' I say, between tears.

'You don't have to. I told you that,' he says.

'I can't stay. It's too complicated,' I remind him.

'Okay, then I make us some tea,' says Lars, brusquely removing his hand from my thigh. He walks down to the kitchen, and I hear him slamming some things around. He is usually so calm, so his anger takes me by surprise. However, it also reminds me that I don't know him well enough to leave my home town behind.

I must be on that flight tomorrow, no matter how hard it is for me to leave.

# Chapter Twenty-One

When you go on holiday, you don't think about how you will feel going home. I am a completely different person to who I was when I arrived. I haven't even had a panic attack in the past week.

I never saw Kristian again, the man I had a little bit of a crush on. However, my adventure led me to meet someone wonderful and a holiday romance that will stay with me forever. I feel like one of those teenyboppers who has met some handsome lad in Ibiza and now wants to hang onto his trouser leg and cry. I have had my first holiday romance at the age of fifty. Good grief!

Like a forlorn teenager, I give Lars my phone number as he drops me off at the train station. I don't expect him to call, but at least he has it. We are both grown-ups who had a fantastic time together but ultimately, it's 'complicated', as they say on those Facebook relationship status options.

Lars squeezes me tight as we say our reluctant good-byes.

'I'm going to miss you, Omelette lady.'

'I'm going to miss you too, Lars. It's been so nice meeting you and your lovely family. How awful that I have to go home,' I say.

'I told you that you don't have to go home,' Lars says, yet again.

'I do. I have my life there. It's easy for you to say when you're in your own country. It's different for me.'

The train pulls up at the station, and we can no longer put this off. The time has come to say goodbye, possibly forever.

Lars squeezes me tightly again, and then I jump on the train with my luggage. I choose to hang around in one of the sections between the carriages until the train moves so that I don't have to sit there awkwardly waving at him from the window. I don't want him to see my tears.

On the train journey to Copenhagen airport, I can't stop thinking about how happy I have been these last few weeks. It is not just about meeting someone wonderful, but everything: the way of life; the Scandinavian food; cycling about the island and living more healthily than I have in a very long time. At home, I mostly sit about drinking sherry and crying. Perhaps all I needed was a holiday, I remind myself. I can find a new way of life back home. I could join a cycling club or see if I can find a Nordic Walking group. That would be fun, whilst also reminding me of Scandinavia. I pull out my iPad and Google 'Nordic Walking groups' and immediately find a local club. For a moment, it makes me feel brighter and more positive. But the feeling doesn't last for long. Who am I kidding? I want to be back in that cottage with my feet curled around Lars.

It's time for a blog entry to take my mind off him.

Sorry I haven't been on here for a few days. I have been writing this blog whilst on holiday, so haven't been able to write every day. But I would recommend a break away to anyone. I can't promise the loneliness won't follow you as it did with me when I first arrived in Copenhagen, but keep yourself busy, meet people, and you may feel a bit stronger after your break away. Try it and let me know how it goes.

I struggle to write positive, encouraging words in my current frame of mind but at least there is an update for the readers. I can see there are a few messages today and a huge ninety-two views.

One message asks if I need a computer expert to help with my blog for just nine US dollars a month. The cheek! Trevor would be livid. The other messages are from my two usual readers.

Hello, you wouldn't believe how much I appreciate your message. Thank you. I told Sparky you'd replied. I'm sure he had a look of relief in his eyes that I had someone else to talk to. I always look forward to your updates on the blog, so I'm disappointed you haven't posted anything in the last few days. I hope you're okay. I can relate to everything you say about grief and how it feels, except for meeting someone else, of course. Nobody would ever replace my Sandra, and I wouldn't want them to. That wouldn't be fair to her memory. Tom.

Next, I read the message from Izzy.

Hi lovely lady, thanks a million for your message. It feels so good to talk to someone who has been through this and understands. The girls I work with don't get how much I loved him. They say we weren't suitable as we were so opposite, but I say opposites attract. How old are you? I'm thirty-nine. Too young to feel like this. I know I'll get over it one day, but it's just

hard. I miss him so much. We were planning the rest
of our lives together. I still expect him to walk through
that door with a big bouquet of flowers like he always
did, but he's not coming back, is he? Wouldn't it be
great if we lived near each other and could meet up to
talk about our amazing partners? I'm in South Wales.
Whereabouts are you? xx

I'm so excited to see that lovely Izzy lives in Wales that I
reply to her immediately.

How wonderful, Izzy! That's amazing. I am thinking of
starting a group get-together in a library. It would be
in the Llanelli area probably – I don't know if you're
anywhere near there? If you are, then it would be
great to meet up and chat. You're right, I do understand how it feels, and it is only those who have been
through it that can truly understand. I have been away
on hols but back in Wales tonight, so let's catch up
soon – if you're not too far away. M X

–

By the time I arrive at Copenhagen airport, I feel a little
more upbeat. But I have one more thing to do before
I leave the country. It's time to leave my Scandi noir
obsession behind me.

*Ooh, Martha. Are you sure? This is quite radical!*

I finish off my cup of mint tea as I wait for the plane to
start boarding (horrifically, there were no PG Tips at the
airport), and I place my Scandi noir book on the table.
When I hear the flight is about to board, I take all my
belongings, leaving the book behind. Hopefully someone

else will read it. I don't want to read about gruesome murders any more; I have a longing to read about love and happiness. I download a romantic comedy on my Kindle and smile to myself. This is what I want in my life right now. No more Scandi noir for me. It was becoming an unhealthy obsession.

I head towards the departure gate and see a souvenir shop, which I am grateful for as there are a couple of things I haven't picked up yet. I grab Legoland and Viking magnets for Angus as a thank you for goldfish-sitting and a tin of Danish butter cookies for the gang at work. I am pleased with my choice and know they will make a nice change to the standard biscuits, even if Trevor pinches most of them.

There is one thing I wanted for myself before I left, but for the life of me I can't remember what it was. I scan the shop, hoping I will remember, but it doesn't come to me. I am still looking around for something to trigger my memory when there is an announcement. It is the last call for boarding, and I can't hang around a moment longer.

I quickly board the plane and look out the window. The sky is grey and dull. Finally, after the safety demonstration, the plane begins to hurtle down the runway. It is then I remember what I wanted to buy so badly.

*A mug, Martha. Oh, flipping heck. You forgot to buy a mug for work!*

# Chapter Twenty-Two

It is always strange when you return from holiday to an empty house. Bills are the only thing waiting for me, and the house feels damp, even though it's summertime. The hanging baskets are crispy and dead, and the whole place feels as though it has lost its zest for life. I have only been gone a month, but the house no longer feels homely. I am further disheartened when I look out the window to see next door's cat doing his business in the rockery.

*Oh dear, Martha. It's carnage here!*

How I miss the deer in Fanø. He never did his business in the garden.

I pop the kettle on, glad that I stopped to pick up some milk on the way home in the taxi when I see there is a message from Suzy. She is incredibly sorry but asks if she can return Gareth after work tomorrow as Angus wants one last sleep with him in his room. Of course, I agree as I know how much he means to him.

I plonk myself down on my favourite reading chair and ring Rosie; that will cheer me up.

'What's up, Mam? You sound a bit down,' says Rosie.

'I'm okay. Just the holiday blues. You know what it's like when you come back from holiday,' I say, holding the phone with one hand and unzipping my luggage with the other. A white cotton T-shirt springs out.

'Aww, I know. You'll be right once you get back to work tomorrow, though.'

'Yes, it'll be nice to see them all. I got them some nice biscuits,' I say.

'Ooh, that's exciting then,' says Rosie.

'Yeah,' I say miserably.

I look at the pretty tub the biscuits are in. It is decorated with an illustrated scene of Copenhagen, which makes me long to be back there.

'Oh, talking about coming back from holiday, you'd be all right if I didn't come back to Wales after I finish here, wouldn't you?' says Rosie.

'Well, umm, I don't know. I was looking forward to seeing you. I thought I only had another four and a half months and eighteen hours and three minutes left until I saw you,' I say.

'Oh, don't be like that now, Mam.'

'Well, I just can't wait to see you again, that's all.'

'Yeah, well, Ben got accepted for a place in York to study veterinary medicine. I'm thinking of applying to the same place. I might do small animals though, can't cope with those big dogs who bite and stuff.'

Rosie rambles on about the animals she loves, and I realise that she has a promising future in front of her. So, of course, it is wonderful that she wants to become a vet. It is just that the thought of her moving to York that doesn't feel very wonderful right now.

'Well, that's great for you, lovely,' I manage. 'Although you do realise that being a vet for small animals means dealing with all sorts of pets? I don't think you can pick and choose what animals you like. It's not all fluffy poodles and bunny rabbits, you know.'

'Huh? Oh, I'll have to ask Ben. Anyway, got to go, Mam. Off tonight to get some supplies in.'

'Okay, you take care, then. Love you, Rosie.'

'Love you, Mam.'

Putting the phone down, I realise that my little girl doesn't need me any more. How did that happen? She used to be so dependent on me to change her nappy, feed her, take her places, and now it's just me alone. I think of Tom and Izzy on the blog. I am not the only one who feels alone. I should be grateful that at least I have had the most wonderful holiday romance, which is more than these two poor souls have had.

I consider unpacking and lift the white T-shirt out from my luggage, but I notice something solid underneath as I do so. What on earth? I dig around and feel a handle. Staring in disbelief, I discover that it is a mug with a big red heart. It says, 'I left my heart in Denmark'.

Lars is the only person who could have put it there. I never left my luggage unattended, except when I put it in the van and ran back to check I hadn't left anything in the cottage. He must have done it then. I hold it tight to my chest. I remember telling him earlier in the holiday how much I needed a mug for work. He must have remembered. What a thoughtful thing to do. It makes me miss him even more.

As usual, I try to take my mind off Lars by going on the blog. I see there are now 179 views, which I am surprised at. Also, I notice that Tom and Izzy have replied to my last message, along with a new reader.

Love ya blog, keep going. Tina x

I check the following message. It's Tom.

Hello, how lovely you've been on holiday. I told Sparky your advice, and he said maybe we should go somewhere. Well, he didn't really, but I imagine that's what he'd say if he had the chance. He'd love to go on holiday somewhere with a beach, and we could go for long walks. Maybe I should think about it. But not Torquay. I'm not ever going back there. The memories are too painful. It was Sandra's favourite place, you see. We used to stay in the same B&B every year for twenty-five years – August 1$^{st}$ for a week. Oh dear, now the thought of a holiday is making me sad. Perhaps I am not quite ready to go away without Sandra. Thanks anyway.

Poor Tom. I hear my phone beep and see that Lars has sent me a message. Tom's words leave me feeling guilty. I should be suffering and more like Tom. I should be sad and missing Anthony. I don't pick up Lars' text and choose to read the message from Izzy next.

OMG, I can't believe you're in Llanelli. I'm in Swansea! I'd love to meet up if you do arrange something and, if you don't get a group started, maybe we could have a coffee anyway. What do you think? I know it's lovely chatting on here, but it would be nice to meet in person too. Let me know when you're back and settled after your hols, and we can catch up. Love Izzy. Xxx

You see, it's not all bad being back home. Perhaps I can make a new friend in Izzy and we can grieve over our partners together. There is always a silver lining.

Finally, I decide to pick up the message from Lars.

I hope you llked your surprise. I miss you
so much, Omelette lady xx

It seems funny being called that now. It's such a world
away.

I decide to unpack before messaging him back. There
is no rush. He will move on soon enough without me.

As I open the drawer to put an unworn T-shirt away, a
pair of Mr Men socks roll out. What are they doing in my
drawer again? If I weren't trying to make such an effort
to control my imagination, I would think that Anthony
put these socks in the middle of my stash of indigestion
tablets on purpose. I'm sure they weren't there when I left.
Quickly moving them out of my sight, another pair roll
out. Mr Grumpy.

Yes, you could be grumpy, Anthony. Like the very
last time I saw you. The time you reversed out of the
driveway, and said you needed some space. The words that
have never left me and the reason that you have haunted
me every single day since the day you died.

# Chapter Twenty-Three

'She has been having bloody hanky-panky, I'm telling you now,' says Mrs Morris to Suzy when she sees me. 'You're bloody glowing, mun. Mind you, I didn't look like that after Gerald had, you know, had his way, like. Oh no, I'd be flushed like a bloody beetroot and look washed-out. But you… You are glowing, Mrs. Go on then, who was he?'

'I've no idea what you're talking about, Mrs Morris,' I say.

'Oh, come on now, bach. Nobody looks like that after a holiday unless they've met someone and had a bit of rumpy-pumpy.'

I try not to blush as I think of Lars and the things we got up to.

'Don't be silly, it's amazing what a new haircut can do, that's all. I think I caught some sun on my face too when I was out cycling,' I say.

'Well, you look bloody marvellous, I tell you. Good for you, and I love your hair. I'm so glad you enjoyed yourself. It looks like it's done you the world of good. Ooh, hey, that book you gave me last time… My grandson saw it in the living room and asked me why I was reading it. I said, I'm not. I brought it back, and Sioned said she didn't think it would be the type of book I'd enjoy. You know I don't ever read the books, don't you?' winks Mrs Morris.

'Shh, our secret. It wouldn't be the same without you coming in. I'm so glad you're here on my first day back. I've missed you,' I say. I reach out to her arm and stroke it. They don't make people like they used to.

Remembering Lars' story about his parents' house, I start to tell Mrs Morris. I think she would find it interesting.

'I met a very interesting Danish man, Mrs Morris. He told me stories about how the Nazis knocked on the door in the middle of the night and took over their house during the war. Can you imagine?'

'Well duw, how awful,' says Mrs Morris. 'His poor family. I was only young then, but I remember my Micky Mouse gas mask.'

'Oh, that's what I told Lars about my mother. She had one too. It's all so awful. Why do people have to go to war? Why can't the world be a happy place with no arguments and...'

I think of Anthony. Why did we have to argue that night? If we hadn't, it would all be so different.

'I know, love. But sadly, we can't change the world... Anyway, what's this Suzy says about you thinking of starting a group for people who've lost loved ones? Suzy was telling me that you said something while you were away,' says Mrs Morris.

'Yeah, well, I started a blog and—'

'A blog?' says Mrs Morris.

She looks around the library and taps the desk with her walking stick.

'Where are the dictionaries? You're talking gobbledygook now,' she says.

'Hello, ladies,' says Trevor interrupting us. 'Need to look at your hard drive, Martha.'

'That's a bit rude to say in the middle of the library, don't you think? You could have waited until she was in the staff room if you want to see her hard drive,' says Mrs Morris.

'Mrs Morris, what on earth are you thinking? He means my computer. I do worry about the way your mind works sometimes,' I say.

We giggle between ourselves, and, as much as I didn't want to come back, it doesn't feel so bad after all.

Unfortunately, the feeling doesn't last long.

'Thanks for the biscuits,' says Trevor in the staff room at break time. 'Blooming lovely, they are.'

'Ooh, they are delish,' says Suzy biting into a pretzel-shaped biscuit. 'By the way, can we bring Gareth around about seven tonight? Before Angus goes to bed? Then he can say a proper goodbye to him.'

'Yes, of course. It will be nice to see Gareth again and little Angus, of course.'

'Brilliant. I'm putting the kettle on. Anyone want a cuppa to go with these biccies?' asks Suzy.

'Yes, please. I'll have one.'

I pull the mug from my bag and pop it in front of Suzy.

'Ooh, that's a fancy mug. Did you leave your heart in Denmark?' she laughs.

'Well, I had a nice time. That's all it means.' I explain.

I try to put Lars and the dream cottage behind me, but then my phone bleeps. I didn't answer Lars last night. Of course, I wanted to thank him for the lovely surprise, but it won't make any difference. I don't want a long-distance relationship.

I look down at the phone, hoping nobody will notice.

Good morning, did you get my message yesterday, Omelette lady? I miss you so much that I drove to the cottage. There are people there, so I hope they didn't think I was spying on them, but I wanted to send you this xx

I look at the photo accompanying his message and see the deer and the bunny in the garden. The following picture is of Lars making a funny face in the van. My heart pangs suddenly for what I have left behind. This is why I don't want to answer his messages. My life is here with this bunch, and I am about to start a bereavement group to help people. Unfortunately, there is nothing I can do about being in Denmark.

'Is that a deer on your phone there?' says Suzy, putting my tea down beside me.

'Yeah, I have a funny story about the first day I saw him, but he was quite the fixture by the end,' I say.

'Angus would love to see him,' says Suzy. 'Would you send it to my phone and I can show him?'

'Yes, of course, I will.' I forward the photo to Suzy.

'Thanks, it's coming through now,' says Suzy looking at her phone. 'Hey, hang on, there's some cute blond guy here, too.'

'I must have made a mistake. Oh my goodness,' I say.

'He certainly doesn't look like a mistake, Martha,' laughs Suzy. 'Come on. Spill the beans.' She holds the phone up beside her face and points to the phone. 'He is lush, lush, lush.'

Trevor comes to see what the fuss is all about.

'Oh, yeah, I would,' he says.

'Trevor,' I snap.

'What's going on here then?' says Sioned, walking in and looking at us all huddled together. 'Who's that? He's bloody lush,' she says, looking at the phone.

'See, told you, didn't I?' says Suzy, looking directly at me.

'Yes, okay, he is a bit "lush", as you put it,' I eventually agree.

'Well, come on then. Who is he?' asks Sioned.

'You'd better make a fresh brew,' I say as I begin the story of luscious Lars.

'Well, I'd go to the end of the earth for someone like that. He's gorgeous. You can't miss out on a happy life with him,' says Sioned.

'Why does nobody understand how hard it is for me? I have a life here with you guys. This is my life. You don't know that we'd be happy,' I say.

'Seriously, Martha. No way can you not message him. You've got to. If you don't go for it, you'll regret it. You could look back in ten years, when you're sixty and alone, and wonder what could have been,' says Suzy.

'Oh, my goodness, you make that sound awful. I enjoy my own company, thank you. I'll be fine,' I insist.

As I say it, I secretly know those words are untrue. I don't particularly enjoy my own company, although I know I should. I was so much happier being in Lars' arms, but, for all I know, he could be some big lothario. He has Dana and the girl in the supermarket ogling him every time they see him. Those are alarm bells, for a start.

'Look, I can't risk giving up what I have here for some crazy holiday romance,' I say.

'It doesn't seem like just a holiday romance from what you're saying, Martha,' says Trevor. 'I wouldn't tell someone about my family history, and I definitely wouldn't allow you to meet my family. No offence, like.'

'None taken,' I laugh.

I think about what they're saying, but then I remember another alarm bell.

'Ah, but also… Now, this is weird. I asked what happened to his wife, and he told me that he would explain when we went for a drink. Long story short, he never did tell me, but when I push for more information, he just says, "she perished". What on earth does that mean?' I say.

'She could have been in a fire,' says Sioned helpfully.

'Exactly, that's what I thought too. See, the problem is, when you meet someone on holiday you know nothing about them. What if he did something to her?' I say.

'I thought you said you'd put all your murder books in the bin. Come on, time to start believing in romance and happiness, you said. No more murdering talk. Besides, I just read that Copenhagen is the safest city in the world,' says Suzy.

'I wasn't in Copenhagen for long. We were out on an island. You've got to admit that saying your wife has perished is a bit weird,' I say.

'Stop! No more of this nonsense. Come on, message him. He seems lovely,' says Suzy.

I finish the dregs of my tea and look at my mug.

'I don't know,' I say.

All three faces peer at me intently.

'Message him,' they all shout together.

'All right, calm down, you lot,' I say. I pick up a Danish cookie and fiddle with it in my hand, and consider what they have said. 'Well, he was rather lush, wasn't he? Let me think about it,' I reply.

# Chapter Twenty-Four

Home from work, I pour the Alphabetti spaghetti onto my toast. I must have a search in the supermarket for some other bits and pieces. I quite got the taste for cooking from scratch while I was away. Perhaps I will stop there on the way back from my first Nordic Walking session tomorrow. I am quite excited about it now. The instructor told us he starts the coastal walk at seven pm and if the weather is nice, we can watch the sun go down whilst getting fit. That sounds so much nicer than a sweaty gym.

I click on the blog before Suzy arrives and update it with my latest post. I think it is only fair I keep my fans updated.

*Fans? Ooh, Martha, what are you like? You're not Adam Ant!*

> Today I went back to work after my holiday. I know nobody usually enjoys going back in after a break, but I work with such a great bunch of people that I had a lovely day. As you know, I had the most fabulous holiday, and I did meet someone very nice. But the team at work think I should message him. I thought it was only a holiday romance. It was fun while it lasted and all that. What do you think? Do I message or not? I was talked into it earlier when I was at work as they were encouraging me, but now I am a bit

Suzy knocks on the front door before I can check the messages, but I see four are waiting for me today. I am getting so much more confident with the blog now I am aware that people are seeking comfort from knowing they are not alone, so I don't mind that the counter is showing 650 hits.

Goodness, I could even be an internet millionaire at this rate! Could this possibly be the start of a new career if this takes off?

Angus is dressed in a checked shirt and smart shorts and looks quite the gentleman standing on the doorstep. I am sure he has grown whilst I was away.

'Hello, Angus. Did Gareth behave himself for you?' I ask as he walks in. He doesn't answer, and I can see he is sulking.

'Sorry, Martha. Angus is a bit upset, aren't you, baby?'

'Yes,' he snaps and stands in the corner, not looking at us.

'He doesn't want to give Gareth back. What was I thinking? I might have known this would happen,' says Suzy.

'Oh, dear. Well, look, do you want to keep him a while longer, then? Would that help?' I say.

Angus's face lights up. 'Yes, please, can I keep him? I want him forever,' he says.

I wasn't quite thinking forever, just a night or two until he got a bit more used to the idea that he has to return Gareth.

'Well, umm, okay. You know what, just keep him, Angus. He's yours. I'm sure he loves you more than me anyway.'

'Are you sure?' asks Suzy.

'Yes, it's fine,' I say. 'Honestly, I can see how attached Angus is to him.'

'Thank you, thank you, thank you. I love him so much. I love you, Gareth,' says Angus to the tank.

'No problem, I'm glad he's gone to a very good home,' I say. 'Ooh, and I have something for you.'

I get the magnets from upstairs and hand them to Angus.

'Here you go.'

'I love them! Thank you,' says Angus.

'You're very welcome. It was just something to say thank you for looking after Gareth so well.'

I pat Gareth's tank and say farewell to the happy goldfish.

'Goodbye, Gareth, you've been great company,' I say, as the tank disappears down the pathway.

I close the door and realise that I now truly live alone, so I grab my phone and consider messaging Lars. I read the message that he sent me earlier and think about Trevor's words. It does seem odd that he would introduce a holiday romance to his sister and brother-in-law. If I wasn't so cynical, I would think Lars genuinely wanted to continue our relationship.

Finally, I press reply and start to write something.

> Hi, I'm surprised to hear from you. I thought perhaps we wouldn't be in touch any longer now I'm back home. Thanks for the mug though…

No, that sounds a bit harsh.

I delete all the words and start over.

> Hello, how are you, good sir?

*Oh, Martha, that's far too formal*, I laugh to myself.

> Hi, how wonderful to hear from you.

Oh, that sounds pushy. I'm not desperate.

> Hello, sorry it took a while to reply.

Yes, I should apologise for the time it has taken me to respond; at least I should have some manners.

> I hope you're well. I've been busy unpacking and getting back to work. Thank you for the beautiful mug. That was so kind of you. What a wonderful surprise. Lovely to see the deer is still at the house. I miss it there.

I ensure I don't say that I miss him. Of course, I do, but I don't really want him knowing that. I'm not some young, foolish girl chasing an unattainable holiday romance.

I press send. There, that will do. I believe that's polite but gives no impression that I am sat at home crying over him.

I wonder what Lars is doing now. A surge of jealousy hits me as I imagine him with another woman. My imagination takes me away for a moment as I picture it. Is he sitting at the bar in town that we go to, talking to the lady who works there? Is he in the supermarket chatting to that pretty woman? I could drive myself insane imagining the possibilities. This is why I have never dated handsome men before. Not that I ever dated anyone except Anthony before. I don't have the confidence to be in a relationship with someone so good-looking. I don't want to fight women off. He could be up to anything with all those women adoring him. This is why I have to try and be realistic.

*Ooh, Martha, I know where he is. I bet he's in bed with Dana!*

'Stop it,' I shout out loud to myself.

I look down to see that Lars has messaged me. *You see, Martha. He wasn't in bed with Dana. He was messaging you, ha!*

Nervously, I pick up the phone to see what he says.

> Hello. It's chess night with Ludwig. The game isn't finished, but I had to leave as up early as always. Agnete was asking after you. It's lonely here without you. Hope you're okay, Omelette lady xx

He's lonely without me. That's excellent news.

'Is it really, Martha? No it isn't!' I say out loud.

'Stop it,' I argue with myself. 'He genuinely likes me.'

'He's just bored,' I say back to myself.

I pour myself a glass of water to collect my thoughts.

It seems I now not only talk to myself, but am arguing with myself! What is wrong with me? To stop myself from overthinking I type back a message immediately.

> It's nice to have a hobby. I'm looking forward to my Nordic Walking tomorrow. It should be fun. I'm sorry you're lonely without me. It's the same here. I do miss your kringle.

I send the message and then realise that might sound rude. I hope he doesn't think it is a euphemism. At least I only said I miss his baking and not him.

Seconds later, he replies.

> Oh, I would love to give you my kringle right now, believe me.

*Ooh, Martha, that's definitely a bit rude!* I throw my phone down on the table. Surely, he didn't mean it like that. I bite at my fingernail. How are you supposed to respond to that? A naughty feeling comes over me, and I start giggling to myself.

> Well, I might give you a nibble of my Welsh cake if you let me get my hands on your kringle.

I press send and cringe. Oh no, does that make me sound as though I have a food fetish? Two minutes later, he replies, and all is okay.

> Ha! Omelette lady, just wait until I see you again. Then, you can have all my kringle. I miss you. Please come back to Denmark now.

How sweet of him that he wants me back there so much. He really does appear to want me to return.

I look at the message and rest back in my chair. His request is tempting now Gareth is gone. There isn't much to keep me here, since Rosie is not coming back. But I want to help others with the grief group; I am even starting a new hobby tomorrow.

> I'm sorry. I wish I could, but it's just not possible. Sounds very tempting, though.

> That makes me sad. I didn't know anyone could make me so happy until we met.

I think back to all the things we did together. Undoubtedly, they were wonderful times.

> I know. We had a great time, but that was on holiday. Real life isn't the same.

> It would be a holiday for the rest of our lives if you come back. I promise we'd have the best times. Jeg elsker dig.

> What does that mean? Have you been drinking?

> No, I was driving tonight. Check your Danish dictionary! xx

I search for my dictionary that I didn't think I needed any longer. It is on the dining table, ready to be given to the church book sale. It means…

> Oh gosh, Lars.

> I mean it. I love you, Omelette lady! You're different to anyone I ever met. You don't know how special you are. That's so attractive to me.

I think of the landlady in the pub. She obviously had a lot of lip filler and thought she was rather special. At least that crosses her off my list of competitors. Hmm. I look down to see another message has popped up already.

I have a confession. I popped in to see
Olaf, and the cottage is free in five weeks'
time. Please let me book it xx

I can't ask for time off again. I'm sorry, it's
not possible. Maybe one day, but not now.

My heart aches as I send the message. My life was easier
without Lars in it. It has become so much more complicated now that I am torn between two countries.

When I go to bed, I dream about being with Lars.
How I wish I were curled around him right now. Perhaps
I should have avoided messaging; it has made me realise
how fond of him I had become in that short space of time.

How much longer can we manage to be apart from
each other? Right now, it feels so utterly sad.

# Chapter Twenty-Five

I keep myself busy with work. I make posters that introduce my new bereavement group. I call it 'Losing Yourself' like my blog and consider that I might even have groups all over Britain one day. Imagine how big this could get, I may even need my own premises! I have decided to hold the sessions on the first Wednesday of every month at seven pm. I figured that would give people enough time to get home from work and then to the meetings. I am excited, our first session will start next week. I hope it will give people enough notice. I will advertise it on my blog later, and pin posters on every noticeboard around the library.

Hopefully, we will have a nice crowd gather, so I decide to search for the perfect venue. I recall a place near the library that loans out rooms for evening classes and give them a call. I choose a room that can accommodate forty people, and consider that sufficient. However, if more turn up, then I suppose I can open the doors and arrange something.

With all the details in place I make up the poster on a simple Word document. I am sticking the last of the posters on the main entrance wall of the library when Mrs Morris walks up.

'Ooh, love. What's this?' she asks.

She pretends to read the poster for the bereavement group. So I read it out loud to her.

'Aww, it's a bit late for me to get home after it finishes, or I'd love to come. I don't like taking the bus after seven thirty, you see,' says Mrs Morris.

'I can give you a lift home, don't worry. Then we can have a chat in the car, and you can tell me what you thought of it,' I say.

'Well, you know I won't beat about the bush, mind. If it's crap, I will tell you.'

I can't help but chortle with laughter. She never fails to make me laugh. 'It won't be "crap", as you put it. I'm thinking this might even get big. Goodness knows what could happen if this goes well. Church halls, hotel meeting rooms, my groups could be hosted anywhere. I have big plans,' I say.

'Aye, there we are, then. Don't run before you can walk now, love. Rome wasn't built in a day,' says Mrs Morris.

'Sorry, I know. I'm getting carried away, but I'm just so excited that this might help people like you and me.'

'I know, bach. I know you're trying to make a difference. Bless you.'

Mrs Morris is not a touchy-feely person, but she touches my arm and rubs it. 'You mean well, don't you?' she says. 'No wonder that hot Danish man wants you to go to see him again.'

'How do you know about that bit of gossip? Suzy, wasn't it? I can't believe she told you,' I say.

'We're just happy for you, that's all. It's lovely that after Anthony's death, you've met someone.'

Mrs Morris always seems to have life worked out. So I can't resist asking her what she would do if it were her.

'He wouldn't have to ask me twice. I'd have already been on a flight to see him,' she laughs. 'If I was your age, of course. Not now, like.'

'I don't know. Let's see what happens. Anyway, I've got my Nordic Walking class tonight,' I say.

'Ooh, what's that, then?' she asks.

'You walk with these specially made poles and… It's so easy,' I explain.

—

Five hours later, I learn that Nordic Walking is nowhere near easy.

'Welcome to the beginner's class. I'm Malcolm,' says a healthy, robust man in full hiking gear. I thought we were just going along the coastal path. Instead, this man is equipped for Everest.

Malcolm sweeps his grey hair from his eyes and tells us he will come around and help us choose our gear. Fortunately, he rents out equipment before we have to invest in any kit.

'Try before you buy,' he insists.

I am relieved as I didn't fancy shelling out £129 for some carbon walking sticks alone.

'So, let me have a look. Hmm, you're not very tall,' says Malcolm, inspecting me. 'Let me make these sticks a bit shorter for you. Now, you have to strap them on your wrists like this.'

Malcolm leans in and straps my wrists to the poles. He is so close I smell the coffee on his breath.

'Push down on the stick. First, you have to get the technique right. Now, let me see,' he says, watching me closely.

I try my hardest to push down, but it feels a bit strange with the straps around my wrists. I feel as though I am in handcuffs and so lose all control of the sticks.

'Like this, for goodness' sake,' says Malcolm. He doesn't seem to have much patience for an instructor teaching beginners.

He demonstrates how you are supposed to hold everything and makes it look effortless. It certainly doesn't feel like that to me. Who knew holding a pair of sticks could be so blooming difficult?

'Right, let's not waste any more time. Are we all ready?' asks Malcolm.

'Yes,' the other people shout, eager to go and as though they are in some kind of cult. There are about ten of us in total. We are made up of a range of ages, although I notice that nobody is under forty-five.

Malcolm turns around to set off, and as he does, my pole flies up in the air. It is as though I have some kind of involuntary spasm that makes me lose control of the stick, and it smacks Malcolm straight on the bottom.

'Oh my goodness. I am so sorry,' I say.

A lady beside me, who introduces herself as Angela, bursts out laughing. Malcolm, meanwhile, gives me a horrified look.

'That's hilarious. He deserved it, to be fair. I'd love to smack him on the bottom with my stick,' she says, waving the stick in the air.

Thank goodness for Angela, or I don't think I would manage the rest of the class. I just want to turn around and go home. I haven't exactly made the best impression.

Malcolm hurries us along for the two-hour session, and aside from some beautiful sunset views, it has to be the worst two hours of my life. The poles fly everywhere, and I can't get the hang of it.

'Would you like me to book you in for next week's session?' asks Malcolm when we finally return after the most arduous workout ever.

I don't think it is my imagination, but I get the feeling he wants me to say no. However, all the class is looking at me, so I feel too embarrassed to say no outright, even though I know that I will never do this again.

'Let me get back to you. I'm setting up a bereavement group at the moment, so it's a bit busy,' I say.

'A bereavement group?' asks Angela. 'My sister and my boyfriend died within six months of each other. I'd certainly like to know more about that.'

'That's great. Oh, I don't mean that's great. I mean... Oh goodness!'

'It's okay. I know what you're trying to say,' she smiles.

It is at times like this that I wish I thought before I spoke. I also wish I had business cards; I might think about getting some further down the line. However, as I don't have any, I tell Angela to look up the blog, send me a message, and I will give her any other information she needs.

I leave the Nordic Walking class pleased that whilst I may have hated the class, at least I did a bit of networking, as Anthony would put it.

On the drive home, I think about the premises I may need if the group continues to expand at this rate. *Steady on, Martha. It's only one new member!*

Despite the sensible me recognising that I am getting carried away, the new, reckless me can't help getting overexcited. Perhaps I should look at commercial rental properties in the area, just in case I get so big that I have to hold meetings at my very own venue. Although that would mean that I would have to charge people for the groups, which would be difficult. I can't imagine them coming in crying and then asking them for five pounds like they are at some kind of slimming club meeting. Perhaps the local government would give me a grant to start an official bereavement charity, or what about lottery funding? They do things for local communities. If I were eligible for lottery funding, it would certainly help me grow the group so that I could reach out to more people. *My goodness, Martha, you are a genius!*

I rush home, slamming the car into the drive, almost scraping the side of the passenger door as I'm so excited, and run inside to check out the prices of commercial properties in the area in case I do expand the group. Even the sight of Mrs Roberts's cat Kevin on the lawn doesn't stop me in my tracks.

I click on the local estate agent's website and notice that one of the properties further down the road is for sale. They're asking £450,000. Goodness me, the prices have gone up around here. Pomegranate View has only three bedrooms; we have four. They don't even overlook any pomegranates.

I might have to get a valuation; I would be highly tempted to sell up at that price. After all, I no longer need four bedrooms when it is just me. Instead, I could use the cash to have an office where people could drop by and chat, until I got the relevant funding. From looking through the adverts, I see that the rates of commercial properties aren't horrendously expensive in the town. I am sure I could manage the rent for a bit.

I think about how people approach projects on programmes like *Dragons' Den* and *The Apprentice*. Every idea begins with some kind of business plan. Isn't this how everything starts, even charities? I would no doubt need something when I show the lottery folk my dream charity organization.

I remove a notepad from Anthony's bureau and start work on my very own plan for a charity. I find myself filling in three sheets of paper with my goals. But as I turn the page over, I notice something written down in Anthony's handwriting. There is no mistaking it. I recognise it immediately and the way he did a swirl on the end of his A.

*FIA, 23rd May, 6:30 pm, Goodwig Hotel.*

I can't believe what I am seeing. The Goodwig was where Anthony died. His anniversary is the twenty-third of May, and the time of his death was 6:30 pm.

Did he have some kind of premonition? And what on earth does 'FIA' mean?

# Chapter Twenty-Six

I am not feeling particularly refreshed this morning. I have tossed and turned all night, wondering what the note could mean. I don't think I slept for even an hour in one go. The day he died, Anthony left the house because he wanted to get away from me, and he stormed off in a temper. I always believed it was my fault Anthony was dead. He wouldn't have died if I hadn't upset him, causing him to drive so carelessly. If I hadn't asked him for money to pay for Rosie's school trip, none of this would have happened. The fact that he had the place and time of his death written down makes no sense whatsoever.

I call Lars to say good morning, then I lock the front door before leaving for work. I spot Kevin in the garden. Mrs Roberts from next door turns her back as soon as she sees me.

I know I should keep my composure, but I can't help take out my frustrations on her and Kevin.

'Kevin is in the rockery again,' I shout across the fence.

'He's a good boy, my Kev. Aren't you, puss?' she says, summoning him back over.

'Then why can't he do his business in his own garden?' I ask.

She turns on her heel and tries to go in the door, but Kevin isn't quite ready to follow her.

'Come on, Kev, inside now,' she says.

'And who on earth calls their cat Kevin, anyway?' I add.

'You can't talk. I heard you called your goldfish Gareth,' says Mrs Roberts.

'I didn't name him, and that's not the point. I'm sick of Kevin using my rockery as a litter tray. Please do something about it,' I snap.

'I can't control a cat. What's wrong with you? And if you fixed this fence, he might not come over so much,' says Mrs Roberts, pulling at the rotten wooden fence panel that I choose to ignore.

'Sort your fence out, yeah? Little Kev could get caught on it when he pops over to your garden for a wander,' she continues. She grabs a piece of the fence and starts shaking it loose. 'See, told you it needs to be removed,' she says, as a fence panel lands flat on my side of the garden.

I look at her incredulously.

'You've just ripped my fence down.' I scream.

'It was so rotten it fell down,' argues Mrs Roberts.

Finally, I snap.

'I can't take any more of you or Kevin. I'm selling up,' I say.

'Good. I'll be glad to see the back of you, quite frankly,' says Mrs Roberts.

'Ditto,' I say.

'You have no idea, do you?' says Mrs Roberts.

'No idea about what?' I ask.

'Your husband,' she laughs.

'What in heavens do you mean?'

'You must have known where he was going when he died,' she insists. 'Everyone else did.'

'Umm, we'd had a bit of a row. I don't remember if there was some shouting before he left… I'm sorry if we disturbed you, but…'

'Yeah, that man was no saint,' continues Mrs Roberts.

'I have no idea what you're getting at. Explain,' I say.

'Well, he was a bit of a ladies' man, wasn't he? Don't know what they saw in him, mind.'

'What are you trying to say, Mrs Roberts? Was he having an affair?'

Kevin sidles up to Mrs Roberts and purrs at her right ankle.

'Aww, come on, Kev. Time for breakfast, sweetie.'

'What are you trying to say?' I insist.

'Goodbye, hope the house sells quickly for you,' says Mrs Roberts as she slams the door.

I am rather shell-shocked on my drive to work. My Anthony, who I thought was a faithful family man all these years, was having an affair and Mrs Roberts knew about it? Are her comments connected to the note in some way?

I ring Basil Jones Estates when I get to work and ask for a valuation. I think I need a new start, even if it is down the road, and not necessarily Denmark. There are too many ghosts of the past, and the neighbours aren't particularly delightful, either. Mrs Roberts has always been odd with me, since the day we moved in after we married. I have never understood what her problem is. I now wonder if she thought I knew my husband was a ladies' man and assumed that I simply turned a blind eye and put up with it. However, I never had any indication that such a conservative man would behave in this manner. I am absolutely devastated and feel as though I have lost my husband for a second time.

I don't know how I muddle through work, but somehow I manage to get through the morning in a daze. Although I do occasionally have to run to the toilet and have a good cry. I am relieved when I get my lunch break and take the page that I have now torn out of the notebook and read it over and over. *FIA*. What on earth could it mean? Is this a woman's name?

'What's that you got there? Everything okay?' says Suzy.

I haven't been able to confide in anyone about this morning's revelations, not even Suzy. I am so embarrassed that I failed to notice my husband was a womaniser.

I think twice about telling her about the paper I have found, but I need someone's opinion.

'I found this piece of paper. Look, it's got the time and place of Anthony's death on it. But what does it mean?' I say.

Suzy takes the paper from me and studies it.

'Well, if I'm not mistaken, that looks like initials or an abbreviation. Don't you think?'

'I can't think of anything. Is there a Federation of International Accountants, or something? I honestly cannot think of anything that it could be, unless it is someone's name,' I hint.

'Hmm, it is strange. To me, it looks as though he was meeting someone. It's as if he's written down a place and time of a meeting, don't you think?' says Suzy.

'But that wouldn't make sense because he was home with me. He left that night because we had a row, and he stormed off. He had no plans that night that he had told me of,' I explain.

'I'm baffled then. So strange,' says Suzy.

'I know, but there's something else. This morning my neighbour told me that Anthony was a ladies' man. I'm so upset,' I say. Telling Suzy makes me burst into tears again. I still can't quite believe it.

'Well, perhaps, she was just trying to stir up trouble. You've said yourself, there's no love lost between you both. But, look, you've always enjoyed investigating things. Perhaps it's time you investigated your own husband. If you actually want to know, that is,' says Suzy.

Her idea fills me with dread. I made enough of a fool out of myself in Denmark thinking those laughing gas canisters were some big conspiracy. I don't want to make a fool of myself again. Finding out the truth makes me incredibly nervous.

'Perhaps you're right. Mrs Roberts is trying to get revenge on me for me reversing into her wall that one time. Maybe I'm jumping to conclusions and getting carried away,' I say.

'Yes, perhaps. Although the note is strange. It's bizarre to have the date and time of your death written down like this. Did you ever go through his things after he died and find anything strange?' says Suzy.

'Oh goodness. No. I left everything just as it was. Though I am thinking of putting the house on the market, so if I was to sell, I will need a good clear-out,' I say.

'To be honest, I think moving to a new home could be just the start you need. It's time for you to move on now. Perhaps you'll find a piece of the missing jigsaw when you clear everything out, and you'll get the answers you're looking for,' says Suzy.

'Perhaps,' I say.

I am absolutely terrified as I think about my quest for the truth – it could be like opening a can of worms. What if there was a secret love child that I never knew about, or he could have even been up to some type of fraud so that he could afford to entertain any lady friends? Is that why he could afford such a good life insurance policy? Surely not. Anthony was a bit difficult at times, but he would never do anything he shouldn't. He was an honest man with his finances, at least. Surely there has to be some kind of explanation to all of this. Am I truthfully a naive wife who didn't know her husband as well as she thought?

For my next blog entry, I know what I have to write.

> Do you think we knew our partners? It's easy to look back with fondness and good memories on our relationships with the deceased, but what if they weren't who you thought they were? What if you found a secret from beyond the grave? What would you do? I haven't found any secrets... Well, not really... But something has come up that has made me think about things. It has made me wonder if I knew my husband. What if he kept secrets from me? Has anyone reading this had a surprise after their loved one died? Please let me know. Anyway, not long until our first West Wales meeting. I hope anyone from the area who is reading this can make it on Wednesday. It would be so great to see your faces.

I click on the messages to see that Izzy has said she can't wait to meet me and again tells me how much this blog has helped her since she stumbled upon it accidentally. She says some things are just meant to be. Tom says he wishes he could be at the meeting, but it's too far away for him to travel. However, if I ever start any groups in Southampton, he would be happy to join them. Perhaps I should ask him if he would like to begin the first group outside Wales. *Ooh, Martha, that would impress the lottery funding folk, ha!*

There is also a message from Angela.

Found you! So great to meet you at Nordic Walking.
Looking forward to coming to the group meeting
Wednesday. Angela xx

The other messages seem to be spam, and one is asking if I want to pay for my funeral now so that I don't leave my loved ones out of pocket. You can even choose the coffin of your dreams, some of which are quite impressive. I quickly delete the message in case I buy anything impulsively. I am here to offer help and not get carried away.

When I finish with the blog, I think about the note once again. What if I was to look in Anthony's side of the wardrobe? Would I find something unexpected? This thought plays on my mind all evening until I can't think about anything else. Even a long conversation with Lars on the phone doesn't take my mind off things.

Eventually, I pour myself a sherry for courage and fling open the cupboard before I can back out.

'Right then, Anthony. What were you keeping from me?' I say to myself as I rifle through his suit pockets.

I don't find anything of much consequence for a while, just a five-pound note, an empty chocolate wrapper, some mints – which are long expired – and a stash of accountancy magazines.

But then, in the pocket of a pair of jeans which are folded neatly over a hanger, I discover a parking ticket for a Pay and Display in Chester. I would think it was someone else's ticket, as he has never been there as far as I know, except that his car number plate is clearly stated on the ticket.

Did he take someone with him? What on earth would Anthony's car be doing in Chester?

# Chapter Twenty-Seven

I put my worries aside for the first meeting of the 'Losing Yourself' bereavement group. My detective work on exactly who FIA is, will have to wait as I am expecting forty lonely, grieving people to show up to my first meeting.

Suzy keeps asking me why I am so sure of the numbers, but, as I have reminded her all day, I have booked the Rosedale Suite, and that is its capacity. Plus, I worked out that at least forty people must want to come as I have flyers everywhere. Surely there are forty people in need of sharing their grief in this town.

I have practiced my welcome speech in the mirror at least ten times. I have never been fond of public speaking, but this is different. I am in charge and chairing the meeting, rather than being asked to stand up and say something I haven't prepared for in front of lots of people. I have also bought a briefcase for this inaugural meeting to make myself look professional. Fortunately, I was passing the Oxfam window when I spotted a brown, slightly tattered one. I couldn't believe my luck.

I have had butterflies all morning, and even messages from Lars don't put me at ease. He knows all about my venture and has sent countless messages wishing me luck and telling me 'I will smash it' all day. Nothing helps though, and as the time draws closer, I find myself a bag of nerves. I try to remind myself that I am doing this for everyone else. I am helping others, not myself.

I place the chairs around in a circle as they would do at any self-help meeting and place a table in the middle with the essentials. I have a box of tissues and some biscuits on hand for anyone feeling emotional.

At five to seven, I feel as though I will vomit all over the trousers I bought in Denmark. Nobody has arrived yet, but I assume they will all reach here in a group. Perhaps they have all started talking downstairs on the way in.

Finally, at 7:01 pm, I hear the familiar sound of footsteps in the distance. I recognise that walk.

'Hiya, bach. You all right? Where is everyone, then?' asks Mrs Morris.

I look around at the empty room and think how I would like to know the same thing.

'I don't know,' I admit.

'Someone was mooching about downstairs. I think she was going to the fashion design class, though. She was very snazzily dressed,' says Mrs Morris.

'Oh, perhaps our group went to the wrong room. Let's wait a little longer before we start. Do you want a biscuit while we wait?' I ask.

'Oh, go on then. Have you got any fig rolls?'

Mrs Morris flicks all the biscuits in the tin until she finds one of her favourite fig rolls at the bottom. 'Ah, lovely,' she says, munching away.

Suddenly a gang of five teenagers walk into the room.

'Hello, welcome,' I say. I was expecting an older crowd, but this is great.

'Umm, where's the guitars?' asks one of them.

Before I can answer, Mrs Morris stops me.

'There was a right bloody racket downstairs. I thought I could hear guitars. On the first floor, boys,' she says.

'Ta,' says one of the gang as they all leave the room.

'I think guitar lessons are going on downstairs,' explains Mrs Morris, taking a final bite of the fig biscuit.

Perhaps that is what has happened to my class. I bet there are a bunch of bereaved people sitting in a guitar class. I should have put arrows to the room, perhaps.

Finally, I hear the clink of high heels.

'Ooh, hello,' I say as two figures approach the door, one of whom is Angela. 'Are you both here for the bereavement group?' I ask.

'Yes, hi. I'm Izzy, so good to meet you,' says a petite dark-haired younger lady.

I remember her saying how she was bereaved in her thirties. She looks fantastic, and I should think she spends most of her days doing Pilates or some kind of bendy thing. She is not how I imagined she would be when we chatted online. She is pretty glamourous, like one of those sickening creatures who get up out of bed in the morning and immediately looks good.

I check the clock on the wall and notice that it is already quarter past seven. My heart sinks at the thought that nobody else is attending. Surely anyone in the wrong class would have realised by now?

The four of us sit and stare at each other, waiting for someone to speak, surrounded by thirty-six empty chairs.

'Well, I suppose we'd better start then,' I say. I look down at my shoes. The embarrassment is making me unable to look the three of them in the eye.

'My name is Martha, as you will probably know' I start. 'My husband has been gone a few years now. As those who read the blog will know, I still miss him and feel guilty for him not surviving and me being here and living my life. It feels like a part of me died that day, but I know I have to keep on living. I try to be strong, and it's getting easier. So, anyway… Please tell me about yourselves.'

Mrs Morris tells us all about Gerald. How he died a long time ago, and one day they will be reunited, and she is looking forward to being with him again.

'Oh, he was a right old boy, my Gerald. He always liked playing pranks on people. One time, I was doing the dishes, and he came in and said… Oh, what did he say now? He said… Oh, that's it! No, it's gone again. Sorry, I forgot, but it was funny.'

The room descends into silence again, apart from the noise one of my posters makes as it falls off the wall and onto the floor.

I want to get the others a little more involved and wonder if Izzy might contribute and help us along a little.

'Izzy, would you like to tell us about your loved one that has sadly passed?' I ask.

'He was my soulmate.' Izzy starts to cry, so I pass her the box of tissues. 'I don't think I can talk about it tonight,' she sobs.

'Oh, please, don't worry. You don't have to talk if you don't want to. You can just listen to the others,' I say. I look around the room and realise we only have one more person that we can listen to.

It doesn't take Angela two minutes to tell her story, and I look at the clock and realise it is only half past seven, and we are all done. I suppose I had planned for forty people to talk, so we finish much earlier than expected.

'Well, thanks for coming. I hope you'll join us again next week. I'm sure there will be more of us then. Once word gets around it will no doubt be packed,' I say eventually.

Angela and Izzy thank me politely and head off together, chatting. At least they seem to have made friends, so it wasn't too much of a disaster.

I stack all the chairs back up and clear the crumbs that Mrs Morris has dropped before taking her home with me in the car.

'Well, that went okay for a first meeting,' I say, putting my seatbelt on.

'I don't know if I'd bother doing another one, though, love. I don't think it's worth the effort, to be truthful,' says Mrs Morris.

I do sometimes wish she wasn't so honest.

'Oh, come on. I bought a briefcase and everything now, Mrs Morris. Don't be silly,' I say.

'You know I'd always support you, don't you? But I don't think I'll be coming to the next one. There wasn't exactly any audience participation, was there?' continues Mrs Morris.

She looks at her teeth in the mirror of the sun visor and then slams the visor shut.

'I think you need to be careful. There's something shifty about that Angela woman. I can't put my finger on it, but I don't trust her one bit. I didn't like her. She's what my Gerald would call a snake,' says Mrs Morris.

'She's lovely, Mrs Morris. How can you say that?' I ask.

'The way she looked at you. It was as if she knew you from somewhere.'

'Well, yes, I met her at an exercise class,' I explain.

'Oh, I don't know. Just keep an eye on her. That's all I'm saying. Watch your back,' says Mrs Morris.

'Okay, but what can she possibly want from me? Surely the worst thing she could do is set up a competitive bereavement group, and she'd hardly be stealing people from me,' I laugh, finally seeing the funny side. 'It was a disaster, wasn't it, Mrs Morris? You can say it.'

'Yeah, it was a bit, love. Sorry to say, but it was a bloody disaster. I know you're trying your best, but I don't know why you bother. Go and live your life with your handsome Viking man. Everyone will be okay. You don't have to save everyone, you know,' says Mrs Morris as we approach her bungalow.

'We'll see. Anyway, thanks for coming tonight. I know you're right,' I say.

'I'm always right,' she laughs.

I think about telling Mrs Morris about the mystery note and what that nosy neighbour of mine said, but she will undoubtedly be keen to get to bed, so I stop myself. I bet she would know how to handle all of this.

'Now, you get home and tell that handsome man you're coming back. Toodle-pip, now off you go,' smiles Mrs Morris.

I drive off with a big smile on my face. My night might have been a disappointing disaster, but she is right. I should be more open-minded about Lars.

However, if there is to be any kind of future, the first thing I need to do is to tell Rosie about him. And I don't think she is going to take kindly to this news.

# Chapter Twenty-Eight

I look at the time and, from what Rosie has told me about her daily itinerary, she should be back from feeding the orangutans shortly. She usually has some free time about now, so this is as good a time as any.

I dial the number with my heart in my mouth. I realise that I am almost scared of my daughter.

'Hiya, everything okay, Mam? You don't usually ring at this time,' says Rosie breathlessly.

'Oh, sorry, is it a bad time?' I ask as I hear some giggling in the background. 'Is that Ben I can hear?'

'Yeah. You're tickling me. Get off,' she laughs.

'Umm, as I said, is this a bad time?'

'No, it's okay. Go on… Ben, stop it,' says Rosie.

Her command seems to quieten him down, and I take a deep breath before I begin.

'So, you know how I went to Denmark on holiday?' I start.

'Yeah, and?'

'Well, when I was there, I met someone.'

I take a deep breath. This is so hard to say.

'I met a really lovely guy called Lars. He desperately wants me to go back there and see him, and I'm tempted.' I say it quickly, so that I can't back out.

'You what, Mammy? Oh. My. God. What about Dad? How can you forget him so easily?' says Rosie.

'With all due respect, Rosie dear, it's been over two years.'

I almost want to snap and say that she has no idea what he was up to. The anger that rises inside me at her response makes me want to tell her about her dad's note and what Mrs Roberts said. Of course, I bite my tongue, but boy am I tempted.

'He loved you and would have done anything for you, Mam. I don't think he'd have rushed out and met someone else. That's all I'm saying. I didn't think this would ever happen,' says Rosie.

'Well, it did, I'm afraid,' I say.

'I'm going to tell Ben. See what he thinks, but I bet it's not just me that thinks you should have other things in your life at this stage and not be looking for a replacement of Dad. I can't deal with this. I'm going now, okay? I need to take this all in,' says Rosie, with the sound of tears in her voice.

I stare at the phone as the line goes dead. She's put the phone down on me. I knew she wouldn't be ecstatic, but I never wanted to upset her.

I see there is a message from Lars asking how my day is going. I burst into tears. I don't want to be torn between him and my daughter; I would never want that. Oh dear, what have I done? Perhaps it was too soon to tell her. I regret the decision instantly and frantically consider how I can put things right. However, an hour later, there is a message from Rosie.

I overreacted. It's just a shock, you know?
Ben says I was hard on you. He says his
gran remarried when she was seventy-five,
and so I shouldn't be so judgemental.
Sorry, I got that bit from you. Ha. Love you.
You deserve happiness. I owe you an
apology, and you know I never say sorry!
Xxx

I am so incredibly relieved that I burst into tears once again. My emotions are everywhere at the moment. Thank goodness she understands. Ben is certainly a calming influence in her life. I do hope we meet soon.

With Rosie having calmed down, I explain to Lars that I would like to take a chance on him. I tell him that my bereavement group didn't work out, and I think it is best I give it up. My house is about to go on the market, so I don't have much to lose except for my job.

Before I speak to Suzy and ask if I can get some unpaid time off, I tell Lars to check with Olaf whether the cottage is still available. Once I know the dates, I can see what Suzy can work out.

As I think about how wonderful it will be to see Lars again, the doorbell rings, and for once, I don't hide. I am expecting the estate agent and have been burning scented candles that I picked up in Asda since I got up. I open the door to him and notice that Mrs Roberts' net curtains are twitching. Of course, it doesn't help when the car parked outside has the estate agent's fancy logo all over it.

'Ooh, nice big entrance you have here,' says the man, introducing himself as Graham.

I think back to Rosie leaving this door to go to school and, years later, the memory of Anthony shouting the last time he walked out. I can see the stripy shirt he was wearing and the new jeans he had bought. It was the first time he had worn them and I was surprised he had been hanging around the house in them all evening. He even had new loafers. He had never been a loafer man before. Anthony always preferred comfy lace-ups until recently. What if that was what caused the accident? Perhaps his new shoes made him slip on the accelerator and kept him plunging forward?

'How many is it?' asks Graham.

'How many what?' I say.

'Bedrooms, Mrs Jenkins. Bedrooms?'

'Oh, sorry. Four. But we do have a study too. Would that push the price up?' I ask.

Graham doesn't answer and continues to make notes in the black folder he carries.

'Nice, neutral walls. Good,' he says to himself as he walks into the lounge.

'Oh, I was going to add a conservatory. I even tried to get on the dark web to find a cheaper one, but... I hope the value of the house won't be affected because I haven't got one,' I say.

Graham gives me a bewildered look and gets a tape measure from his pocket.

'Would you mind holding this?' he says.

I'm glad Mrs Morris isn't here now. She'd be giggling rudely. I do as I am told until I am allowed to let go.

'Would you like a cup of tea or anything?' I ask. I haven't been very hospitable to him.

'No, I'm all right. Thank you. Better get around the house, I have another viewing to do after this. Now if you can point me to the master bedroom,' says Graham.

I lead him up to my bedroom that has been tidied in anticipation of his visit. I look around the room that I shared with Anthony for so long. It looks cluttered and I don't think any feng shui expert would be impressed. Perhaps that's where our marriage went wrong!

Next, I lead him into Rosie's room. Graham takes notes and measures the walls with their One Direction posters on. I look at a poster of Harry Styles, feeling guilty. She has no idea I am doing this.

'Right, think that's it,' says Graham as we head back downstairs.

'I'll do some calculations back at the office, but I think we're looking at somewhere around £490,000. You might get half a mil,' says Graham.

'Half a mil!' I say.

'Yes, I think we'll shift this pretty quickly, to be honest. In fact, I have a family looking for something right now. This fits their requirements. Would you have somewhere to go if we sell fast?' asks Graham.

I think of the cottage and hope it is still available.

'I suppose I'd have to put my things into storage, but… Yes, I have somewhere I can go,' I say.

A feeling of liberation comes over me. So many things have happened in this house, some good, some bad, but what feels right is letting it go. I am excited about leaving it behind.

In fact, I am so excited that once Graham leaves, I grab some bin bags and start sifting through more things. If the house were to sell quickly, I would certainly need to be organised. I start on Anthony's drawer. I should have taken his stuff to the charity shop a long time ago, maybe I would have found something was amiss much sooner.

As I start to rummage, I feel as though I am violating his privacy going through all his bits and pieces like this, but it has to be done if I want to find out the truth.

Before placing his items in the bin bags to take to the Heart Foundation, I look at every piece of clothing for clues as to what he has been up to – even the golf shoes and jumper he bought, which still have the tags on. I remember him buying them, as he said he might take up the sport so he could do a bit of networking on the golf course. To my knowledge he never did and the new clothes confirm this.

I look at his socks. The cartoon characters on them stare back at me. Does the fact that such a serious man wore cartoon patterned socks and underwear subconsciously represent that he was not all he appeared to be?

A brand-new pair of khaki chinos surprise me. Anthony always told me off about spending money and yet here at the back of the drawer are jumpers, trousers and a shirt, all unworn. How careful I would be buying second-hand clothes while he was spending on all these new clothes that he never even wore! This discovery annoys me, so I scrunch up his underpants into a ball and throw them against the wall in a temper.

I then empty three drawers quite quickly. It is surprising how much faster I work in a bad mood. Finally, I start on the last drawer. I almost give up on finding any clues of who exactly he was involved with and throw the things in the bin bag carelessly. But then I see something that makes me stop. In front of me is a printout. I carefully unfold the sheets of paper and read the words in front of me.

Oh, my goodness, it is a boarding pass for a flight to Rio de Janeiro dated for the day after Anthony died.

Was he going to take me to Rio? Was he guilty about something and planning a surprise to make my dream come true?

I am heartbroken as I clutch the boarding pass. What if he was going to take me on the holiday of a lifetime and I had no idea? Perhaps that is why money was tight and he was acting so strangely the day he died.

I look at the second page of the paper to confirm my name, but drop it in horror. My heart rate quickens and I feel a panic attack begin. Something which hasn't happened for a while.

It is not my name that is on there, but someone else's.

He was supposed to be travelling with a Ms. F. Andrews.

# Chapter Twenty-Nine

Sometimes it is easier to talk to strangers when you have a crisis. Part of me wants to pick up the phone and confide in Suzy, but I can't quite say the words out loud yet. The name that has sent the world I knew into a spin – Ms. F. Andrews.

I would like to look up social media for the culprit, find out more about who she could possibly be. But what does the F stand for? Felicity, Faith, Fay? It could be anything. I don't know where to start with any of it really, so I confide in the people who read my blog.

> I am so sorry to be writing this, but today I really need YOUR help. I have discovered something shocking about my husband. I will come straight out with it. He was supposed to be taking someone to Rio with him the day after he died and I had no idea. Why would he have a flight booked to Rio with another woman? I mean why? Was it a business trip? Do accountants have business trips to Rio? Do you think it could be an innocent work trip? Or was he having an affair? I know it's obvious but I don't want to accept the truth. I still keep looking for other reasons. I guess it just helps telling you all. Anyway, hope you're all well and please tell me what I should do next, because I have no idea. M x

I check the messages that are waiting for me. Tom has sent me a lovely message asking how the meeting went. I don't think I will tell him what a disaster it all was. There are the usual spam messages and a message from Izzy.

> Hi Martha,
> Just wanted to thank you for the meeting the other day. It was nice to meet a new friend and Angela and I have a lot in common. I wanted to let you know that I won't be attending any of the further meetings as it wouldn't be appropriate given the circumstances. I'm sure you'll agree.
> Wish you all the best,
> Izzy.

Circumstances? What circumstances? Because nobody turned up at the meeting? I want to ask what she is on about but she seems to have blocked me after sending the message. I can't reply. Goodness, was I that awful at the meeting? I know sometimes you can meet someone online and think they are nice and then meet them and not get on, but surely I wasn't bad enough to block? Her tone is completely different too, what happened to 'Hi lovely lady' and all the kisses? At least I can still get in touch with Angela, even though Mrs Morris warned me not to trust her. Perhaps Angela knows something.

I message her to find out what's going on.

> Hi Angela,
> I am sorry the other night was such a let-down for everyone. I expected a lot more people to turn up so I was very disappointed with the turnout.
> I hope you don't mind me asking you this, but is Izzy okay? This is a bit embarrassing but she seems to

have removed her account, or more likely blocked
me. I wondered if I had done something to upset
her? She also said that she couldn't attend another
meeting 'because of the circumstances'. Do you have
any idea at all what she is talking about? Has she
said anything to you? I wouldn't mean to offend her,
if I have then please send my apologies to her.
Hope to hear from you soon.
Martha x

I am quiet for most of the day at work as I try to put all the
missing pieces of this jigsaw together. I was right; I am no
Gretchen Rasmussen – she would have solved this in no
time at all. I can only deduce that Anthony was having an
affair with Ms. F. Andrews. But quite why Izzy is so odd
with me doesn't add up. Perhaps it's a coincidence and
I am looking into everything too much. It isn't exactly
surprising when I have had the shock of my life. Nothing
is as it seems any more.

Unfortunately, it isn't Mrs Morris's day to come to the
library today or I would ask her what she thought, since
she met both Angela and Izzy.

I must ask her when she is in tomorrow. I do consider
checking with Trevor if perhaps I have the wrong end of
the stick and Izzy hasn't blocked me, but done something
to her device. However, it's obvious her tone was different
and she wanted nothing more to do with me.

I have only been blocked once before and that was by
someone in school who blocked me on Facebook. I wasn't
wearing my glasses and had pressed a laughing emoji on
a sad story she posted and by the time I realised what I
had done, she had blocked me. I don't think I pressed any
wrong buttons on my blog.

Thoughts of Izzy and what I have done to her go around in my head all day. I can't wait to get home to see if Angela has responded to my message. I don't even let Suzy know I am leaving work as I am in such a hurry.

As I get home, I notice the 'For Sale' sign has already gone up on the lawn. They don't waste any time. I bet Mrs Roberts' eyeballs were on stalks when she saw that. She probably lent them the hammer to make sure the stake was firmly in the ground.

For once, Kevin isn't roaming around the garden. Perhaps the sign will scare him off, like a scarecrow for cats.

Rushing into the house I pop the kettle on and open my laptop. *Please let me have a response from Angela.* Unfortunately, there is nothing from her. There is a message from Tom though.

Hi Martha,

I am sorry to hear about all these secrets that are coming out. I have to tell you what I think, as you seem to want to know. I think he was having an affair and running off to Rio with the lady in question. Apologies if this isn't what you want to hear, but I think you will appreciate me being truthful with you. I know it must be a shock, and I did ask Sparky if he thought I should tell you. He wagged his tail so I took that as a yes. I hope you can find peace if you have the answers. My Sandra would never have had an affair and I am so thankful for that. Some people don't take their marriages seriously nowadays, makes me mad. Now make a nice cup of hot chocolate, with marshmallows if you must, and have a cry. Hopefully you'll feel a bit better in the morning. Take care of yourself, love, Tom.

Bless him, such a lovely man.

Lars calls me and we chat about our day. He sold out of his *spandauers* today. It's not surprising, they are delicious. I then attempt to watch TV but even the sight of Alan Titchmarsh doesn't help. I can't concentrate on anything until I hear back from Angela. What if she doesn't message me? How will I cope?

I check the messages again at nine o'clock. Surely, she will be home by now and had a chance to read my message.

Finally, at 9:30 pm, I see her message. I can't open it fast enough.

> Hello again!
> Sorry that Izzy blocked you. I guess you didn't deserve that. She said you knew? I don't understand. She said that your husband had told you. I know the circumstances have been difficult, but you're such a trooper. I admire your strength. I don't think I will be at the next meeting, btw. I feel a lot better after everything. It made me realise there is always someone worse off.
> Take care
> Angela x

That is as clear as mud. What does she mean?

I type back furiously, even though Angela seems to be caught in the crossfire.

> Angela,
> Just come out and tell me. It's obvious Izzy, or my husband, haven't told me anything. What's going on? Did she know him? Just tell me the truth. I deserve that, at least! x

A frantic hour later Angela finally replies.

> Hi Martha,
> I shouldn't be the one having to tell you this. What if
> I arrange a meeting with you and Izzy? It really isn't
> my job to be getting involved like this. You need to
> hear it from Izzy. Regards, Angela x

Immediately I type back.

> Yes, please arrange a meeting. Tomorrow if you can.
> I need to know the truth x

It is probably too late for Angela to message back and arrange it at this time in the evening, so I go to bed. I am going to need a clear head tomorrow as I figure out if Izzy was also having an affair with my husband. But if Izzy was having an affair with him, it still doesn't make sense who Ms. F Andrews is. Izzy doesn't begin with the letter F.

I begin to drift off to sleep but jolt up in my bed. The puzzle is starting to join up.

FIA.

What if the 'I' stands for Izzy? Is she F. Izzy Andrews? She has to be! It's the only explanation.

# Chapter Thirty

I consider asking Rosie if she ever noticed anything odd about her father's behaviour, but, as Gretchen does on TV, I must uncover more evidence first. There is no point worrying Rosie if my overactive imagination is to blame for all of this, and there is a perfectly reasonable explanation. Somehow that is certainly not looking remotely plausible at the minute, but who knows? However, I need to find out everything before I am willing to accept these devastating revelations.

Angela still hasn't messaged me back with a time for the meeting and the only message I have today is from Lars. He is asking if I have booked my time off work yet, but, quite honestly, it is difficult to think of anything else when you find out that your marriage was a sham. I will not be going anywhere until I know exactly who Anthony was involved with. I don't tell Lars about my situation. It would be difficult to explain to him until I have all the facts. I simply tell him that I haven't had a chance to speak to Suzy yet.

*Well, hurry up, Omelette lady. Olaf wants to know if you're booking the cottage and I'm desperate to see you xxx* replies Lars.

It makes me smile that he is desperate to see me. But right now, I have other priorities. I think again about Gretchen. Wouldn't she have an ally that she would discuss her suspicions with? Everyone needs an ally and it's time to confide in the perfect one.

'Hello, Mrs Morris. How are you this morning?' I say, rushing straight up to her as she walks into the library.

'Hiya, bach. Not so good today, sciatica's playing up.'

'Oh, no, come, sit down. Let me get you a chair.' I grab the nearest chair and Mrs Morris winces in pain as she sits down.

'Oh, bless you. Can I get you anything? Paracetamol?' I ask. I don't like seeing Mrs Morris struggle.

'No, I'm all right. Just need a sit down. I'll be right now, in a minute.'

I bring two teas from the staff room and pull a chair up beside Mrs Morris. I know I should be working, but I can't focus on work in my frame of mind, plus Mrs Morris is in pain.

Mrs Morris takes a sip of her tea.

'Ah, that's better. I'm right now. So, what's news then, bach? When you off gallivanting to see that hunky man again?' she grins.

'I've got to tell you something. I've got a bit of a problem. Well, more a mystery really,' I start.

'Well, tell me, what's troubling you? But before you do, can I be cheeky and ask for a biscuit to go with this tea?' says Mrs Morris.

I run off to the staff room and search for something for her. All the nice Danish biscuits are gone and I realise I should have bought a tin for Mrs Morris too, but it was difficult to carry everything. When I go back, I will make sure I bring her some.

Eventually, I find a Garibaldi. Trevor must have bought them.

'Sorry, this is all we have today,' I apologise.

'Not fussy, don't worry. Just nice to have something sweet with my tea,' she says.

Mrs Morris munches on the Garibaldi quickly, washing it down with the remainder of her tea.

'Now, go on then. What were you saying?' she says.

I explain about the note, how Izzy blocked me and how I messaged Angela.

Mrs Morris leans into me and lowers her voice.

'I bloody told you I didn't trust that Angela, didn't I? I'm always right. It's instinct. I was born with it. Runs in the family, so I'm told.'

'Well, maybe you're right. But what made you think she couldn't be trusted?' I ask.

'You could see what she was like. Body language and stuff. The way she was playing with her ponytail and swishing it about the place. I couldn't work it out, but she knew you somehow and I don't trust her.'

'But Angela didn't have a ponytail – that was Izzy. Are you sure you have the right person here?' I ask.

My eyes turn to a man who has just walked into our section of the library. I pray he doesn't ask me for anything, I can't be interrupted right now.

'What? The one in those tight little trousers. She looked as bendy as a pipe cleaner. Oh, do you remember those? Gerald always had his pipe cleaner handy.'

'Yes, I used to make things with them. But, please, Mrs Morris. Stay with it for a minute. Izzy, that was. You're describing Izzy.'

'I thought she was Angela and the one with the short hair was Izzy?'

'No, you must have got their names mixed up. You're definitely talking about Izzy. Okay, so it's Izzy I can't trust. Not Angela.'

'Sorry, love, yeah. The bendy-looking whipper-snapper. Must have mixed up their names, then. Definitely the bendy one I didn't like. The other one was nice enough. I think you can trust her. Yeah, definitely, now I think about it she was all right.'

'So, what do you think was going on, Mrs Morris? Do you think Izzy was having an affair with Anthony?'

'Well, who knows? You'll have to ask her, isn't it? Do you know where she lives or anything? I'd bloody turn up and ask her what she's playing at. You can't block people when they turn up at the door. In my day, you said what you wanted to say and got on with it, none of this blocking nonsense,' says Mrs Morris.

'I know. But I've no idea where she lives – all I know is that it's somewhere in Swansea. Could be anywhere. Oh, well, Angela said she'd arrange a meeting. I suppose I'll have to wait. But it's affecting things with Lars. I'm so distracted with it all,' I say.

I notice the man who walked in has been hovering and finally he won't wait any longer.

'Excuse me for interrupting, but do you have any books on Liberace please?' he asks me.

Liberace, that's a random one.

'Oh, goodness, I'll have to have a look on the system for you. Give me a moment.'

I say goodbye to Mrs Morris and promise to keep her updated on the developments with Izzy.

I start to search on the computer for books about Liberace, but I can hardly focus. In fact, I feel another of my panic attacks come on and suddenly become dizzy. This business with Izzy is affecting me more than I realised. Fortunately, Sioned walks by as the panic attack begins to consume me.

'Sioned, sorry, can you take over here please? I don't feel too good,' I manage, before running out down the corridor, through the double doors and out into the fresh air.

*Martha, breathe. Come on, it's a panic attack. You've had them before. You can get through this.* I crouch down onto the floor. Somehow it feels safer down here. People on the street start to stare and I am conscious of the spectacle I am making of myself. I get up and stand against the wall.

'Are you all right?' shouts a man farther up the road.

'I'm okay. Just a dizzy spell. I'm fine. Thank you,' I say.

Distracted by the man, I manage to get myself together and go back inside to avoid any further attention. I grab my things and tell Suzy that I am going to have to leave. I need to be safe at home.

–

When I arrive on my street, Graham's car is parked outside the house. In my rush to get home, I had forgotten there was a viewing today and that I had left the key under the mat to let them in. That's all I need.

'Hello,' I shout, as I see the front door has been left open.

'In here, Mrs Jenkins,' replies Graham.

I look at a young couple who are smiling at me.

'Hi, I'm Amina. Oh, you've such a lovely house. We love, it, don't we, Ahmad?' says the trendy woman in a pretty pink leather jacket.

She reminds me of the young woman in the super-market who was always talking to Lars, and I am hit by a wave of jealousy. I try to smile.

'Yes, it's exactly what we've been looking for. We were just discussing what we're prepared to pay, weren't we?'

says Ahmad. He puts his arm around his wife. They look so happy as they search for their new home. That part of my life is well and truly gone. I want to tell them to make the most of each other.

'Oh, good. It's been a happy home mostly. The woman next door is a bit of a...' I almost say 'pain', but then realise how ready I am to say goodbye to this home. 'A character. Yes, she's quite the character,' I say.

Amina and Ahmad smile at each other.

'Aww, it's great to have good neighbours. Means a lot, doesn't it, Ahmad?'

'That's brilliant, yeah,' says Ahmad.

I feel terrible about bending the truth and so have to ask them something. 'Do you like cats?' I ask.

'Oh, we love cats,' says Ahmad. He pulls out his wallet to show me a photo of three beautiful Persian cats.

'Great, you'll all get along fine then,' I say.

That's a relief.

'Oh, fab. Yeah, we have three cats and three daughters,' laughs Amina.

Ahmad flicks back his wallet and shows me a photo of three lovely girls under the age of six.

'Oh, how wonderful. They must keep you busy, then,' I smile.

'Never a dull moment in our home. Oh, and I see you've a daughter,' says Amina pointing to a photo of Rosie on the mantelpiece.

'So you've two daughters, have you?' she says.

'No, just the one,' I say.

'Oh, sorry, it's just that we were looking in your airing cupboard. I hope you don't mind – Ahmad wanted to check the insulation. He touched something and a photo fell out from behind. I assumed it was your husband with

233

your daughter, though I did wonder why they were both banished to the airing cupboard,' laughs Amina. She walks over to the sideboard and picks up a photograph. 'Sorry, we didn't mean to be snooping, I promise. It fell out, so I left it here safe for you.'

She hands me the photograph and I lose all focus as I try to take it in. I feel hot and start to retch.

'I'm sorry. Excuse me. I'm going to be sick,' I say.

'Oh, did you eat something?' says Amina, kindly.

I can't answer. I run to the nearby cloakroom and am violently sick. I scrape my hair back from my face, when I hear Graham's voice.

'It's okay. We'll let ourselves out, Mrs Jenkins,' he says.

'Hope you feel better soon,' shouts Amina.

After looking at that photograph, I am not sure that I will be feeling myself for some time to come.

# Chapter Thirty-One

It takes me an hour to compose myself and be able to look at the photograph again. First, I have to pour myself a sherry and sit down to steady my nerves. Leaning over to the coffee table, I pick up the photo. I notice the two of them are standing in front of a cathedral. It looks vaguely familiar. I recognise it from somewhere, and something tells me that Rosie went on a school trip there once. I'm sure she stood in the same place – or do all cathedrals look similar? I type in photos of Chester cathedral on my phone for confirmation.

Immediately, an identical cathedral flashes back at me on the screen. That is why he had kept the parking ticket. If it was taken around the same time as the date on the ticket, this photo is six years old. Six years! How long were they together, if it is indeed her name on the boarding pass? They must have been together until the end. I try to think back. Did I notice anything odd six years ago? Rosie would have been twelve. I remember she had trouble settling into secondary school. She found the work more challenging than she'd expected, so I was busy helping her with her homework every night. Was I so busy that I didn't notice the husband I loved was meeting up with a younger woman behind my back? Was he planning on leaving us? How I wish I could confront him right now.

I have so many questions that he can't answer. The only person who can answer anything is Izzy, the woman who is looking back at me in the photograph. They look so comfortable together that it is easy to see why Amina mistook the closeness for a dad and a daughter, especially as Izzy looks so young. Did he realise that people mistook her for his daughter?

I don't particularly want to see Izzy ever again in my life, but I want the truth. I need Angela to fix up this meeting and the sooner the better. I log onto the blog to remind Angela to chase Izzy up, but see a message has finally come in from her.

> Hi,
> She says she'll meet you at the café around the corner from the library. Five pm, Monday. Would that work for you? Hope you're okay. Angela x

It means I will have to wait all weekend, which is going to kill me. However, it is better than nothing. At least she will see me.

Immediately I type back.

> Thank you so much for arranging this. You've been fantastic. Can I ask, would you come with me on Monday? I don't know if I can face meeting her alone. Sorry to ask you. I appreciate you've already done enough. Have a lovely weekend, Martha x

I am about to message Tom to see how he is getting on, when my phone rings. I recognise it as the estate agent's number.

'Hello, Mrs Jenkins. It's Graham. Hope you're feeling better now?' he says.

'Yes, thank you. I'm sorry about earlier. How embarrassing. A bit of food poisoning, I think,' I say.

'Glad you're okay as I need to chat to you. It's about the couple who were at the viewing earlier. They've put in an offer and it is the asking price, £495,000. They said they don't want to mess you about to-ing and fro-ing and they need to move to the area quickly. There is no chain, finance is sorted, so all seems very straightforward. It's almost too good to be true. We don't often get offers like that. Makes my job easier,' he laughs.

'Oh goodness. That's fast. I know it's all very perfect, but would you mind giving me until Monday to get back to you? I have a lot on my mind at the moment and it's a bit of a shock that the first viewing went so well. I'm sure it's fine. I do want to sell. It's just that... Oh, I don't know. I should snap it up and I will but...'

'No, of course. I understand. It's been your home a long time, Mrs Jenkins. Get back to me on Monday, then. I'll let them know.'

I put the phone down and begin to panic when I remember that I still haven't even told Rosie that the house is for sale yet.

I put our family home on the market without even consulting her; what sort of mother am I? I suppose it was the thought that she wasn't coming back here and then Kevin and Mrs Roberts made me finally snap. Now I have an offer, it all seems very sudden and it will be another big change in her life.

I can't face a fight with Rosie about selling the house, not when I am still coming to terms with my suspicions about her father. Would I ever tell her, or let her think he was the perfect dad? It is something I must think about.

I pick the phone up to ring Lars. I feel the need to speak to him.

'Omelette lady,' he says as he answers.

Hearing Lars' lovely Danish accent floors me. His voice sounds so soft and kind and I try hard not to burst into tears with relief at the sound of it, but it's no use.

'I miss you,' I start to cry.

'Ah, my little Omelette lady, I miss you too. So does this mean I can book the cottage for you?' he laughs.

I don't answer immediately. Instead, I look around the living room at everything I will leave. For a moment, my grandfather clock in the corner is the only sound. I fiddle with the blue tartan Welsh wool throw on the sofa, stroking the fabric in my hands. The time has definitely come to leave this house.

'Yes, I'm ready,' I say.

I realise that hearing Lars' voice makes me feel stronger than I have all day.

'Can I come out next week?' I ask.

'Yes, that would be fantastic, but did you speak to work yet?' says Lars.

I don't tell him how I left work earlier with a panic attack, and so Suzy will understand that I need some time off. She has already tried ringing me twice, presumably to check that I am okay, but I couldn't face explaining everything to her after the discovery of the photograph.

'I think she'll be okay. I'll give her a ring later and explain,' I say.

'Well, Omelette lady, you made me very happy. Which day do you think you'll get a flight?' he says.

'I have some important business to attend to on Monday, so how about I fly out later in the week? I'll check what's available,' I say.

'This is so great. Agnete and Ludwig will be happy to see you too,' says Lars excitedly.

As soon as I finish my phone call, I ring Graham back. *Please let him still be at the office.* I am almost breathless as he picks the phone up. Rosie will have to understand. I am doing this for my own sanity.

'Graham, I want to sell. It was silly of me to even have to think. Please tell that lovely couple it's theirs. I'm more than ready to leave.'

'That's wonderful, Mrs Jenkins. They'll be absolutely delighted,' he says.

I have spent far too many years doing things for others. I even wasted my time on a man who hid a barrage of secrets from me. From his brand-new clothes, hidden in the back of the wardrobe, to the flight ticket and photo of him and Izzy, I had no idea who I was married to. Now I just need to know quite how much of a sham it was, and only Izzy can provide the answer to that.

## Chapter Thirty-Two

Izzy is looking as bendy as ever when I see her walking towards the café. I decided not to go in and wait for her, choosing instead to watch her from a distance. I suppose I wanted to have a good look at her, see what she had that I didn't – apart from the bendy legs, of course. She wears a silk scarf tied in a fancy knot around her long thin neck. She is a good six inches taller than me, I'd say around five foot ten. She looks taller than Anthony was. I wonder if he had to stretch up to kiss her? This thought fills me with anger. My husband kissing someone else. I wouldn't ever have believed it.

I watch Izzy walk into the café and give myself a moment to compose myself. I wait enough time for her to order and sit down. I don't fancy waiting beside her in the queue. Eventually I open the door to the café. Angela made excuses, so I face Izzy alone. She is already sitting down, probably with a skinny latte. I would guess that she wouldn't have ordered the hot chocolate with cream and a Flake like I am about to. If I am to find out the truth about my husband, at least I need chocolate in front of me.

'We're closing in half an hour,' says the lady behind the counter.

'It's okay. I won't be here long,' I say.

I approach Izzy's table. It is shocking to think this is the same lady I communicated with and got on so well with before I knew what had been going on behind my back. Would we be friends if circumstances were different? Who knows? But the atmosphere is certainly very different now.

'Hi,' she says, her hands wrapped around her mug as though she is cold.

'Hello,' I manage. I reach into my handbag to pull out the photo of her and Anthony. 'Someone found this in my airing cupboard,' I say, throwing it down on the table.

At least Izzy looks embarrassed. She averts her eyes, looking down at her coffee, as though she is searching for what to say in there.

'I'm so so sorry. I promise, I had no idea,' she says eventually.

'You had no idea of what? That he had been married forever?' I ask.

'Look, he told me that it was over. He said you knew all about me. I even came to your house once when you were out. I met your neighbour and we chatted. He told me the marriage ended years ago, but you were religious and that's why you wouldn't let him get a divorce. He had a pretty miserable life, from what he told me. He said his daughter was a spoiled brat and always wanted clothes and was expensive. She sounded dreadful, if I'm honest. Sorry, that's your daughter. I shouldn't have said that. I guess I felt sorry for him and was glad I could give the poor man some happiness.'

I bite into a chunk of my Flake angrily. Crumbs of chocolate spread all over the table and I take satisfaction as a piece lands in Izzy's skinny little drink. I hope her hips expand in front of me.

I am devastated as I think how Anthony betrayed not only me, but Rosie too. Izzy had even been in our house, with all our things. How dare he say such terrible things about our precious daughter to his lover? Any feelings I had left for Anthony are instantly shattered. My marriage was indeed a complete and utter sham. What a toad!

I look around to see that the waitress has moved from behind the counter, and is pretending to clean a table near us. She puts her head down and quickly sprays disinfectant as she realises I have caught her eavesdropping.

'Well, for a start, I'd have rather he asked for a divorce than live a lie. I would never have made him stay if he didn't want to. Rosie can be demanding, but she isn't that bad. I never knew about you, until things started to unravel over the past week. I'd never heard your name mentioned before, not even in passing.'

'I'm so sorry. You have to understand. I'd never have had an affair with him if I'd known. It's just that he told me so many nice things. He was kind and loving to me. He said I was his true soulmate. We even had our own song.'

'I don't suppose it was David Bowie, was it?'

Izzy looks at me, shocked. 'Yes, "Absolute Beginners".'

'It was our song too.' I explain.

The waitress stands with her mouth open, gawping at both of us.

'Don't you have things to do? Aren't you closing soon?' I ask.

I realise that meeting somewhere public was perhaps not the best thing to do.

Izzy begins to cry and for a moment I feel sorry for her. Anthony, it seems, lied to both of us. She is simply another of his victims.

'How long were you together?' I ask. I need to know.

'Eight years,' she says.

'Eight years!' I shout.

So, the photograph in Chester was taken when they had already been together for two years. Poor Rosie was still in primary school when they got together. My goodness. This just gets worse.

'So, you'd been together for all this time, until the day he died,' I say.

'Yes,' says Izzy. She looks down again at her coffee and sighs.

'I was the last person to see him. He was meeting me at the Goodwig. He saw me waiting and lost control of his car. I called the ambulance. I tried to save him but it was too late. He... Well, he died in my arms. I'm sorry.'

'He was meeting you? You were the one who called the ambulance?' I repeat.

He died in his lover's arms.

The police didn't say who had called the ambulance when they came to tell me the news.

He wasn't even supposed to be out that night. He started the argument; that's the only reason he went out. How did they even arrange to meet so quickly?

'Yes, I'm so sorry. I saw it all happen in front of me. He was meeting me for dinner,' says Izzy.

I sit back on my chair. My goodness, I had the slow cooker on for him.

'You must be mistaken. I had dinner ready for him,' I say.

'No, we had a reservation there. It was one of our favourite places to go,' says Izzy.

That night, I remember Anthony looking at his phone. I thought it was for the time, but he must have been reading a message from Izzy. People we knew must have spotted them. Mrs Roberts knew. How many more people did? I feel such a fool.

'Listen, ladies, I'm closing up now,' says the waitress.

'No, please. This is important. Just give us a few more minutes,' I beg.

'No, I can't, sorry. I've got to pick my son up from his dad's. I've already let you stay longer than I wanted. I should have locked up by now,' she says.

There is so much I want to know. Did Anthony hate me? Did he find me so unattractive he had an affair with someone much more glamourous?

'Look, we have so much to find out from each other. How about we go for a walk and chat some more? There are so many unanswered questions.' I say.

We let the lady lock up the café and head towards the park. It is quiet and the breeze is refreshing. I was struggling to breathe inside, and I fought hard not to have a panic attack in front of Izzy.

'So, what other lies did he tell you?' I say.

'I don't know how much of what he said was lies. I mean, he used to be a golf pro and he listened to the same music as I did. He loved Stormzy. He enjoyed reading books and—'

'What? He bought golf clubs and never used them. He didn't have a clue about golf. I doubt he would even have known who Stormzy was if Rosie hadn't mentioned him. And the only thing Anthony ever read was his accountancy magazine,' I say.

Izzy loosens her scarf from around her neck. She is looking increasingly uncomfortable.

'Okay, but he definitely liked flying small aircraft and he had a pilot's license. I saw a photo of him with a small plane. He told me that one day he'd fly me to Paris and—'

Ha! I burst out laughing.

'What's so funny?' asks Izzy.

'He was claustrophobic and terrified of small planes. No way would you get him up in one of those. I'll bet the photo you mention was from when we visited an air show. It was hard enough to get him to fly to Majorca. That's why I was surprised when I found the tickets for Rio,' I say.

'Ah, you know about Rio, then?'

'Well, yes. I am guessing the tickets were meant for you?' I say.

I remove the piece of paper from my bag with the initials 'FIA' on and show her why I have come to that conclusion.

She reads the paper carefully.

'As I said, he was meeting me that night. He must have written the time of our meeting down. And, yup, that's me. FIA. Everyone calls me Izzy, but my full name... Well, it's Fiona Isobel Andrews. We were flying to Rio to celebrate and do some samba dancing. Anthony loved dancing.'

'Dancing? He hated dancing! And celebrate what?' I ask.

'He said you'd finally agreed to a divorce. We were going to get engaged in Rio.'

I clutch my chest as I hear this. The final piece of the puzzle is in place. I feel myself gasping for breath. Leaning against a tree, I stop for a while to compose myself, but I don't quite manage and everything around me starts to fade.

# Chapter Thirty-Three

I wake up to find myself lying on the ground wrapped in an unfamiliar jacket. My legs are elevated. A woman is watching me and I can instinctively tell that it isn't Izzy. I try to focus on the face. It blurs in and out of sight.

'Hello. How do you feel?' says a voice.

'Giddy. What's happened?' I say.

'I was walking past and saw you slumped against the tree. Did you fall? Do you remember anything?' asks the stranger.

I begin to recall what Izzy said to me.

'No, someone told me something terrible and then I don't know...' I pause for a moment. 'Where is she?' I ask.

'Who? I found you alone,' says the kind lady. 'Shall I help you up? Are you okay to move?' she continues.

As my eyes focus, I realise that Izzy is nowhere to be seen. She left me. She watched me drop to the ground and walked away. She tried to help my husband, but not me.

Gingerly, I get up. My toes tingle as the circulation makes its way back through my body. The lady looks at me, concerned.

'Don't worry. I'm fine. Honestly. Thank you for looking after me,' I say. 'This must be yours.' I hand over an orange coat.

'Are you sure you don't want me to call anyone?' she asks.

'No, really. I'll just go home and have tea. I'm okay.'

Even if I did agree for her to call someone, who would she call? My unfaithful dead husband? My daughter, thousands of miles away in Borneo? Lars in Denmark? Suzy is busy with Angus; there is not really anyone to call. So, I make my way back home alone. I will be okay – it was just shock that made me hyperventilate and probably faint. As I drive home carefully and slowly, the feelings of apprehension about meeting Izzy have been replaced with disappointment and sadness for the man I thought I knew.

When I enter the house, my emotions change. Looking around the home we brought Rosie up in and shared so many memories, I feel rage. All of this was built on lies. A strength possesses me like a demon. I don't want anything of Anthony's in this house. Frantically, I feel the need to remove every piece of evidence of him. I hope the Heart Foundation will make a fortune with his stuff.

I rip his boarding pass up into tiny pieces. I get some scissors and cut every pair of his underpants into bits. It feels comforting. I throw his golf clubs into the boot of the car ready for the morning. I notice Mrs Roberts staring from her window at the commotion but ignore her.

I continue throwing everything out until anything remotely reminiscent of Anthony is either in a bin bag for the charity shop, or in the bin in smithereens. When everything is done, I smash our wedding photo. The glass from the frame shatters all over the floor and I cut myself picking it up. The pain from my finger is a fragment of the pain that is in my heart.

I am sucking at the blood on my finger to try and make it stop when I see that Rosie is calling. It's very late for her. I decide to call her back later as I have to deal with my injury first. I don't know that I can speak to her right now and remain upbeat. However, a message from Rosie flashes up as soon as she stops ringing.

> Mam, call me back. It's urgent xx

I attend to my bleeding finger and take a deep breath before calling her back. It must be an emergency at this time of night. I hope I can deal with whatever it is. I am not sure I can manage much more.

'Hi, Rosie. What's up?' I ask.

'Oh, Mammy. It's Ben. We had a big row and I think it's over.'

'Aww, you two were great together. I'm sure it's something that can be worked out,' I say.

'I don't know. One of the other girls – Ella – she said she wants to be a vet, so she's been hanging around Ben. I told him she doesn't want to be a vet at all. I caught them all cosy, chatting together and I said to him, "My father would never behave like this. He wouldn't have looked at another woman." Of course, he said he didn't look at her, he was only helping her with her choice of uni, but I don't believe him,' sobs Rosie.

Her words about her father make me feel sick to the stomach. At that moment I decide that I will protect her from the truth. She must never find out that the father she has always thought of as a faithful, family man was none of those things. What good would it do to her to tell her the truth?

'Oh, well, I'm sure it's a mix-up. You know how passionate Ben is about being a vet. Even if this Ella girl does have an ulterior motive, I don't think Ben would be interested. From what you tell me he is smitten with you and quite rightly too,' I say.

'I don't know. I honestly could have locked Ella in one of the enclosures when I saw her with Ben,' says Rosie.

'Well, there's no need for that. Calm down and see how things are tomorrow. I'm sure there's nothing going on. It's not like he's bought her a ticket to Rio,' I say.

'What are you on about, Rio?' asks Rosie.

'I'm just saying, it's not like he's going away with her. He only helped her look at universities. Try and calm down, okay?'

'But I love him so much, Mammy. I'm so scared I'll lose him,' says Rosie.

'If he's a good person and meant for you then that won't happen. I promise. If it's meant to be, it will be.'

I feel like a charlatan giving her advice when my own relationship was such a mess.

'I know I'm being really insecure. It's just, after Dad, I'm so scared of people leaving me,' says Rosie.

'I understand. Perhaps have a word with Ben and explain how you feel, eh? What do you think? He seems quite sensible and understanding.' I say.

'Yeah, you're right. I feel so much better now. Thanks, Mam. You're the best.'

I smile. Perhaps my grown-up daughter does still need me after all. This gives me a sense of purpose as I realise that some of the people, like Tom, on the blog need me too. So, I open up the laptop and type my latest post.

I am going to start with an apology. I have had so many issues at home that I don't think I have helped

249

as many of you as I should have. This blog was created to help us share stories of grief, but you have been helping me! The truth is, I am probably not very good at blogging. I have had some lovely messages of encouragement from you, but let's face it, I am not an agony aunt like Denise Robertson off This Morning, RIP. I am just a widow battling her own issues. So, I apologise to you all and thank you for being so kind to me. I am now considering closing the blog down, and starting a WhatsApp group instead. Would anyone be interested in that? If so, please message me privately (we don't want the whole of the internet to get your details!) and I will do that instead so that those who want to can still stay in touch. Hugs to you all, M x

The inbox shows me that Tom has sent me a message. I will definitely add him to the WhatsApp bereavement group.

Hello! Are you feeling better today? I hope you are. Did you find out if your husband was cheating? I do hope I was wrong. Anyway, just to say me and Sparky are here if you need a shoulder to cry on. Feeling good today. Took Sparky for a walk and he played with a friendly labradoodle in the park. His owner was such a lovely lady, a widow called Lucy. We spoke for an hour while our dogs played! I went to Sandra's grave after to have a chat with her. I told her that I felt guilty talking to Lucy and then the sun came out from behind a cloud, as if she was giving me her approval. Isn't that odd? I bought Sandra some lovely flowers down the market as I was feeling a bit guilty. What do you think? Here's a photo. Tom, x

I look at the photograph of the pink and white roses that decorate the immaculately kept grave. The headstone tells me that Sandra was only fifty-five. Poor lady. Tom has never told me how old he is. I suppose everyone is different, but I hope he does find happiness again, perhaps with Lucy. It would be sad to think that Tom could spend the rest of his life grieving over Sandra otherwise. I am going to message him back to tell him that he should not feel guilty whatsoever. He shouldn't spend his life feeling guilty for living. He has always done the best by Sandra and now he deserves some happiness.

I think about how lucky I am to have met Lars. I haven't known him long, admittedly, but something tells me that I am doing the right thing by taking a chance on him.

Sitting back, I consider the day I have encountered. I have felt shock, sadness, disappointment, anger and I have even fainted! I have felt unloved and unneeded. *Oh, what a day, Martha!*

However, as the day draws to a close, I realise that I am also very lucky. I have a daughter who needs me and a wonderful man who says he loves me. Sometimes you have to count your blessings and not your losses.

I smile as I pick up my phone and type a message to Lars. There is something very important that I have to tell him. Now that I no longer have any guilt about Anthony, I can be honest about my feelings for Lars.

Jeg elsker dig x

# Chapter Thirty-Four

I had thought of phoning Suzy to explain I was having some kind of breakdown and would have to take sick leave for a while. However, I realise that I am not sick, I am okay. I have survived the truth about my husband. So, it would be unfair of me to not turn up for work, on the pretext that I am ill. Instead, I decide to go into the library and explain the situation. Suzy has been so encouraging about Lars that I hope she will understand why I want to head back to Denmark. I will miss this gang, but I don't know that I belong in Wales any more. As my mug says, 'I left my heart in Denmark'.

'Morning,' says Trevor, as I bump into him coming out of the staff room. 'You seem in a bit of a hurry, Martha. You got a flight to catch?'

If only he knew what I am about to announce.

I wait for Suzy to arrive; she is late this morning.

I hang around the staff room for her until she finally runs in, trying to take her coat off as she hurries.

'Sorry, being late is not a good example,' she says breathlessly.

We all know she is a fantastic boss and understand that she must have a good reason to be late. She is always so punctual that she doesn't need to apologise.

'The teacher wanted a word with me about Angus when I dropped him off, so I couldn't really leave school this morning,' explains Suzy.

'Gosh, it's not a problem. We all know you don't make a habit of it. Hope everything's okay?'

'Yes, it's fine. It's just that they have a no nuts policy and Angus has somehow been smuggling cashew nuts into his lunchbox. He must have stolen them from my secret stash. I only eat them when he's gone to bed. They're too expensive to share. I was horrified when the teacher told me. Thankfully nobody in his class has a nut allergy.'

'Oh dear, well, hopefully he'll learn his lesson,' I say.

'Yeah, definitely. Anyway, better crack on,' says Suzy.

'Sorry, I know you're not having the best start to the day, but I really need a word please? In the office?' I ask.

Suzy agrees and we sit down in her office. I look at the photo of Angus on her desk. I notice it is a new one and Gareth is in it too.

'So, you know how I met Lars in Denmark and...' I start.

'Don't tell me, you want some time off?' asks Suzy.

'Yes, sorry. I know it's last minute. But ideally, I'd like to leave this week. A lot has happened that I haven't told you about.'

I explain about all the things that have gone on and why I had a panic attack and had to rush out. Suzy is incredibly sympathetic as always.

'You poor love. Of course you need a break. Honestly, it's fine. We are still a little over staffed. To be honest, I'm sure Rebecca would be quite happy if I let another staff member go. Why don't you take unpaid leave for a while? If you decide not to return then we can deal with your notice somehow. Would that work?'

'Oh, Suzy, you are the most incredible boss ever. You know that?'

'Well, I have been told that, yes,' she laughs. 'Now, I'd better get on with these emails waiting for me. Why don't you work today, get everything in order, and then take from tomorrow onwards off?'

'Oh Suzy, thank you.' I give her a big hug and am so grateful that my boss is also my best friend. I will miss her when I am away.

Mrs Morris walks in at lunchtime and I am surprised but pleased to see her.

'Hey, it's not your day to come in. This is a nice treat seeing you,' I say.

'I had to go to the market to get some bird seed, so thought I'd pop in,' says Mrs Morris.

I am always happy to see her but today especially so. I now get the chance to say goodbye.

I sit her down in the library to tell her the news.

'Aww, I'm going to miss you again now, bach,' she says.

'I know. I'll miss you too. Why don't we get Trevor to see if he can set up something on your phone, or on a computer so we can still see each other? Are you on Facebook?' I ask.

'Facebook?' laughs Mrs Morris.

'Okay, never mind.'

'Well, I'm glad you're going back there. You've been a different person since you came back. You were always bloody gloomy before you took that holiday, to be honest. A bit miserable, like,' says Mrs Morris.

'Mrs Morris! Do you always have to be so truthful? Can you not sugarcoat anything?' I laugh.

She does have a point, though. I was a different person before I went. And now, as I head back to Denmark, I have changed further. Finding out the truth has in some ways been a relief. All this time I have been thinking it was my fault Anthony was dead, when he was rushing to see another woman and she was the one who held him as he died.

'Anyone there?' asks Mrs Morris.

'What? Sorry. What you saying?' I ask.

'You've a habit of drifting off, don't you, bach? I was saying, don't forget to pack some condoms, now. You can still get pregnant at your age, you know. One of my mother's cousins gave birth at fifty-two.'

As usual with Mrs Morris's comments, I blush. An eighty-two-year-old is giving me advice on contraception. Oh goodness!

'Mrs Morris. Stop being so naughty,' I laugh.

'I'm just saying. Well, unless you want to go back to nappies at your age. But hey, perhaps you do. In that case, maybe try one of those ovulating sticks. You pee on them, you know?'

'No, thank you, Mrs Morris. I have a grown-up daughter and that's enough. How do you even know about ovulation kits?' I ask.

Mrs Morris pulls her stocking that is crinkling around her ankle. 'I never told you I was a midwife before I retired, did I?'

'No, I didn't realise. I bet you were brilliant. How did I never know that?' I say.

'Ah, there's a lot about me you don't know, bach. People look at me and see a little old granny. I did have a life before I got old, you know,' smiles Mrs Morris.

'I don't see a little old granny. I see the most interesting, wise lady I've ever known,' I say.

We both sit in silence for a moment.

'Bless you, dear. Right, I'd better go. Things to do, people to see and all that. I've got a busy day, actually,' she says.

We all know Mrs Morris won't see anyone until her next visit to the library, or her grandson comes down from Scotland again, but she seems in a hurry to leave.

As we say goodbye, I spot tears in her eyes. It makes me fill up too.

'Now then, no crying, Martha. Bugger off to that hot young man of yours,' says Mrs Morris gaining her composure. She toddles off with her stick and I can't help but sob. I truly love Mrs Morris and the friendship we have. I couldn't bear to lose touch with her. I will make sure that Trever sorts something out for her so that we can keep in contact.

Before I leave work, I have a chat with him and get him to promise me that he will fix something up for Mrs Morris.

'We're going to miss you. It won't be the same without you complaining about my Garibaldis,' he says.

'I know, I'll miss you all, too. Who knows? I might be back before too long,' I say.

'Well, I hope not. I hope it all works out for you. I really do. You deserve it,' says Trevor.

I give him a hug and we say goodbye. I have no idea if I will be back or not, but I hope, even if I stay in Denmark, that I will visit sometimes.

The last time I walked out of the library for my holiday I was apprehensive. This time feels different. I am much more confident, as I know what is waiting for me on the other side of the airport.

I look back at the library doors for one last moment. I have loved my time here, but hopefully today is the end of an era.

# Chapter Thirty-Five

'Mammy, you're having a breakdown, aren't you?' says Rosie, when I explain that I am leaving for Denmark in the morning.

'No, I'm not having a breakdown. Your mother is quite sane, I promise,' I say.

Looking around at the boxes that are packed and ready to go into storage, I can't quite believe how much I have accomplished in such a short space of time. Apart from my gran's vase, family photographs and a few of Rosie's teddy bears from when she was young, there wasn't anything much of any sentimental value once I had cleared the last of Anthony's things out. Even my trusty worn-out sofa isn't worth keeping, but I don't have time to organise a new home for it right now, so it is off to a ten-foot shipping container that I have hired by the week until I know whether I will return or not. I realise that all the possessions I have hoarded over the years are not really worth anything. My whole life is contained in these boxes and they don't mean much to me when I look at them.

I still haven't broken the news to Rosie that I have accepted an offer for the house and that the things she left in her bedroom are now all in a large cardboard box, marked 'Rosie's Room'. I know I should have discussed it with her before even having the valuation but I couldn't face it. Finally, I summon up the courage to tell her that she won't be coming back to the house and give her a call.

'Rosie, love,' I start.

'You only call me that when something terrible has happened. Like when Dad died. That's what you said then. What's going on?'

I take a deep breath to steady my nerves.

'Rosie, there is no easy way to say this—'

'You said that when Dad died too. Just tell me,' interrupts Rosie.

'Okay, okay. Now don't go off your head, okay, but I have sold the house.'

'You sold the house? Why would you sell our lovely home? I can't believe this. Do you have a gambling problem? What is wrong with you?'

'Nothing is wrong with me. Look, things happened a bit faster than I imagined. You said you didn't want to come back. That you'd be going to York with Ben and—'

'Yeah, but that doesn't mean to say I won't be taking the train back home to see you and stay with my mam. Oh my God. Is that too much to ask for? I can't even speak to you. I'm fuming.'

'Come on now, Rosie, love. Don't be like that,' I say.

'Don't you "Rosie, love" me. How could you do such an evil thing? What about all my stuff? Where is it?'

'It's all safe in boxes, don't worry,' I explain.

'Don't worry? Don't worry? What about my jewellery? The necklace Dad gave me when I was small? All my teddies and stuff? I don't believe this. You've made me homeless and stolen all my things,' shouts Rosie.

'I have not made you homeless. You weren't even staying here before you left, and I have not stolen your things. I'll rent a smaller home when I get back from

Denmark for you to visit, okay? And all your things are safe in storage.'

'I'm fuming, absolutely fuming. I left thinking I'd be back there and now I won't be. I bet it's that man you've been hanging around with. He put you up to it. Lars. What's his name again?'

'Lars Nielsen. But it's nothing to do with him, I promise. I decided to cash in on things whilst prices were high. It's not to do with anyone. I didn't want to live here alone, after Dad. I didn't want to wait around for you to come home from uni every now and then. I'm sorry, but mothers need to live their lives too, you know,' I say.

'I can't believe my own mother would do this. Dad would never, ever have left me homeless,' shouts Rosie.

'Dad... Yes, Dad. The perfect father and husband,' I say sarcastically.

'Yes, he was. Nobody will ever be like Dad,' she says.

I hear her voice begin to crack and I feel dreadful as she breaks down in tears.

'You should take a leaf out of Dad's book, Mammy. He always put his family first,' she cries.

'Well, look, I'm sorry I'm not as fantastic as your dad, Rosie. But it's just incredibly lonely living here all by myself. You know me and Mrs Roberts have never particularly got on and between one thing and another, I have to move on,' I explain.

'Well, you should have asked me first if it was okay to sell the house. And I would have said no,' says Rosie.

'Come on. Don't be like that,' I say.

'Don't be like that? My mother has made me homeless. Homeless,' she screams.

I figure that it will take time for her to come to terms with losing the family home, but she was staying with her friend Amy when she left for Borneo so I know she is definitely having one of her more dramatic moments.

'Well, I want to know more about that man you're seeing. Send me a photo of him. I want to see what he looks like. Perhaps he's an evil monster. I want to make sure my mother is safe and that he isn't after your money, or something. Right. I'm going now. I'm off to tell Ben. He won't believe it,' says Rosie.

'Oh my goodness. He's not after my money. Well, at least I don't think he is… And I haven't done anything to you,' I say.

Rosie slams the phone down without her usual goodbye or telling me she loves me.

It makes me feel sad and for a moment I wonder if I am doing the right thing after all. Surely, Lars isn't after my money? He's just a quiet baker.

But then I remember that Lars still hasn't explained how his wife 'perished'. Perhaps I have been a little impulsive and rushed into this relationship.

*Oh, Martha. Is it all too soon?*

I decide I need some reassurance. I need to speak to Lars.

On the third ring he answers.

'Hej, all ready for the flight tomorrow, Omelette lady?'

'Yes, I am. Well, sort of,' I say.

'What do you mean, sort of? I hope there's not a problem. I'm desperate to see you,' says Lars.

'No, not really a problem. I have to ask you something. It's silly, I know, but I need to know something from you.'

'Sure, what is it?' he asks.

'Well, you know how you said your wife perished? What did you mean by that?' I ask.

'You know I don't really like to talk about her because she perished,' says Lars.

'I know, but it's just a funny word to use. Perished. Why do you say that word? What exactly do you mean?' I ask.

'Well, okay. You know, in the bakery, food perishes, right?' says Lars.

'Umm, okay. I don't quite understand though,' I say.

'She perished. Like milk does. She went off, you know. She left me.'

I laugh so hard. So, Lars did not do anything remotely gruesome. The relief is immense.

'Oh, silly sausage. It's the way you said it, I thought you'd murdered her or something!' I say.

'Why would I murder her?' asks Lars.

'Oh, never mind. I must tell you about my overactive imagination one day. It's a curse, really.'

'Right, okay. So does that mean you will still be here tomorrow?' says Lars.

'Absolutely. Too right I will be there tomorrow,' I say.

'That's fantastic. I'll pick you up from the train station in Esbjerg as planned,' says Lars.

'Perfect,' I say.

As we tell each other how much we love one another, I realise how excited I am about seeing him. I would never want to upset Rosie, but she has Ben and her forthcoming career. She needs to understand that it is time for me to make the most of every moment I have left on this planet, and Lars is part of that plan.

# Chapter Thirty-Six

This time I don't need to ask for directions at the airport. I remember exactly where to go. I feel like a seasoned traveller, as I confidently make my way to the platform for the Esbjerg train. It is only my luggage that holds me back a little, as I try and steer the trolley with two huge suitcases. It is much more than I had previously, but then I have brought every material thing that is important to me – my whole world.

When the train pulls up at Esbjerg station, I see Lars immediately. I'm not sure if it is his handsome, kind face or the huge bouquet of flowers that he is holding that makes him stand out. I feel like the luckiest woman alive as I step off the train and he greets me, lifting me off my feet, squashing the bouquet between us.

'Hello, Omelette lady,' says Lars.

The flowers don't look quite so plump now and a few carnation leaves fall to the ground as Lars places the bouquet on top of my suitcase.

'Ah, come here, I've missed you,' he whispers, leaning over to kiss me.

The kiss is perfect. Absence has certainly made our hearts grow fonder. It is fantastic to be back in his arms again. I hadn't quite realised how much I had missed this.

Fortunately, my luggage fits in Lars' van and we drive off, happily chatting, his hand on my leg.

'So, how was your flight? All good?' he asks as we turn the corner towards the ferry terminal.

'Great, this time I had two empty seats besides me. Everything was perfect,' I smile.

The ferry to Fanø comes into sight. I can already picture the cottage, the deer and the bunny. I don't even mind that the woodpecker will probably wake me up early in the morning. I am about to arrive at the place where I feel most at home.

The twenty-minute drive to the cottage goes fast as we catch up on everything that has been happening. Lars tells me that Agnete has had a famous client come to her for help, but she isn't allowed to divulge who it is. I can't help wondering if it is Kristian.

When we finally arrive at the cottage, it is incredibly emotional. Apart from the freshly cut grass, everything is just as I left it, even though other people have been staying here since my departure.

As we open the front door, Lars picks me up and lifts me over the threshold of the cottage.

'Are you supposed to do that at this age? I don't want you to put your back out,' I laugh.

'Shush, Omelette lady. I'm a strong Viking,' laughs Lars.

He kisses me as he puts me back down and I feel so alive and happy. Lars even knows that I like my cup of tea when I get in and so he rushes to put the kettle on.

'I hope you brought those teabags you like. I couldn't find any in town,' says Lars.

I open my bag and remove the box of teabags, which I had left at the top for easy access. As I hand them over, I see there is a message on my phone. It's Rosie.

> Having trouble with WiFi here today. Hope you get this in time. Don't go to Denmark, Mammy. Don't get on that flight. Ben found something out about Lars. Message me when you get this.

Another two messages follow.

> Mam, confirm you got this. Did you go to Denmark?

> Mammy, where are you? Message me so I know you received this.

I almost jump out of my skin as Lars leans in behind me, kissing my neck.

'I hope I didn't put too much milk in it for you,' he says, handing me a cup of tea.

'Oh, what? No, umm...' I say.

'Are you okay?' he asks.

'Yes, just need the loo,' I say.

Running to the downstairs bathroom, taking my phone with me, I quickly lock the door.

Furiously, I type a message to Rosie.

What do you mean? I'm in Denmark already. What did Ben find out about Lars?

I feel sick. I might have known this was too good to be true.

I talk to myself again, something I haven't done for ages.

'Ooh, Martha. What did you do now?'

'Sorry. What are you saying?' says Lars.

'Nothing!' I shout.

I have to find a way of getting rid of him until Rosie messages back. What if it is something terrible that they have discovered?

Lars has always made me feel safe until now, but I begin to doubt everything. I have to make an excuse to get him to leave.

I come out of the bathroom, rubbing at my temples.

'I have the most awful migraine. It must be all the travelling,' I say.

'Oh, no. Can I do anything? I know, how about a nice massage?' says Lars, coming closer. For the first time, I back away from him.

'No, I think I need sleep. I need to rest in a dark room,' I say.

'Poor you. Let me get your room ready for you,' says Lars. He runs upstairs and I hear the noise of the curtain hooks clanging against the rail.

'Shall we go to bed then? Your room is waiting,' he smiles when he returns.

'Look, I'm sorry but could you leave me for this evening? I don't want to sound miserable, but I don't feel

266

too good. I think I need some peace and quiet. Alone, you know?'

Lars seems taken aback at this news.

'Oh, I thought we would stay together tonight but… Well, okay, I can still make the ferry back, I guess,' he says.

'Great, thanks. I'll let you know how I feel in the morning, okay?' I say.

Depending on what Ben has found out, I might have to escape the cottage by tomorrow. What a dreadful thought.

Lars kisses me goodbye, but I struggle to return the warmth of his embrace.

'Are you sure you're okay?' he asks.

'Yes, fine. Honestly, just a nasty migraine,' I say.

'Okay. I'll check on you tomorrow. Take it easy,' says Lars.

'I might have a lie-in, so please don't worry. I'll message you when I feel up to it, okay?' I say.

Lars jumps into his van and waves as he drives away. I close the front door and lock it, leaving the key in to make sure nobody can come in. I don't know what sort of news to expect from Rosie and Ben. It could be absolutely anything.

I am relieved that Lars has left, but disappointed that I am now here alone. I assumed we would be spending our first night reunited wrapped in each other's arms and not apart like this.

Sitting in the lounge, I reach for my phone. I desperately need Rosie to message me back, but there is nothing.

I can hardly keep still and so I run upstairs and pull one of the Danish books out from the bookcase on the landing. I don't understand any of it, but, for a moment, it takes my mind off the anxiety I have about Lars.

Finally, my phone bleeps and I almost jump out of my skin.

> Hope you feel better in the morning my
> lovely Omelette lady. Sweet dreams xx

I decide I won't reply until I know more. For all he knows I'm asleep by now anyhow.

I message Rosie again.

> Rosie, you have to tell me what's going on
> before it's too late. Is he evil? Has he done
> something bad? I need to know now.

I look at the time and realise that she will probably be sleeping by now, but hopefully she will get this as soon as she wakes up.

As I press send, a message from Rosie comes in.

> Typical, WiFi a nightmare here. Sending
> you this before I go to bed. Looks like Lars
> is on every dating site out there.

Rosie seems to have tried to send it a few hours ago but, as there are photos attached, it must have taken a while to get through.

I look at the profile of him. All of them say the same thing.

Lars Nielsen, 43 y.o. Skads, Denmark. Romantic Capricorn, looking for fun and

good times. Sensitive, spiritual soul who likes
to meet new people from different cultures.
Get in touch to find out more.

My heart lurches as I read it. He likes to meet people
from different cultures. Oh, my goodness, that's me. Did
he simply want to meet someone from a new country?

I look at the photograph. Examining it closely, I see
that the background is the garden at Agnete and Ludwig's.
Perhaps he even asked Agnete to take that for him, especially for this purpose.

I don't even understand why he is on dating sites when
he has so many women around him. I am quite sure there
is no need.

The thought that he could get me all the way over here
and do this to me makes me feel sick. How could he do
this and why did I trust him?

I cry myself to sleep. Lars Nielsen is a serial playboy
and I fell for it.

# Chapter Thirty-Seven

I manage a few hours of sleep and then it starts. *Tap, tap tap.* I grin to myself as I hear the noise. I am no longer fearful of it and am pleased to hear that my little woodpecker still lives here.

However, my grin quickly subsides when I remember Rosie's messages. I still can't believe Lars could seem so genuine and do this to me. What a rotten egg, as my nan would say.

I pop on my glasses and head downstairs. I notice there is a message from Lars on my phone that has been buzzing away in my dressing gown pocket. I choose not to read it. Instead, I walk to the window and spot bunny eating grass again. It is nice to see him. I look around for the deer, but he is nowhere to be seen. It is then that I hear the noise of a vehicle. No cars come up this lane and so it can only be either Lars or Olaf.

Please let it be Olaf, I pray. But then I see the white van approach. Oh no, I told Lars that I would get in touch when I was ready. Why is he turning up again?

I step back from the window and run to the back of the cottage. I hide by a wall, hoping he will leave when he has no answer.

'*Hej*, where are you? I brought breakfast for you,' shouts Lars through the front door.

I hear his footsteps walking around the cottage. They are distant at first and then I hear them get closer and closer, until he reaches the back door.

'*Hej*, are you in there?' says Lars.

I don't reply.

'Ah, I see you,' says Lars. I look up as he watches me through the kitchen window crouching down by a table. 'What are you doing down there? Did you lose something?' he asks.

He has caught me and I now have to open the back door and let him in. What a disaster! I don't particularly want to shout through the back door that I know what he has been doing. However, I suppose I should explain that I know and that he can't get away with such terrible behaviour. Perhaps it will stop him doing it to someone else.

I open the door to him and he gives me a big smile.

'Are you feeling better today? I was worried about you,' says Lars.

'I'm fine. It was just a migraine. Nothing to be concerned about.' I notice how my tone has changed with him.

'That's great. I thought we could go for dinner in Esbjerg tonight, if you feel up to it. Agnete and Ludwig could join us, if that's okay for you?'

'I don't know that I am up for dinner, to be honest, Lars,' I say.

'Are you okay? You seem a little weird. Are you tired?'

I sit down at the kitchen table and consider where to start. I pull my phone from my pocket to show Lars what is troubling me. There's a new message from Rosie.

I'm sorry, Mam. We had to tell you. It's better you find out now than later. Love you. Xx

I scroll back to the previous message. 'This is what's wrong,' I say, showing Lars the dating profile. He seems as shocked as I am about them.

'But I didn't do this! I don't understand,' says Lars. He looks at the pictures again. 'Why would I be on a dating site when I met someone so special? This is not me.'

'Well, it clearly is. Look, it's your face,' I say sarcastically, holding the picture up to his chin.

'I don't even know of these dating sites. I don't understand,' says Lars.

'Look, please don't insult my intelligence. It is you and there's no point denying it,' I say.

'Yes, I see it's me, but I didn't do this. I wouldn't know how to if I wanted to. Not that I want to,' says Lars.

'Well, if you didn't, then who did?' I ask.

I stare at him, waiting for an answer, but he looks puzzled. He is certainly good at acting; perhaps Kristian taught him well.

'Please, you must understand I wouldn't do this to you. It must be someone having a joke. Perhaps my ex-wife? We didn't part on good terms, but I don't think she has this photo of me. Where would she find it?'

'Well, who took the photo?' I ask. I don't even know why I am giving him the time of day when he surely knows full well he put this online himself.

'Agnete,' he says loudly. 'Yes, Agnete took it. I remember. It was last summer. I was at the house and she took this in the garden.'

He sits down and rubs his forehead.

'Agnete put this on dating sites? I don't believe it,' he says.

'No, neither do I,' I say sarcastically.

'I mean it, you have to believe me. It must be my sister... or someone else. But I didn't do it. Please don't let this make you think less of me. I didn't know anything about it until I saw this with you,' insists Lars.

I look at him distrustfully. If I didn't know what my husband of all those years was up to, I am not exactly going to trust someone who has just walked into my life.

'Let me find out some more. I'll speak to her. I'll pick you up for dinner tonight and we can talk. At least let me find out who did this. It's upsetting for me too that I'm on here. I'm also angry with whoever is responsible.'

Lars tries to take my hand but I snap it back. Gosh, he's good at lying.

'Please, you have to trust me. It's not something I'd ever do. Give me until tonight to find out more. Can I pick you up and you'll agree to dinner with me? I'll find out everything by then and prove my innocence, I promise.'

Part of me wants to say no, but being a sucker for solving mysteries, I find myself agreeing.

'Thank you. I promise I will get to the bottom of this,' says Lars.

He leans over to kiss me, but I turn my face. A kiss lands awkwardly on my cheek.

—

I make myself some tea and walk around the garden after he has left. I search for the deer. Surely he must be around here somewhere. The fresh air hits my face as I look around. Whatever happens between me and Lars, I decide that I will stay in the cottage. I came to this place before I met him. I am not going to let our relationship change anything. It is beautiful here regardless.

When I have exhausted the garden and its surroundings, I consider whether I can get my bicycle back from Morten, the man I rented it from last time. Perhaps he has my lovely blue bike available again.

I decide to take the long walk to his corrugated iron shed, where I see my bike leaning against the side. Morten is busy outside, oiling the chain of a child's bicycle.

'Good to see you again,' he says.

'Thank you. It's so nice to be back. I see the bike is here. Can I rent it?' I ask.

'Ah, I'm sorry, it's reserved for someone. I have this one?' he says.

I look at a silver bike with scratches. It is nowhere near as sparkling as my blue bike but it will do the job.

'Okay, can I take this one for now and if the blue one comes back, can you let me know?' I ask.

'*Ja*, of course,' he says.

I pay the deposit one more time and Morten gets my seat into position. I wobble off in the direction of the shops.

The wind blows relentlessly and I fight to steer the bike. I don't know if it is the weather conditions or the bicycle, but it feels harder to ride this time.

I am relieved to reach the town. However, before I venture into the supermarket to stock up on all my necessities, I feel the need to speak with Dana about Lars. I don't know her well, and she might not divulge anything, but at least I can try and find out what he is like. Perhaps she knows something. Anything at all would be a help.

I park the bicycle in the rack outside the pub. The warmth inside hits me as I open the door. It would be stifling if it wasn't for the little fresh air coming through the open windows.

'Martha, welcome back,' says Dana.

'Thank you. It's so great to see you again,' I say.

'I'm so glad you're back. I can't listen to Lars talk about you any longer,' she laughs.

Her comment takes me by surprise.

I look to the table I was sitting at when I first met Lars and see it is empty. Even though I don't know what to think of Lars right now, I am drawn to sit there.

Dana follows me as I sit down.

'So, what can I get for you? Menu? Are you eating today?' she asks.

'No, I don't have anyone to share my omelette with, so just a Faxe Condi please,' I smile. Amazingly, I can still pronounce my favourite Danish soft drink.

'One Faxe Condi coming right up,' says Dana.

She starts to walk away but stops and turns around. 'It's funny how life works out, hey? Lars always complained how we should make an omelette for one person, but look what happened! It led him to meet you. A match made in heaven.'

She walks away to get my drink, but I wish she had said more. How could she possibly think he is so happy when he has all that stuff going on online?

Dana comes back with my fizzy drink and I have to stop her before she rushes to the next table.

'Can I ask you something? Why do you think we are a match made in heaven?' I ask.

'Well, he's changed so much since he met you. He's happy now. He was so sad before. I always believe that the broken fixes broken. When you came in here, you looked the same as he did. Something in your eyes. You both looked broken and both needed putting back together.'

I never thought I looked broken before. Tired, worn out, sad, perhaps, but not broken. Perhaps it was more obvious than I thought.

'Wow. I didn't know he was that broken. He seems to be quite self-assured. I mean he's even on dating sites. Did you know that?'

Dana bursts out laughing.

'I don't think he uses dating sites; he's far too serious and old-fashioned. No, he believes that you meet someone and you know right away if she's the one. He doesn't mess about.'

'How do you mean?' I ask.

'Did he tell you his parents were married within three months of meeting each other?'

'I didn't know that.' I admit.

'Yeah, look. I thought he was quite cute when we first met. I tried to get a date with him. He was having none of it. He said he didn't date anyone unless he thought it was going somewhere. Lars was devastated after his wife left him. She was a really bad person.'

'Will you tell me what happened?' I ask.

'Everyone here knows she walked out on him and left him for the baker, Pedr, who was his competitor. Lars' enemy, shall we say. She took all his recipes and left overnight. Lars was so shocked. He had no idea. Some say she only married Lars to get all the recipes so she and Pedr could have the best bakery around. But many didn't like the way she did this so they... what do you call it? They "boycott" the bakery.'

'Oh, that's awful.' I say. 'Poor Lars.'

'*Ja*. Poor Lars. Ever since that, he didn't bother with anyone. That's why I don't see why he would be on dating sites. He said next time, he would know when it was the right person and he wouldn't get involved with anyone, unless he knew. And… He finally met her, right here,' smiles Dana.

I sip my drink and think about what she has said. I want to believe her but what if she has been told to say this? Surely, Lars wouldn't be that devious.

It is as though Dana can tell I still have doubts.

'I promise, he adores you. You're one very lucky lady. He has a good soul. There aren't many people that are so genuine. He didn't deserve his ex-wife, but perhaps it was because he was too trusting.'

I consider how I was also too trusting of my marriage partner. We certainly have that in common. My head is in a spin as I try to work everything out. He does sound as though he is genuine, but I still need to find out for myself. The only way to get to the bottom of this is to meet for dinner tonight and see what he has found out.

Exactly why he is on a dating site and who put his profile on there is a question that still remains to be answered.

## Chapter Thirty-Eight

As I get ready for dinner, it doesn't feel as though I am preparing for a date – although I guess it isn't a date, but more the outcome of an investigation into Lars' true nature. I know that Agnete and Ludwig are joining us, as Lars has messaged me to let me know that they will meet us at the restaurant. However, I do think we should have met alone tonight as we have far too much to discuss. I don't fancy having a huge barney in front of Lars' sister and brother-in-law. I am worried Agnete might put it all down to the fact that we are not having enough sex or something.

Looking in my wardrobe, I don't find much inspiration for tonight. I must visit Louisa's shop again and treat myself. Finally, I pull out some plain black trousers and a white blouse.

-

Lars turns up early and catches me by surprise as I struggle with the waistband of my trousers. I must have put on weight while I was back in Wales. I blame all those biscuits at work.

He is jumping with excitement.

'I know who did it!' he shouts as he runs through the front door.

'Agnete?' I ask.

'Yes, I won't say anything more, but I hope tonight you'll have all the proof you need that I knew nothing about it.'

If it is Agnete who has caused all this trouble then I must admit that I am not so excited about seeing her. Does she hate me? Is that why she did it? I knew it was a bad idea to meet them tonight.

I walk into the restaurant in silence. Agnete smiles over as she sees me and Ludwig bobs his friendly head around and grins from ear to ear.

'*Hej*, so happy you are back,' says Agnete.

'Are you?' I ask.

'Yes, of course. I'm so happy, because Lars, he missed you too much. Isn't that right, Ludwig?' says Agnete.

'*Ja*, thank you,' says Ludwig.

Normally, Ludwig makes me smile but I am a little apprehensive about them both tonight. I don't know who I can trust around the table.

Lars can obviously sense there is tension in the air as we sit down.

'Let's order some drinks and then Agnete has something to tell you, don't you?' he says.

'*Ja*. I have an apology to make,' she says.

I order a bottle of lager, just as Lars does. Perhaps we are more similar than I imagined. I remember what Dana said about us.

I can see that Agnete wants to speak, but I need a drink first before I listen to her. However, it appears that she is eager to get her story across.

'Martha, I am sorry. So sorry. I don't know how you found these dating sites. I made it two years ago. I forgot it was on there. Lars was having a hard time when his wife left. I hated to see him so lonely. He was so down and—'

'Okay, that's enough, Agnete. She doesn't need to know how hard it was for me,' says Lars.

'I'm trying to explain why I did it. I think now maybe it was a stupid idea but I wanted to help and now Lars told me how upset you are. I don't want to make you two break up because of my mistake. Please, believe me. Lars knew nothing about this,' says Agnete.

Lars smiles at me and I start to soften a little. Perhaps she is telling the truth. Between her and Dana, Lars certainly has some good character references.

The waiter interrupts us with the menus, but I don't have much of an appetite. Even if this is true, Rosie still has it in for Lars. If I tell her what I have been told I don't know that she will even believe it. Perhaps she needs to meet Lars for herself, then she might see that he isn't necessarily the monster she thinks he is.

'So, do you believe me now?' asks Lars.

Agnete looks at me hopefully and Ludwig smiles.

All three of them stare at me.

'I never meant harm. I don't remember the password so couldn't delete it, but I will try and get to the account. I promise,' says Agnete.

'Okay, I believe you.' I say eventually.

'I am so thankful,' says Agnete, raising her glass.

'*Skol*,' the three of us say together.

'You two were made for each other. I knew that when I first met you,' says Agnete.

'*Ja*, thank you,' says Ludwig.

We all laugh and it feels as though I am back at their house and I am one of the family again. Perhaps I can trust this family after all.

'It's great to be back,' I say.

'Please don't leave my brother again. He's been so miserable without you,' says Agnete.

'Ah, I was okay. She exaggerates sometimes,' says Lars.

For the first time I notice the shyness under his cool demeanor. I see what Dana meant about him. I am incredibly lucky to have met someone so special.

For the rest of the evening, we get along well. We discuss Agnete's work, what Rosie has been doing in Borneo and I tell her all about my position at the library, which is very tame compared to her job. I can't think about going back to work at the moment, but I still have plenty of time to decide. I asked Suzy to give me until the end of October for my final decision. It is still a risk as I won't have known Lars that long, but I have a feeling that I won't want this adventure to end.

When we finish dinner, we say our goodbyes to Agnete and Ludwig and I promise I will see them soon.

'*Ja*, thank you,' says Ludwig as we hug.

I wasn't sure where tonight would end, but Lars and I feel closer than ever. I have no doubts about his faithfulness.

He puts his arm around me when we leave and holds me so tight it is as though he is putting all my broken pieces back together again. I hope I can do the same for him.

As we head off to leave the mainland, Lars turns to me and says, 'So does this mean I can stay over in the cottage tonight?'

Goosebumps take over my body as I think about the two of us being together as one again.

'Of course you can.' I say.

# Epilogue

## The Following Summer

It has been almost a year since I first came to Fanø yet it feels as though I have been here forever. In that time, I have made new friends, learnt how to knit at the annual knitting festival that the island holds, and today, I will help Lars fly a giant kite at the kite festival. It seems there is always something to celebrate on this glorious island.

Lars has been busy in his shed making his kite for months. He refused to let me see it, and says it is a surprise. Last year he had his eagle, but this year he won't give me any clues. I wonder if it is a giant omelette, or perhaps something he sells in the bakery, like a loaf. I can't imagine that would be the most impressive kite though, from what I have heard about previous events, some of the kites sound pretty spectacular.

I know from watching the videos Lars has shown me that these are no ordinary kites like the plastic witch I had when I was a child. Last year there were giant bees, colourful crabs, sinuous seahorses and colossal sharks. Lars tells me that people come from all over for the event and that it is the largest kite meeting in the world. I can't wait to finally see it with my own eyes.

We leave the cottage we recently bought on the island early so that Lars can set up his kite. I have been told that I must keep my eyes closed until it is well and truly up in the air and there is to be no peeking allowed. Lars bundled it in the van so fast that I was unable to even get a sneak peek. I am dreadful with surprises and the suspense is killing me.

I tried to get Agnete to give me a hint but her lips were sealed. Nobody has divulged anything. So, by the time we arrive at the beach on Fanø where the festival is taking place, I can hardly contain my excitement.

'Will you tell me now what you made?' I beg Lars.

'We're here now. You have to wait,' he laughs.

'I can't wait any longer,' I say.

Like an impatient child waiting to open a present, I am desperate to know what it is.

'You must. I have to get everything into place,' says Lars.

Looking around, I can see many of the kites are already set up. There is a huge turtle flying above us. Further along the beach flies a magnificent kite of a scuba diver and as the wind blows, her legs move as though she is kicking through the air. It amazes me how cleverly made these kites are.

'Right, now close your eyes,' says Lars.

'Do I have to?' I say.

'Yes, you do. I don't want you seeing it until it is in the air,' says Lars.

I grumble and complain and then do as I am told.

I keep my eyes closed until finally Lars says I can open them.

'Now, open your eyes. Can you see it?'

Looking up I see a kite shaped like a baker. He has blue trousers and a little baker's hat with blond hair poking from beneath it.

'Oh, that's so cute! It's you,' I say.

'He has a message,' says Lars. He unties a rope from in front of the van and a banner flies up into the air to join the baker.

I read what it says twice to be sure I am correct.

'*Will you marry me?*' I say.

I look at Lars to be sure this isn't a mistake.

'Is that for me?' I ask.

For a moment I worry that his kite is tangled with someone else's and the message isn't for me.

'Of course it is for you, Omelette lady. I love you more than anything. So, what do you think?' smiles Lars.

'Oh, Lars. I would love nothing more than to be your wife. I love you more than anything too,' I say.

'That's a relief because I have another surprise for you,' he says.

I rub at my eyes as I look at who has suddenly appeared in front of me. It can't be, surely!

'Mammy, so, did you say yes?' asks Rosie.

'Rosie. What on earth are you doing here?' I ask.

I give her the biggest hug and step away to look at her once more in case my eyes are deceiving me. She looks well and has the remnants of a golden tan from Borneo. She looks so much more grown up and confident than when we said goodbye at the bus station.

'Hi, I'm Ben,' says a young lad standing next to her.

'Ah, yes, I recognise you from all the photos Rosie has sent me,' I say.

'Mammy, I haven't sent that many,' says an embarrassed Rosie.

'No, but you have told me a lot about him,' I tease her.

Lars shakes hands with Ben. It is as though we are all one big family, meeting again after an absence.

'I can't believe it. I never expected this lovely surprise. What are you doing here? How did you find us?' I ask.

I see Lars wink at Rosie. 'It's okay, you can tell her,' he says.

'I was worried about you being here with someone I hadn't yet met. I was wrong about Lars. I was scared he'd hurt you. So, I got in touch with him on Facebook last year and asked him what his intentions were. Sorry, but I didn't want to see you hurt again, after you took Dad's death so badly.'

I look at Lars and Rosie in astonishment.

'You both kept your communications secret from me?' I say.

'It wasn't a mean secret, Mam. When I realised he was a good person, we got along great. He asked me if I would mind him proposing. He explained that he didn't want to step into Dad's shoes, just that he loved you and wanted to spend the rest of his life with you. So, then he asked if we'd like to come and see you. He even paid for our flights. I wish Ben was that romantic,' says Rosie.

Ben shuffles about on his feet.

'I did tell you we'd get engaged one day. I just need to save for a ring,' says Ben.

I think about the jewellery box that I brought over with me. I still have my engagement ring from Anthony. Rosie always loved it. I don't know if it is appropriate given what went on in my marriage, but I should perhaps ask Ben if he would like to give that to her. After all, one surprise deserves another.

'Gosh, you lot have got up to so much without my knowledge. I can't believe it,' I say.

'Well, I wouldn't want to miss this next bit,' says Rosie.

'What bit?' I ask.

I notice Lars coming around from behind me with a small box in his hand.

'I hope you like it. Rosie helped me choose it,' says Lars.

I open the Georg Jensen box to see the most beautiful silver ring with a glittering blue topaz stone. It is absolutely incredible. I put it on my finger and it fits as though it was made for me.

'How did you find something so perfect?' I ask.

'Well, I know the type of thing you like and we have the same ring size, so it wasn't difficult,' explains Rosie.

My eyes begin to fill up. What an emotional morning.

'Goodness, I still can't believe all of this,' I say as I look at everyone. 'Where are you even staying?' I ask Rosie.

'Your friend Olaf sorted us a cottage. Ben was most impressed to find a deer in the garden when we arrived. Now I see why you love it here so much,' says Rosie.

Ben nods. 'Yeah, it's fab here, isn't it?' he says.

'Even Olaf knew?' I laugh. My goodness, I really was the last to know!

'*Hej*,' comes a voice. 'Are we too late?'

I see Agnete and Ludwig rushing along the beach towards us.

'Ah, you couldn't wait, Lars?' says Agnete.

They both start chatting in Danish and I recognise some of the words. It sounds as though Agnete and Ludwig were in on the plan too.

'We got tied up at the restaurant, sorry,' says Agnete.

'What restaurant?' I ask.

'We have lunch booked. To celebrate your engagement. We prayed you'd say yes,' laughs Agnete.

'We were a bit worried that you'd say no and it would be a huge disaster,' laughs Rosie.

'We had a plan B though, didn't we, Rosie?' says Agnete interrupting.

'Yeah, we were going to turn it into a birthday celebration. Because you didn't really celebrate your fiftieth last year,' says Rosie.

'Hang on. So you two have already met?' I ask.

'Yes, we picked them up from the train station and took them to the cottage last night. You could say we helped with the arrangements,' says Agnete.

'How many secrets did you guys have?' I ask.

They have all gone to so much effort on my behalf. I am extremely grateful to be surrounded by such wonderful people.

I look across and see Morten from the bike shop; he is holding hands with Yasmin from the supermarket. We know each other well now and she saves me a bottle of my favourite wine whenever it comes in. I had nothing to be afraid of.

'So, did she say "yes", Lars?' shouts Yasmin.

I hold my hand up to show them the ring. Even they knew of Lars' plans. It's a good job I agreed to marry him!

'Congratulations,' they both shout over.

I am so incredibly happy and our extended family walk along the beach together to look at the rest of the kites. The sky is jumbled with different designs. There are huge rainbow ones and even a replica of the *Titanic* and a sports car, all fighting for space in the sky. Around us, the atmosphere is buzzing with excitement. Strangers smile and compliment each other on their imaginative creations.

'I can't believe how friendly everyone is, Mam,' says Rosie.

'I know, it's fabulous, isn't it?' I agree.

'Hey, have you seen the time?' says Agnete.

'Lunchtime,' says Rosie.

Lars remains quiet and looks at me with the shy smile that I love so much. He takes my hand and adjusts my ring slightly.

'It suits you,' he says.

'It really does, thank you,' I smile.

I lean over and kiss him, but a voice interrupts me.

'Ugh, Mammy. No need for that at your age.'

We laugh and head to the restaurant.

They have chosen Dana's pub for us to celebrate. As soon as we walk in, I realise that she was in on the secret too.

'You said yes?' asks Dana.

'I did, indeed,' I smile.

'Wonderful. I wanted to be there, but I had to get your table ready. I have a private room booked for your party,' says Dana, leading us to a bigger room to the side of the pub.

'That's very kind, but there are only six of us. You didn't need to book a private room,' I say.

Sitting down at the table, I take a photo of my ring to send to everyone back at the library. They will be so excited to hear the news. As I send the photo to Suzy, I hear something that takes me right back there. How bizarre that someone has the same message tone as Suzy. I didn't think anyone else would have part of the Welsh national anthem as their ringtone.

'Turn your phone off,' says a Welsh accent.

I get up from my chair and look outside the room, where I can hear the voice is coming from.

'Suzy, Trevor? I don't believe this,' I say looking directly at them.

'Sorry, it wasn't supposed to happen like this,' says Suzy.

'Yeah, we were supposed to come in and surprise you, but this one had that blinking ringtone. I've told you so many times it's time for a change, haven't I?' says Trevor.

'Well, Angus likes it,' says Suzy.

Suzy and Trevor are so funny. They've worked together for so long they are like an old married couple sometimes.

'Never mind about your ringtone, come here. Give me a hug,' I say.

Suzy hugs me first and then Trevor. I step back to see if they have brought anyone else with them.

'Where is Angus? Is he here too?'

'No, Lloyd is looking after him. He told me to come and have a short break. It was such a surprise when we got the message from Lars inviting us out here,' explains Suzy, as we walk into the private dining room.

'Yeah, what a lovely thing for him to do,' says Trevor.

I look at Lars who is watching me with a big smile on his face. I am the luckiest woman alive.

'Well, I'm so pleased you could both get away. I'm amazed there's any staff left at the library!' I say.

'Sioned said she'd hold the fort, plus we have Alex in now, just part-time. We couldn't quite stretch to a full-time member.'

'Nothing changes, then,' I laugh.

'No, same old,' says Trevor.

'And Mrs Morris. How is she?' I ask.

Trevor never did manage to get her online. She said she thought the laptop might give off radiation.

'She's still good old Mrs Morris. Her sciatica's been playing up a bit more, so she can only come in once a week now. She's getting less mobile. But, anyway, she gave me something for you. We told her we had been invited over and...'

Suzy takes an envelope from her bag.

'I had to write it for her, as she couldn't see to do it herself. But, well, anyway, here,' says Suzy.

I begin to read the letter.

*Dearest Martha,*

*Suzy and Trevor are coming out to see you, so I asked them to bring this letter.*

*I'm sorry I haven't been able to 'Moon' you, or whatever they call this thing where I can see you over there by computer. Trevor tried to be helpful and said he'd do it all for me, but I made an excuse. The truth is I am not good at goodbyes and things. I don't really like them. So writing to you is easier – even if I did have to ask Suzy to help me. I think it must be cataracts, about time I visited an optician! I'm not very good with opticians either. But anyway, this is not about me. It's about you, my lovely.*

*You were always a pleasure in the library (except when you had that miserable mopey time, of course) and it's not the same without you. I only go in once a week as nobody chats to me like you did. I do miss seeing your friendly face, I must say. But there we are, my loss is Lars' gain. Sorry, I'm talking about myself again.*

*Right, so what I wanted to say to you was this. It seems that your husband wasn't a very nice man, Martha. Not after you found out what he did to you. You didn't deserve that. I'm sorry to say it like that. But you met someone much better and I am so happy for you. I have sorted everything back here. I sent the fishmonger around to that*

*Izzy woman (I have ways of finding out people's addresses that I won't put on here) and I asked him to dump all the fish he didn't sell on her doorstep. Of course, he did it in the dead of night when nobody was watching and I gave him an extra fiver for his troubles. So, now she's sorted I want you to have closure.*

*Now onto that lovely boy you met. What Gerald and I had was so special that nobody could ever come close to him. I see something similar in Lars from what I have heard. I hope one day you might bring him to Wales for me to meet. I know I would love him as though he was my son-in-law, because you, Martha, feel like the daughter I never had, if I'm honest.*

At this point I have to stop reading. My eyes fill up. I take a glass and pour from the water jug that Dana has placed on the table.

'Oh, my goodness, Suzy,' I say.

'I know, I was getting emotional trying to write it,' says Suzy.

*So, I want you to know that I hope you make the most of every day with Lars. Suzy tells me you help him at the bakery now. Well, don't work too hard because life is very short and then it's gone. Enjoy every moment with your second chance in life. This is your time now; make the most of it.*

*With lots of love,*

*Margaret (Please stop calling me Mrs Morris)*

*xxx*

'Wow, I'm gob smacked. What a day. So many revelations and surprises,' I say.

'You must be a little overwhelmed,' says Suzy.

'I am a bit. I'll take Lars to meet her. I'll write to Mrs Morris and tell her we'll visit soon. I just hope there aren't any more surprises today. I don't think my heart can take it,' I say.

I look over to Rosie who is chatting animatedly to Ludwig. How on earth can she be chatting to him? She can't speak Danish now, surely? What are they saying to each other? I strain to listen in.

'If you want to grow a big cucumber then I can tell you how. Gardening is good for the soul. Great relaxation,' says Ludwig.

'I don't think I'm quite ready to get into gardening, but thanks for all the tips you've given me,' says Rosie to him.

What on earth? How can Ludwig be speaking English so well? I can't help but interrupt them.

'Ludwig, you speak English now?' I say.

Ludwig blushes.

'Only a little,' he says.

'Ludwig has been taking English lessons, especially for you,' explains Agnete.

Ludwig, Agnete and Lars look at each other.

'It was to be your surprise for our wedding day,' smiles Lars.

'I'm sorry I spoilt it,' says Ludwig.

'No, not at all. It's wonderful that we can converse now. But I'm amazed you would do that for me. Gosh, you guys are just… Wow, I have no words.'

Dana comes along and pops open a bottle of their house champagne.

'Enjoy,' she smiles.

Everyone around the table lifts their champagne glasses for a toast.

Lars places his arm around me and I snuggle into the comfort of his body.

'*Skol!*' says Agnete.

'Congratulations, and welcome to our crazy family,' says Ludwig.

# A letter from Helga

I am so delighted to have written this story featuring a beautiful island in Denmark. It has always been a magical place to me, and I hope to take you, the reader, on that journey to the island with me. With my Danish ancestry, it was important for me to show the world what a wonderful and special place Denmark is. I hope you will agree and enjoy some hygge when reading *A Scandinavian Summer*.

I worked on this story for my Creative Writing MA. Whilst it is a romantic comedy, I wanted the story to feature real-life issues, such as bereavement, along with empty nest syndrome, that many parents face. Reaching fifty is a milestone when people often face changes in their dynamics at home, and I wanted to reach out to anyone facing these challenges and remind them that they are not alone.

I hope you will enjoy meeting Martha and her friends at the library. Also, look out for Mrs Morris, who was my favourite character to write. Perhaps she needs her own book!

Once again, thank you so much for your support and for choosing to read *A Scandinavian Summer*.

I am always very responsive on social media, so please feel free to contact me if you enjoy the story. You can contact me via:

www.twitter.com/HelgaJensenF
www.facebook.com/helgajensenfordeauthor
www.instagram.com/helgajensenauthor

# Acknowledgements

As always, the biggest of thank you's to Keshini Naidoo at Hera Books, who has allowed my stories to come to life. She is one of the most fantastic people to work with, and I will always be grateful for the opportunities she has given me. It is always an absolute pleasure to work with you, Keshini. Also, a huge thank you to everyone involved in helping this story come alive and the excellent editor, Jennie Ayres. Thank you to Dan O'Brien at Hera also for your invaluable input.

An individual thank you must be said to my lovely cousin, Marianne. I am so sorry for the countless panicked messages you have had regarding Danish spellings. You deserve a medal, and I promise you a honey rum the next time I see you, or maybe even a bottle of something sparkling! *Tak for hjælpen.*

Of course, a huge thank you to JK as always for the smiley faces and yet more fish fingers as I juggled my deadlines. Thanks to the fantastic 'Aunty Lisa' for keeping the dog amused.

As ever, the biggest thank you to my gang. Suz, Susan, Nicola, Sam, Lisa, Eleri, you are the best. Also, thank you to all my other amazing friends, special people, and writing buddies. I have the best people in my life, and I am so grateful for that.

A special mention to my Danish family and my father, who died when I was a child. I always wanted to make him proud, so this book is dedicated to his memory.

Thank you to every reader who takes their time to pick this book up. The wonderful readers mean so much to me, and I can't thank you enough for choosing to read my stories.

Happy reading X